P9-DXT-019

HENRY
SUTTON

CHARTER
NEW YORK

A DIVISION OF CHARTER COMMUNICATIONS INC.
A GROSSET & DUNLAP COMPANY

THE PROPOSAL

Charter Books
A Division of Charter Communications Inc.
A Grosset & Dunlap Company
360 Park Avenue South
New York, New York 10010

2 4 6 8 0 9 7 5 3 1
Manufactured in the United States of America

The Proposal

"Thought strives to become action, the word to become flesh, and, marvelous to relate, man, like God in the Bible, needs only to express his thought and the world takes form."

—H. Heine

"Nothing but a wish can impel our psychic apparatus to activity."

—S. Freud

PART ONE

ONE

Surely, Victor thought, it had to be a joke. And not a very good one at that.

He had listened to the pious nonsense about the aesthetics of depravity and had heard the songs, one or two of which were not entirely without merit. But still, the idea of a musical comedy based on the life and works of Baudelaire was asinine. There was nothing to do but sip one's drink, produce from time to time a rictus that might be construed (by an idiot) as a smile of pleasure, and wait until it was over. Victor was Ormsby's guest, after all. He knew that Ormsby's motive in inviting him had been kind. A quiet evening at a backer's audition? *Of course, you'll come. Do you a world of good! Must get about, mustn't one?* All that fake cheerfulness that people produce for the sick, the insane, or the bereaved, as if they believe that the pain turns sensible men and women into kindergarten students. (It does, of course.)

How long, O Cicero, are we to endure your orations here in the senate? Victor looked about the room, admiring the Matisse, deploring the credenza, curious about the tea service on the tray behind him. Was it actually Georgian or a recent copy? Hard to tell, without picking it up and actually looking at it. (Later, after the audition was over, he did look and discovered it was authentic.) It wasn't just the tea service that had fascinated him, but the question of which would be more in character for Ormsby. He'd guessed it would be a copy.

The young man at the piano, the composer of the proposed show's tunes, finished his introductory blather and went on to the next song. The girl began to sing. Victor noticed—and noticed himself noticing—her ecru blouse. The third button had come undone. Again. He had thought, at first, that the effect had been deliberate, a part of—what had Ormsby called it, the aesthetics of depravity? Anyway, a calculated come-on, the button of the blouse left undone, the shape of the breast and the swath of lighter skin showing below the tanned, publicly visible area exposed in a peekaboo routine as old as the—as those very same—hills. He even allowed himself to invent a scenario in which she was not calculating at all, but innocent and poor, owning but the one blouse, and unaware of the defect of its closure until the very last minute, too late to do anything about it. He doffed his barrister's wig, took his place in the jury box, and dismissed the suggestion as improbable. She was, more likely, a sloven. Then, up on the bench, he smothered a yawn.

She was not such a gorgeous little piece as to warrant the attention he was paying her. He knew that. It wasn't such a stunning breast, not so large nor so tantalizing as many he'd seen. But she was slender, with delicate arms and a graceful neck, so that the blossoming of the bosom seemed to have taken rather a good deal of her *elan vital,* and had a poignant quality to it. Rather pointy and wanting to be rounder, it would have, he had no doubt, a nipple of pale candy-pink.

She couldn't really punch out the song, but she was on key and she enunciated well enough so that the audience of prospective investors could understand the words. That was perhaps a mistake on Ormsby's part. The lyrics were idiotic. What girl would sing that she was *waiting for the dirty old man of her dreams*? And the girl was unlikely to be very much concerned whether the investors put up the money or not, whether the show was ever produced or not. She had been hired for the evening to sing the songs, take her pittance, and disappear. No point, then, to this titillating display.

He was annoyed with himself for having wasted so much attention on . . . on what? A rather lean, almost lanky girl. She would be all shoulder blades and hipbones in bed. She wasn't worth this psychic investment. It was the tediousness of the evening. When, he asked himself, would he learn to be blessedly, savagely, surgically rude, as apparently it was necessary to be to avoid such torments as this pointless soiree? It was his own fault for coming. Still, he felt a welling-up of anger toward Ormsby, toward these sleek, chic patrons of the arts—who in their daytime lives were dreary businessmen—and even toward the girl. Especially toward the girl. As a drowning man feels rage at the frailty of the straw at which he clutches, even while clutching it, he nursed his petty annoyance. Open the goddamn blouse, then! If you can't sing "Melancholy Baby," show us your tits! He conceived the lovely idea of getting up from the chair, walking toward the piano, wrenching the flimsy fabric from her body, mopping his face with it, bowing, perhaps, to the assembled guests, and taking his leave. The theatre of cruelty. Ormsby, no doubt, would explain that it was regrettable, that he, Victor, had been under an awful strain. Excuses would be invented. He could probably get away with it. (A reason, therefore, not to do it.)

Free fall. There are times when one just doesn't care any more, when one loses all sense of consequence. A consequence, sometimes, of loss. Victor had not yet recovered from the loss of his wife, Margo, and in fact he did not expect to recover. Didn't want to. The miserable healing of time depends mostly on our frailty, our infidelity, he thought. He wanted to be able to function, of course, but not to heal entirely. He would have liked the hard lump of a cyst somewhere in his emotional organization, a tough-tender place to which he could reliably refer any time, a month from now, a decade from now. He was not a stupid man and he realized that there was at least an element of masochism in this desire, and that there was more than a little guilt involved in it. He had wanted Margo to die, had wanted her to be released from the pain and the terrible disfigurement. It had been a slow, messy death, its tortures only extended and made more exquisite by the cunning of modern medical science. For her sake (but for his, too, because he had hated to watch it) he had begun to wish that it could come mercifully to an end.

And now? Brittle, bitter, angry, he also felt liberated, not merely from the agony of Margo's death but from a whole set of moral imperatives that only made sense in relation to her. His mood, curiously enough, was cynically cheerful as a result of his having seen through the great dirty joke of the world. He felt a giddy irresponsibility, a mild mania, so that the temptation to rip off the girl's blouse was not altogether unserious. Or so that, after the last number of the audition, while the guests were drinking, smoking, nibbling canapes, and mingling in the pretense that this was a social evening rather than a commercial occasion, Victor answered Ormsby's inquiry about the production by suggesting that the show ought to tour prisons.

"Prisons? Why?"

"As a punishment."

"You're in a foul mood," Ormsby chided.

"Yes, of course," Victor answered cheerfully, proud of it.

"That's why I asked you to come, this evening."

"Oh, was it? I was in a fine mood until I arrived."

"How very droll," Ormsby said. He turned, found a rather plump and very severe woman behind him, introduced Victor to her and her to Victor, and ducked away.

"Are you one of the producers?" the woman asked him, looking belligerent.

"No," he told her. "I'm a friend of Ormsby."

"I see," she said grudgingly, as if she didn't quite believe him. "And what do you do?"

"I own pornographic magazines."

"Like *Playboy?*"

"Oh, no. Mine are hard core. You wouldn't have heard of any of them. The most successful is *Hot Come.*"

She hesitated, glared, and then turned away, which was exactly what he had wanted. He felt rather better. Not all better, but a little.

It was a small and mean triumph, but it was nonetheless gratifying. It would have been unimportant, had it not been for the shooting. That was the occasion; the conversation with the woman—whose name he had not caught—was only the precondition, a transaction to set and define his odd mood. The shooting was not even important in itself—except to the gunman who was apprehended, and to the doorman, who was shot and bled copiously from a flesh wound of the upper thigh. Why the gunman had shot the doorman was never clear. What mattered to Victor was that, having decided the party was as much of a bust as the audition had been, he'd left early. And on the way down to the lobby of Ormsby's building, he'd realized that his companion in the elevator was the girl who had been singing, the girl whose blouse he had been thinking of ripping from her body. This amused him. He did not speak to her, however. Better the memory of a legitimate impulse, however slight, than the dreadful tedium of her ambition, her complaints, her ordinariness . . . She had smiled at him. He had nodded ever so slightly. They had ridden down together, just the two of them. And then, when the door opened, they had seen the face of the gunman, had heard the two shots, had heard the doorman's guttural grunt.

Victor had pushed the "Door Close" button. The door had closed, but then, stupidly automatic, it had begun to open again. The girl had pushed "P"—for the penthouse. To get as far away from the gunman as possible, Victor thought, only a beat later realizing that Ormsby was in the penthouse.

"We must call the police," the girl said.

"If you like," he said. Those were the first words he ever spoke to her.

Later, remembering it, or remembering them—the words—he supposed that even they had had a dash of contempt for her innocence and earnestness. Gunfire? One calls the police, of course. Perhaps, in some more ordered world, one does or did. But he had long ago outgrown all that. A New Yorker, he knew that fallen bodies are to be stepped around, or, if absolutely necessary, over. But one doesn't volunteer. Or get involved. She, at twenty-three, had her code, a mélange of tips from the Girl Scout Manual, Amy Vanderbilt, and Heloise, along with the "Don't Litter" signs on sidewalk trashbaskets. She was not uneducated (or no more uneducated than most Americans of her time and place), but . . . innocent. Stupid. A man is shooting a gun? You call the police. A synthetic a priori proposition, like not flushing while the train is in the station.

It was not necessary, however, for her to give her name. Or to tell the police, when they arrived, that she—and Victor—had seen the face of the gunman.

"No," Victor protested, "I only got a glimpse of him. I'm sure I'd never recognize him."

"You could look through some mug shots and

try, couldn't you?" the lieutenant countered.

"I doubt that it will do any good," Victor said.

"We can try," Emily said.

It was what he deserved for not having acted on that impulse earlier. He'd have been home and in bed now if only he'd ripped her blouse off and then walked out of the party. Now, he'd have to go down to headquarters. She'd turned him into a supporting character in *Kojak!*

The dumb snit!

In the police car, on the way to the station, she talked, starting correctly with an introduction; indeed, almost a dossier. Her name was Emily Howland, and she came from Shaker Heights which was just outside Cleveland.

"Yes, I know," Victor said, looking out of the window.

"You remembered my name?" she squeaked.

"No," he said. "I meant that I know where Shaker Heights is."

"Not many people do."

"Nor are they any worse off, I shouldn't suppose."

"Anyway," she said, and she continued with more information: her school and college, her arrival in Manhattan, her engagement to a young writer who was, she said, "utterly brilliant and utterly broke, but an utter dear."

"You don't utter!"

"Oh, yes. I do. That's very funny, actually. His name is Larry. You'd like him."

"What makes you think so?"

"Everyone does."

"But what do *they* know? *They* don't even know

where Shaker Heights is."

"They? Who?"

"Everyone."

"You're teasing me," she decided.

"Yes, but that's only because I never hit women in a police car."

"I don't remember your name," she said.

"I don't remember telling you."

"All right. Touché. What is it?"

"Victor. Edmunds."

"How do you do?"

He raised an eyebrow. He wasn't sure he could stand much more of this. "Why do you . . . run on so?"

"To be friendly. For its own sake, and . . . well, you might be important. In publishing, perhaps. You could help Larry. Or . . . or me. You might have important connections in show business."

"Very very few."

"Would you rather I kept quiet?"

"Yes."

Had the police not taken up as much time as they possibly could, punishing Emily and Victor for her confession that they'd seen the gunman's face (which was the only punishment they were likely to cause), it might have ended there and been nothing more than a mildly unpleasant evening. But for two hours they sat there, Victor on the left and Emily on the right, looking at mug shots of various ruffians and malefactors. She smelled faintly of Camay, he thought. From time to time, a sergeant brought unspeakably bad coffee—as in *Barney Miller*. But there were long stretches of uninterrupted page-turning. During which, inevitably, she chattered. She apologized for having got Victor into this, expressed contrition for his time being wasted, and promised next time to avoid the same mistake.

"Just so long as I'm not with you, I don't care what you do," he said.

"That's not very friendly."

"No, it isn't. I don't feel very friendly."

"How sad."

"Don't patronize me, young woman. You can't carry it off, anyway."

"I said I was sorry."

"I know. But we're still here, aren't we, still looking at these thugs . . ."

A long silence. More mugs of thugs. More coffee. New albums and more pages. Then, "Wait a minute!" from Victor.

"You recognize somebody?" the sergeant asked.

"This is the district attorney. What's his face doing in here?"

"Oh, there are a few ringers. To see whether people will pause at a familiar face. To see if they're really looking."

"I'm glad I've passed the test."

"How did you know what the district attorney looks like?" Emily asked.

"I was at a dinner party with him about two months ago," Victor explained—to Emily, but for the sergeant's benefit. Eventually there would be some prospect of release.

It worked. The sergeant thanked them. The doorman would be looking at the same pictures in a day or two, when he got out of the hospital.

"He's all right?"

"Oh, he'll be fine," the policeman said.

"We can go now?" Victor asked.

The sergeant nodded.

"You couldn't give me a lift home, could you?" Emily asked Victor. "I'm afraid of subways at this hour. And I only have a dollar and change. Not enough for a cab."

"Didn't they pay you for singing?"

"A check. I don't know of any cabs that take checks."

He hesitated. She had been a great nuisance, but even so . . . "All right, why not?"

"I appreciate it," she said.

In the cab, he felt less put upon. He was going home at last, even allowing for the detour to drop the girl. She continued to babble, apologizing yet again. "Still," she said, "it must have its good part. It might be useful to Larry."

"Larry?"

"My fiance. I told you about him."

"Oh, yes. The writer."

"Yes. It would be a way for two people to meet. The way they do in the movies. The two strangers, thrown together. Like us, except that they like each other . . . I mean, it isn't that I don't like you. But you don't like me, much."

"I haven't thought about you much," Victor admitted. "I was just a little annoyed. I'm sorry."

"That's okay."

The driver stopped for a red light. A streetlight lit Emily's profile. She had good clean features, a little delicate, but . . . poignant. That neck of hers appeared almost fragile. It was a trick of the light, perhaps, but the performances of nature, however slight, produce their effects. One does not need an earthquake or a typhoon; a wash of light can transform one's world, too. He thought of what she had said about their meeting.

"All right," he said, "the two people meet. And she is engaged, as you are, to a struggling young artist. He—the man she meets—is older and comfortably fixed. He finds her attractive. He suggests . . . that they get married. So that, when he dies, she will be left as a wealthy widow, and can marry Larry and keep him in the comfort and style he deserves."

"What?" she asked. "It wouldn't work," she decided. "What if he didn't die?"

"No problem. They could have some reasonable arrangement. A marriage settlement. She'd get so many dollars a month for every month the marriage lasted. He'd prefer that, anyway. It would discourage murder plots by the young woman and her fiance. She wouldn't inherit a penny, you see. It would gain them nothing to kill him."

"But would a nice girl do a thing like that?"

"Why not?" Victor asked, amused now. It was a better game than he'd expected.

"It's . . . it's whoring, really."

"It would be a marriage. Perfectly respectable. With the blessing of the state. Unless you disapprove of marriage."

"Without love?"

"There are people who marry without love. For all kinds of reasons."

"I expect there are."

"And there would be love. Her love for Larry."

"Would he know about that?"

"Why not? I do."

"Are you proposing?" she asked, smiling. But it was a nervous smile, on edge, ill at ease.

"Who knows? I might be. I'd have to think about it. Would you accept if I were?"

"I don't know. I'd have to think about it."

They stared at each other, trying to figure out the angle of the joke. Whose joke upon whom?

TWO

Later that night, he found himself considering it. *It,* still, rather than *her*. What was intriguing was the shape of the idea rather than the actual being to whom it might or might not apply. She was an occasion, a glimpse in lamplight. But the proposition —or the proposal—had its own appeal. And there was, of course, the shape of her breast.

Victor was no youngster. He was impressive rather than handsome, plump, sleek, well-tailored and well-groomed. His hairline was receding at a slow but inexorable rate. His health was good. His outlook mixed. He had been twice married, once divorced (eight years before) and once bereaved (only two months before). He was subtle enough to understand that jokes, even the most bizarre, had some germ of seriousness to them. Or the good ones do. And this one was good enough to engage his attention, not continuously, but insistently, like a rough place on one's cuticle that kept catching on silk.

So, he had seen something in the girl, had responded to her more than he might have liked to admit. But that wasn't all of it. There was the financial intricacy of the arrangement. It would be a way of infuriating Adolph and Arnold, his two grown stepsons, whom he detested and who detested him in return. Margo's children, they were her residuary legatees. Victor was the beneficiary of a trust fund from which he derived income, but which would vest, after his death, in the stepsons. He had, therefore, an incentive to spend every nickel he could. Anything he left unspent would go to them. As would the apartment, a condominium of considerable value which he had the right to use during his lifetime.

More to the point, however, was Victor's fragile emotional condition. Having lost Margo, he did not want to put himself in the position where, ever again, he could lose someone he loved and feel as bad as he had felt. On the other hand, two months of almost absolute celibacy had been enough to suggest that he would sooner or later be propelled into some kind of relationship. He had supposed there would be a series of them, trivial encounters that were more or less satisfying, physically, but that were frustrating and frustrated emotionally. There were always contradictory demands—of the man for an uncomplicated sporting fuck, and of the woman for a for-God's-sake relationship. One could learn to promise as little as possible, to deny at the outset even the frailest hope. But they never really listened. They were sure that fate, or chemistry, or their own irresistible charms would change one's mind.

With this young piece of goods, however . . .

There would be a kind of safety. He could not possibly get involved with her in any way that would leave him vulnerable and hurting. And he could do good things for her—assuming, of course, that she was clever enough to understand that and not to look for more. It was clever and it was clean. Both of these qualities were appealing to Victor, whose own aesthetics of depravity were as well developed as anyone's. He looked around the elegant desolation of the apartment. The idea of bringing a girl like that into it—and into his life—and of redecorating the apartment—but not the life—to her taste was irresistible. And her taste would be dreadful, not bold enough, too modish. If she had any at all.

But suppose he woke up one morning, a month or so after the wedding, and discovered that he loathed her? It would have to be part of the arrangement that he could divorce her at any time. Fire her, essentially. It would be an incentive for her to be pleasing. Greed and the dislike of failure were a better basis for marriage, anyway, than sentiment and compatibility. It would be fascinating to see how far he could push her without having her quit. A delicious series of experiments, or more accurately, a process of training, like the breaking of a horse, could well turn her into a perfect slave. He could make something of her. It hardly mattered what. The point was to take her as she was and turn her into something else, making her his creature.

He realized that the girl herself had been less important than the timing of their meeting. He had been quite numb for two months, stunned by

Margo's death, and at the beginning barely able to gather the energy to get out of bed in the morning and select a costume for the day's charade. His appetites had deserted him, even for food. It was a matter of time, of course. His nervous system had begun to recover in its stupid almost vegetable way. He was delighted to feel again, but appalled that she should have been the one to arouse his feelings.

The sensible thing, he knew, would be to ignore it. It and her. In a week, he would forget her. Besides, they'd just been joking, passing the time in the taxi. On the other hand, if the joke had stuck in his mind, then it might have stuck in hers, too. She had not dismissed the idea. She might be willing to test herself against it. Out of greed, or pride, or for the adventure of it. The way people climb mountains or swim the Channel.

He could call her. He could find out how serious he was.

He didn't have her telephone number.

He felt a kind of relief. And realized that he had been anxious. Afraid that she would turn him down. Nervous as a young boy. Not because of her, but because of the idea, he had been breathing just a little faster.

How could he have been so stupid as to have failed to get her address and phone number?

On the other hand, Ormsby would know how to find her. And as he realized that, he felt the excitement returning. It made him feel young.

And she?

She told Larry, of course, about her wild evening, her performance, the guests, the gunman, the police, the trip to the station, and her conversation with Mr. Edmunds.

"Who's he?" Larry asked. Larry was getting ready to go to work. He wrote during the afternoons and evenings, and drove a taxicab at night, from two in the morning until ten.

"A producer type. We'd been talking about you, actually. About your being a writer. And I said that the way we met—I mean, the way he and I met—would be a good start to a story."

"Oh? A lot of machinery, isn't it?"

"Is it? It didn't seem to be. Anyway, he didn't think so. He even suggested that they should get married."

"Who should get married?"

"The man and the girl. Us, essentially."

"Us?"

"No," she explained, "he and I."

"You and Mr. . . ."

"Edmunds."

"Should get married? I don't get it. You mean, as the ending of this story? The cute meet, and then the happy end?"

"I don't think that was what he meant. I think . . . It was a way for me to help you."

"Me?"

"Your writing. You wouldn't have to drive a cab any more. I'd marry Mr. Edmunds. And then he'd die. Or we'd get divorced. But there'd be so much money for every month that the marriage lasted."

"That's the dumbest idea I've heard all week," Larry said. He grabbed the big crowbar he carried with him under the front seat of the cab to use on muggers, and his cabbie's cap.

"I don't think it's so dumb!" Emily protested. She wasn't sure whether it was dumb or not, but that wasn't the point. She didn't like Larry to think of her as dumb. And they had been having a difficult time of it, which wasn't surprising in the light of his strenuous regimen of work at the desk and then work in the cab, and the exhaustion and frustration that went with both kinds of employment. He often snapped at Emily, who lately had begun snapping back, or at least defending herself. "I don't think it's so dumb at all. We could use . . . fifty thousand dollars." That was the largest sum of money she could imagine. It was what her parents had paid for their house in Shaker Heights when she had been a junior in high school.

"Well, it'd be whoring."

"It'd be marriage."

"What would happen? You'd probably fall in love with him, or he'd fall in love with you."

"You sound like you're jealous."

"Well, sure I am!"

"You shouldn't be. He doesn't even like me. He was terribly annoyed about my telling the police we'd seen the gunman's face. He thought I was an idiot. And I guess I was."

"What about you? Did you like him?"

"Did I? I don't know. I hadn't thought about it."

"It's nuts! Screwy!" Larry said, and he went off to work.

Left alone, Emily continued to stare at the closed door, not quite transfixed perhaps, but absorbed by the question. Did she like Mr. Edmunds? Did she really like Larry? She liked the downy red hair on his arms, and his bare chest, and the way he freckled in the sunshine in the summers. She supposed she admired his mind, although it was sometimes a pain to be talked down to, which he did a lot, even though he said she was imagining it. She could get angry at him, at the things he said and did, and then forgive him because of the way his collar bones stood out at the base of his neck, and because of the way his hair mopped down on his face when he slept. She was used to him. She hadn't ever asked herself whether she liked him. He had courted her, told her he loved her, picked her out. She had been the passive one, responding to his demands. And when she was depressed, she had been able to imagine the possibility that one day Larry would cast her away. It had never crossed her mind that she might be the one to leave, or that he would care much if she did.

Mr. Edmunds was . . . innocuous. He was round, rather pinkish and not at all frightening. He had been joking, of course. To embarrass her. But she hadn't been embarrassed. She had been pretty good, she thought. It was Larry who had been disappointing. He should have been . . . cooler and laid back. Or hotter, declaring his love for her, and his rage. That he'd been just a little bit jealous and just a little bit annoyed was unsatisfactory. He wasn't taking her seriously, which was finally what she wanted and had almost forgotten to hope for.

Or maybe he'd been right. The idea of going off to marry that funny pink man for the money, for Larry, for their future . . . was screwy, wasn't it? A skinny girl, she had grown to slender womanhood without making any connection at all in her mind between the angularity of the fashion models in the magazines and her own body. Still, she knew she was young. She had good skin. She was long-waisted and wore clothes well. And she knew she looked great in a bikini, with her hipbones sticking out and her abdomen flat as it was. She'd had crude propositions, had heard the off-color remarks, had been pinched in subways. But this was different, not a proposition but a proposal. It was even flattering.

She tried to make excuses for Larry. He was tired, had been working hard, had to face a long night in the cab, and hadn't been able to get the point of what she'd been telling him.

She decided it would be fun to tell him that Mr. Edmunds had called back, had repeated his suggestion. In a day or two, when Larry was more himself, she could tell him that and see him wriggle a little.

She had no expectations that there would really be a call. He hadn't even asked for her phone number.

And if he had? Would she have given it to him? Probably yes, she thought. And she blushed.

In the morning, when Victor arose to the music of Vivaldi and the smell of fresh perked coffee that his electric timer produced for him promptly at nine, he was surprised to find that his first thought was of his scheme. It was still there, and increasingly insistent. He realized how dull his mornings had been, how tiresome. He had expected, with Margo's death, that there would be a new page, a new freedom. But he had been setting the machines out of habit, and arising because they clicked into action and required him to do so, too. There should have been something exciting, something interesting . . . Was she? Was it? Interesting? Oh, yes, as interesting, at least, as Clarissa had been to the poet, Lovelace. Her innocence was like a blank canvas begging to be marked up.

He would make her his slave, nothing less. It would be an exquisite process to see how he could bend her to his will. Sexually, of course, but in other ways as well. If Kant was right, and the worst sin was to treat another human being as an instrument rather than as an end in himself, then it ought to follow that there should be fun in violating that categorical imperative. It should be the most fun of all possible naughty things to do. It ought to be absolutely delicious.

He showered, shaved, drank a second cup of coffee, glanced at the paper's reports of fires, holdups, and random violence, all of which struck him as being crude and extremely banal. The truly original crime was one the legislators had never imagined and therefore had never thought to prohibit. Not that Victor thought of himself as a natural criminal, but he liked to believe that he had about him some originality, that there were still new things to do, new thoughts to entertain, and new feelings to experience. No matter what came of the encounter of the previous evening, he owed something to Emily for an invigorating morning.

He telephoned his lawyer, who was also a friend. George Kern might disapprove of the idea, Victor realized, but he would not ridicule it. On the contrary, he'd take it seriously, if only as a legal gamesman. And to protect Victor, his client.

"Any question that's an excuse for us to have a drink together is worth discussing," Kern said.

"I've got a busy day, but I'll be free at five. Can you come by here?"

"Fine! I appreciate it."

"See you then," Kern said.

He supposed he could call her, Emily, to find out whether she had made up her mind. But, no, strategically, it would be well to let a day or two go by. So as not to appear too eager.

He realized that he was scheming like a schoolboy. He loved it.

George poured whiskeys from the impressive crystal decanter, produced ice from a concealed ice-making machine, handed one of the glasses to Victor, and sat down to hear the ridiculous question. Victor hesitated for a moment, and then, secretly pleased with himself for the twinge of discomfort he had discerned, he asked George whether one could make a pre-marital agreement that would in effect pay a woman so many dollars a month for each month the marriage lasted, but exclude her from any alimony or death benefits.

"Yes, of course. Why?" George asked. "You thinking of marrying again?"

"I'm thinking about it. It's not likely to happen, but . . . an odd thing happened to me last night."

"Oh?"

He told George about his encounter with Emily. "It isn't anything serious. It's not likely to happen. But the subject came up. Of marriage."

"You'd never met her before?"

"That's right. And . . . I don't even like her very much. But she's attractive in her way. It's like . . . like some perfectly innocent, vacuous face one simply wants to smash, to see transformed by terror—

or lust. It hardly matters which. Does that make any sense?"

"Oh, certainly. But not as a basis for a marriage, I shouldn't think."

"But why not? We don't have slavery any more. The only arrangement left by which, in any sense at all, one owns another human being . . . is marriage. She'd be an amusing toy."

"All right, fine. Have her move in and make her your mistress. But why marry her?"

"Why not?" Victor countered. "The rules have changed, after all, as you know better than I do. Divorce used to be a difficult and expensive business. It isn't now. It's nothing at all. And if I had an agreement beforehand that limited what she could get, then there'd be even less nuisance. The trouble with the law, most of the time, is that it lags behind popular opinion and seems antiquated. In this, it's ahead of its time. Public sentiment still operates on an idea of marriage that the law hasn't maintained in years. It's at least arguable that the laws as they are presently written better fit my kind of marriage than they do the romantic and sentimental varieties."

"An interesting view," George said. "And as I think of it now, it may be correct. I'd have to think about it for a day or two, turn it over in my mind. There might be some risks that are not immediately apparent."

"But on its face, it looks plausible?"

"Oh, quite. As a matter of fact . . . now that I begin to play with it, I can see some benefits that you may not have realized."

"Such as?"

"Assume you remain married for . . . let's keep

the arithmetic simple and say ten months, at ten thousand a month. That'd be a hundred thousand, right?"

"Ten times ten, yes."

"That'd be a debt. Which your trust fund would have to pay on your death. It'd be a way of getting more money from your stepsons."

"But it would be an incentive for the girl and her fiancé to kill me. No, no. That won't do. It's absolutely necessary that there be no benefit at all to her if I die."

"She has a fiancé?"

"Oh, yes. If she did this, I'd think it would be at least partly for his benefit. That makes it for love, rather than for money. She's too dumb to be greedy for herself."

George Kern raised his glass. "You sly dog," he said. "Freshen that for you? I think we need it."

"I don't know whether we need it or not. I rather think I deserve it."

Dressing for dinner that evening, Victor realized that he would not have to call Ormsby, after all. He could, but he could also get the information just as readily from the sergeant at the police station. What could be more reasonable than a call to ask for the girl's telephone number? He could say that she had left a scarf in the taxicab. Straight-arrow types who come down to headquarters to spend hours looking at mug shots also return lost items, don't they? And that way, he would not have to endure Ormsby's condescension. Ormsby would assume that he wanted only to fuck the girl, no matter what clever story Victor fabricated for him. Ormsby was far too dirty-minded. Ormsby, after all, was a reasonable fellow. Victor had to consider what he would think, himself, if the situation were reversed.

In no way was he ashamed of himself. On the contrary, he could not have been more delighted by the prospect or proud of himself for having conceived it. Still, he was aware that the odds against his success were long enough so that there would be risks in confiding too much of his plan to anyone too soon. To any man, at any rate. To a woman, on the other hand, to the right woman, under the right circumstances . . . He thought about Irene Tarashoff, with whom he was to dine that evening.

Victor and Irene had once been lovers. Before he had married Margo, and before she had married Tarashoff, they had toyed with each other, bemused, diverted, for the better part of a year. And they were still friends. Victor did not take credit for that persistence of the friendship. He considered it a matter of great luck. At the most, he would have maintained that both he and Irene had been sufficiently civilized and graceful—or perhaps just sufficiently polite—as to keep the possibility of friendship open. It was what one wanted to happen and what very seldom did. Disengagement, for humans, is as tricky as it is for black widow spiders—or trickier, for with humans the likelihood is that *both* participants will get wounded. But with Irene, he had been lucky. She had divorced Torello (or Torelli, or whatever his name was), and Victor had gone to London and had married Margo, but the timing had been such that neither could suppose the other had betrayed the relationship. Neither could suppose that there had been a rejection.

This dinner invitation had concerned Victor, for

he had seen a certain danger to their meeting. Irene was alone again, having divorced Tarashoff a year or so before. He was alone, now that Margo was dead. It was unlikely, but for all he knew, she still might have some interest in him, might consider the occasion now ripe for the renewal of their connection. Victor was ambivalent about this possibility. Irene was still an attractive woman. But she was too headstrong, too sure of herself, too much her own person ever to live with. And her sexual voracity, while pleasant indeed to encounter, would be impossible for him, or for any one man, to satisfy. She was remarkable but intimidating. Among other things, Victor remembered how she had once inserted a corked wine bottle into her vagina and pulled the cork out by her muscular contractions, masturbating to produce the contractions. It had been a game, a kind of bet, and when she had managed to get the cork off the bottle, Victor had kept the bargain by lapping the wine that spilled out of her. (She had had to go to the gynecologist the next day to get the cork removed. Victor always had wondered what she had told the doctor.)

A splendid woman, but to be kept at a distance. And he could do that, tactfully and gracefully, by telling her about his designs on Emily. It would be a declaration of his intentions. And for all Victor knew, she might have useful suggestions to make. After all, vicarious wickedness is better than no wickedness at all.

THREE

Irene's apartment was in the same building as Victor's but on the other wing. The apartments were actually mirror images of one another, so that Victor felt a disorientation whenever he went there. Architecturally, she lived through the looking glass, so that instead of simply adapting, he had expectations that were always diametrically wrong. Her furniture was different, of course, and her paintings—he particularly admired the three Russian icons on the wall in the dining room—so that he found himself better off by concentrating on small areas. The little corner in the living room, for instance, with the wine-colored Tabriz rug, where they sat and drank pastis before dinner, was in no way disturbing. He could steady himself by staring at the Tabriz.

He had thought it was going to be a dinner party. Another couple of couples, at least. But she had only two places laid at the table. So, a tête à tête. She had offered drinks. He had come with her into the kitchen to help. Then, in the living room, they had sat down to talk.

She was solicitous. She spoke of Margo and of his loss, particularly the process of recovery, in which, as she said, "one feels a little better, and then feels guilt about the improvement. It keeps swinging back and forth that way. It happens to everyone."

"It was like that, yes. But I've begun to . . . to recover," he told her.

She was glad to hear it. She had invited him, in fact, to see how he was coming along. And to offer whatever help she could.

"Help? How do you mean? It's kind of you, of course, but . . . One must work through these things. What it mostly takes is time."

"You've had a couple of months. That should be time enough for you to go on to the next remedy."

"Which is?"

"A change of scene. A change of air."

"Oh?"

"I thought we might go on a trip together."

"Ah, I see," he said, taking a sip of yellowy drink.

She was a good looking woman, a bit leathery to look at but soft to the touch. Her figure was still delicate, and her features were even more clearly defined than they had been years before. Her slender nose and her high cheekbones looked to be carved from stone. Her lips, on the other hand, were full and soft. She was wearing a simple dark green dress, cut low to show off her full breasts and her emeralds. He had to admit that it was a pleasant prospect. If only he had not bumped into Emily, or if the bump had not produced this bizarre fascination . . . "It's kind of you," he said.

"Of course, it's not," she said. "If I didn't want to do it, I shouldn't have made the suggestion. Nevertheless, your tone was such that it suggested a following 'But'." She smiled, ruefully. "Well? Am I wrong?"

"We are old friends," he began, and relying on that old friendship, he told her about his meeting with the girl, their conversation in the taxi, and his idea about what might happen next.

"I should have called you a week ago. What shall I do? My timing used to be more reliable."

"I can't tell you what an ass I feel like."

"As well you should. She'll bore you, you know."

"But that's the gorgeous part of it," he explained. "If she does, as she very probably shall, I'll divorce her. Fire her—which is what it will amount to. That's the beauty of it. It's her job to keep me from being bored."

"The other risk is that you'll become involved. Grow fond of her."

"Not likely. I really don't think so."

"Stranger things have happened. You're at an odd place, you know. It's a vulnerable time . . ."

"Of course. Otherwise, I'd behave sensibly and . . . and accept your offer."

"That's not terribly flattering, but it's probably true. Take your drink in. I think supper's ready."

As they ate, Irene discussed plays she'd seen, paintings she had admired, new restaurants she'd been to and had disliked. She was poised, charming, lively . . . All the things that Emily wasn't. And she retrieved what otherwise could have been a very awkward occasion, making the meal a rite of its own. He was being such a fool, and yet the folly pleased him. He realized that even if there had not been any particular kindness in her invitation, there was kindness now, as she avoided any allusion to his contemplated marriage—all through dinner and afterward, when they took their coffee into the living room.

But she had not forgotten his declaration. It was only that she had her own way of testing it. She excused herself for a moment, then returned to the living room and seated herself at some distance from Victor, in a hardbacked rocker that did not really fit in with the other pieces in the room. Victor supposed it was an American note in the otherwise French statement. She was perhaps ten feet from Victor, and in a darker corner of the room. For her back? Her eyes? He wondered, but did not ask, having no wish to pry.

"So, tell me about her," Irene commanded.

He told her a little more. He described Ormsby's backers' audition, and her performance of some of the songs. He made fun of the idea—the aesthetics of depravity, indeed!—and of the execution. *The dirty old man of my dreams.* He described her voice, thin and reedy, just barely adequate for a living room, and utterly hopeless, he was sure, in filling a theater. She listened, saying nothing, just rocking. He went on, as she seemed to want him to do, talking about the way the button of her blouse kept coming undone, which was, of course, an obvious trick, but still effective. Maybe effective, come to think of it, because it was so obvious. Perhaps it was effective because it was she. Another girl with the same blouse and the same recalcitrant button . . .

She sighed. Or groaned?

"Are you all right?" he asked.

"I'm just fine. I came, actually."

"You came? I beg your pardon?"

"I came. When I went into the bathroom, I put in my ben-wah balls. They're little plastic balls with heavy steel balls inside them. When I rock, they whirl around and . . . stimulate me. While you've been talking, I've been rocking."

"Good Lord!"

"Come here," she said.

He got up from the Windsor chair, crossed the room, and came up to her rocker. She took his hand and put it in her lap. Against her crotch. "Push. Hard!"

He pushed. He could feel the mound of her pubis. He could feel the muscles of her abdomen ripple. He could feel her hand on his cock, hard now, holding him through the cloth of his trousers.

"Haaah!" She had come again.

"Now, go sit down."

"What are you doing?" he asked, utterly bewildered.

"I'm helping you make up your mind. About the choice you must make. This waif-like girl or me."

"You're helping me?" he repeated, feeling like a dull schoolboy.

"That's my intention. I make you hot and then I refuse you. You go home. Almost certainly to masturbate. If you find yourself thinking of her, then you'll probably go ahead and . . . propose. If you find yourself thinking of me, or of . . . of anyone else . . . then my advice would be to forget her. It's a way of getting in touch with your unconscious."

"How extraordinary!"

"Oh, it works. I've made decisions that way. And it's even easier for men."

"I suppose . . . it could work."

"Call me," she told him. "I'm eager to know how it comes out." She smiled, blew him a kiss, closed her eyes, and started to rock again.

He found his own way out.

He tried it.

He thought of Emily.

Vividly.

He imagined her with those ben-wah balls stuck in her cunt, her eyes narrowed in inward pleasure . . . And of himself, observing her.

Before he fell asleep, he telephoned the police station. It was not difficult to get the information he wanted—her address and phone number. He wrote them down on the pad on his nightstand. He took a couple of aspirins, prophylactically, to counter the headache he sometimes got from drinking more than two glasses of wine at dinner. He turned out the light and fell immediately into a sweet, dreamless sleep.

Emily did not really expect him to call, but during the day following their meeting she found herself wondering whether he might, and if he did, what she would tell him. It was a wistful sort of thought, for while she was quite prepared to lie to Larry, she would have preferred to be able to tell him the truth. She wanted to tweak him, to prod him a little, to make him notice her.

But he didn't call that day. As, after all, she had known he wouldn't. She'd given it up, had even given up the idea of fabricating a communication in order to tease Larry. But then, late that afternoon, there he was, on the telephone, talking to her. "Victor Edmunds. You remember me, I trust. We met at Ormsby's, or in the elevator, actually. And we shared a taxi from the police station?"

"Oh, yes. Of course, I remember. I remember you proposed."

"I did. I did, indeed. And have you an answer for me?"

"I think we ought to discuss it a little further."

"I quite agree. Over lunch, perhaps?"

"Would it be all right if . . . if I brought Larry along? My fiancé?" she asked. She hardly expected him to agree. But Larry was there, at his desk, not ten feet away. She saw his head come up at the sound of his name. Good, just what she wanted.

"By all means," Victor said. He was spontaneous and gracious, so that she felt just a little bit ashamed of herself. But then, why should she? It was his crazy idea! "Shall we say tomorrow? The *Veau d'Or?* One o'clock?"

"I think so . . ."

"You wouldn't stand me up, would you?"

"No, no. I . . . I'll be there."

"With Larry?"

"I hope so."

"I'll be looking for you."

He hung up. She stared at the phone and slowly replaced it on its cradle. "Larry?"

"Yeah?"

"That was Mr. Edmunds. He wants us to have lunch with him tomorrow. I accepted."

"Who?"

"That man I told you about. The one who wants to marry me."

"What?"

She had understood that some sort of argument was inevitable and had found herself looking forward to it. It was an opportunity to vent some of the frustrations and resentments that had been building for the year and a half they had been living together. It would precipitate some sort of decision about where they were going, would be a storm to clear the air. Also, with her ambitions as an actress, she liked dramatic scenes. They felt real, as much of the routine of her life did not.

Larry objected, of course, to the proposal—not only of marriage but of lunch. It was either ridiculous or obscene, or possibly both. And he wanted no part of it.

"What a stick you turn out to be. Where's your sense of fun?"

"It isn't fun to see you make an ass of yourself. Or to be made ridiculous, myself."

"It'd be a good lunch. And . . . and interesting. It could be something you'd be able to use. I mean, for God's sake, the whole thing started out with you. We were talking about your work, and how the way we'd met could be the beginning of a story."

"Not a story. A bad movie, maybe. You haven't the vaguest understanding of what I'm trying to do."

"Your stories are boring and pompous. And that's why nobody buys them."

"I see," he said, coldly, hiding the hurt. But she saw it, and took some satisfaction in seeing it. If only he cared as much about her as he cared about his writing. . .

"Well, I'm going. You can come along or not.

As you please."

"No, I won't. Why should I?"

"Because you care about me? Because you trust me? Because it's a joke and we could enjoy it together?"

"If it's a joke, then I don't have to come. And if I trust you, I don't have to come. And if you cared about me, you wouldn't go. It's reversible, after all."

"How clever! But that's Harvard talking, isn't it?"

Larry had gone to Harvard and was proud of it. Emily teased him about it, in an affectionate way when she was feeling affectionate, but with real animus when she was angry. He lowered his head and jutted his lower lip in a sulk that Emily generally found appealing. But not this time. His physical attractiveness was beside the point. What good was it to her that he was tall, that he had red hair, that he had clear, pale skin so that he seemed in some lights to be made of porcelain, if he was not hers?

"Aren't you bored with that old joke?" he asked.

"I'll tell you what I'm bored with. I'm bored going on the way we've been. If you don't want me to marry him, then you marry me. And I won't go to lunch."

"That's insane."

"I don't think so."

"We can't get married now because we can't afford it."

"But we could. It's only two dollars."

"That's not what I mean."

"We still can. I can marry him and then we'll have money."

"What makes you think I'd still want to marry you? Or that you'd want to marry me?"

"Well, if we change our minds, then we change our minds. That could happen to us any time, couldn't it?"

"That's my point," he said, as if it were a tennis match.

"And mine, too."

"Are you . . . are you serious about this?"

"No," she said, "but you could make me get serious about it. All you have to do is just keep on saying the wrong thing every time you open your mouth, and it could get serious."

"Then my mouth and the subject are both closed."

"Like that!" she said. Just what she didn't want.

While Larry and Emily were bickering, Victor was talking to Irene, whom he had called to inform of his success. "I'm having lunch with her tomorrow. With them, actually. She's bringing along her young man."

"Well, good luck to you," Irene said. It was not quite eleven. Irene was still in bed, dawdling over coffee and the *Times*.

"You don't seem terribly pleased for me."

"Why should I be? What's in it for me?"

"I don't know. Perhaps the young man. Would you like to come to lunch?"

"I think not."

"I don't mean actually at the same table. But. . . across the room. In the same restaurant."

"Why don't you let me know what happens. And what he's like. We'll talk about it after the fact, perhaps."

"I thought you'd be amused."

"Oh, I suppose I am. But I never laugh out loud before noon."

"I'll call and let you know," he promised.

He was disappointed. He had no idea exactly what he'd expected, or why he'd even asked her to come to the restaurant. To see the girl? To contribute to the situation? It was a strange thought, perhaps the result of her strange test of the previous evening. He had the idea that the game might go on longer, might be somehow better if he had Irene's participation. He had no idea how he saw her participating. Maybe just as an observer. But without her, no Emily could keep him entertained for more than a month.

More likely a fortnight.

As an entirely idle speculation, he decided they'd make a fine combination in a *ménage à trois.*

What about the girl, though? He could hardly remember what she looked like.

What he could remember was the quality of the pang she had caused in him. In the taxicab. He had to trust in that.

The aesthetics of whatever it was . . .

FOUR

He had strolled over to the restaurant early, not so much for the punctilio of good manners as to enjoy the warring of eagerness and apprehension. He was shown to a corner table and took a seat with a view of the entrance. He looked about him at the starchy white napery and the gleaming crystal and flatware, all of which suggested the formal neatness of a made-up and turned-down bed in a good hotel, the crispness only an invitation to mess, demanding to be rumpled and stained. He ordered a Negroni and sat back to enjoy his unease.

He looked up and saw them. She was . . . not disappointing. She looked around, uneasy, self-conscious, but still graceful, like a cat in a room strange to it. She pleased him. Her fragility came back in a rush of cues—the narrowness of the wrist as she touched her hair, the lean long-waisted body, the slender neck and the delicacy of her chin. She was wearing a denim skirt and a blouse of blue polyester that was trying to pass itself off as silk. Her young man looked red, beefy—lanky, and therefore not even prime beef. He hung back a half step behind her. Victor rose so they could see him. There was a delicious tremor in the backs of his knees. Emily waved. They approached.

Introductions and orders for drinks. A glass of white wine for Emily. Bourbon for Larry. Of course, bourbon, Victor realized with satisfaction. A two-fisted bully-boy pose. He drove a taxi, didn't he? Victor could imagine him at home in one of those awful vest undershirts, a can of beer in his fist.

"I have no idea what will come of this, but at least we should have a diverting lunch," Victor said as the drinks were served. "Let's drink to that."

"Larry didn't want to come," Emily announced. It seemed a good place to begin the conversation.

"Then, why did you?" Victor asked him.

"Partly, she forced me. And I guess I was curious to see what kind of a nut you were."

"As you see, a harmless enough nut. I'm not violent, at any rate. I'll do her no physical harm. You may rest easy on that point."

"I'm resting easy, believe me. This is the dumbest thing I've ever heard of."

"Really?" Victor asked. "Perhaps it is. But that's one of the reasons it appeals to me. Isn't it something of a strain to be intelligent all the time? I'm not sure we were meant to."

"Larry went to Harvard," Emily announced.

"How nice. I went to Princeton," Victor told them, "but it isn't terminal. One recovers from either institution. Or most of us do."

"It won't work, you know. You can't get away

with this . . ." Larry glared at him.

"But I'm not trying to get away with anything. This is a fairly straightforward proposition. Proposal, actually. And it's something that Emily will have to decide for herself."

"But we all have to decide, don't we?" Larry asked. "I mean, I won't let her do it. Or if she does it, then that's it, as far as she and I are concerned."

"You won't let her?" He turned to Emily. "But you aren't married to him, are you?" he asked her. "I expect you've already discussed that aspect of it. Did you suggest he marry you?" It was a happy moment of intuition. Of course, they would have to have discussed marriage. So, no matter what happened here, at lunch, there had already been . . . a result. A resonance. He was hollering into the right cave.

"Yes," she admitted. "And he said we couldn't afford it."

"But you could. In a year, say. You could set a date now," Victor said. "I'd be agreeable."

"I don't give a damn whether you're agreeable or not. I'm disagreeable."

"Yes, I see that."

"Please, Larry. There's no point in behaving badly," Emily said.

Victor realized that she was enjoying this. He gazed at the delicate clavicles he could see at the opening of her collar.

"Would you like to see a menu?" Victor offered. "The *palourdes* are fresh."

"Palourdes?" Emily asked.

"Clams, that is," Victor explained. "It seems to me," he said to the young man, "that we ought to be able to discuss the question intelligently and reasonably. After all, it's Emily's decision."

"There isn't any question, and there's nothing to discuss," Larry insisted. He glared at Victor, who noticed that the hand on the table was clenched into a fist. Would the boy turn violent, after all?

"If I were you," Victor said, "and if I were so strenuously opposed to the idea we've met to discuss, I'd be a little less blunt about it, and perhaps a little more effective."

"Would you now?" Larry asked, glaring.

"Oh, certainly. I'd . . . I'd appear to favor the idea, even sell it hard, so that the effect would be to implant doubt rather than generate annoyance and determination. You should be telling me how grateful you are that I'll be helping to support your work. You should be telling me what a wonderful girl Emily is, and how terrific she is in bed. Is she, by the way?"

Larry took a long pull at his drink, put the glass down hard, and said to Emily, "Come on. We don't have to listen to this filth!"

"I'm not going anywhere," Emily said.

"There, now," Victor warned, "you see what you're doing? You're alienating her, which you can hardly afford to do. It's her decision, after all. If you're not careful, you'll drive her to accepting my suggestion. And you'll have only yourself to blame."

"When I want advice from you, I'll ask for it," Larry said, pushing his chair back and standing up. "I think you're sick."

"What an impoverished imagination you have," Victor taunted. He realized that Larry was unlikely to hit him, or unlikely to hit him very hard. And more important, he saw that the effect of this gaucherie was to drive Emily into a posture of apology, or even further—and better—to force her to disown the young man entirely. How very well it was working out! "Don't be such a stuffy little prig. Sit down. Have another drink. Look at the menu. Enjoy your lunch."

"I'm not having any lunch," Larry said—as Victor had known he would. "Come on," he said to Emily. "Let's get out of here."

"I said I'm having lunch with him. I'm going to stay."

Larry hesitated. It was lovely. Victor could see him struggling in the tight little corner he'd backed himself into. He could sit down and look foolish. Or he could leave and look foolish. And risk losing the girl. He started toward the door, seemed to get stuck, like a piece of machinery not quite in gear, and then lurched forward again. He turned back at the front door—realizing, perhaps, the enormity of his error and the hopelessness of his position—and then he fled.

"I'm terribly sorry," Emily said. "He didn't behave well."

"Don't worry about it," Victor assured her, smiling pleasantly. Larry had behaved perfectly. "He's a very earnest young man. One can't hold that against him."

"It can get tiresome."

"Yes, I should imagine. Perhaps this . . . arrangement might help him in other ways, too. Loosen him up, maybe? By the way, are you terrific in bed?"

"Less experienced than you might like," she

said, not blushing or making a great business out of it. "I'm not really the one to judge. I enjoy myself—or try to."

"Splendid."

"And you?" she asked. "How are you?"

"Adequate," he replied. "But it will be your task to convince me that I'm superb. That's one of the fine things about this arrangement. . . It's so wonderfully clear. We are not approaching it from a position of equality. You are getting paid in dollars. This establishes, first of all, your fundamental superiority. You have what I want. Just as the doctor or the lawyer or the actress gets paid by the patient or the client or the admiring audience, you will be paid—and while you will have superiority, I shall have the say as to how you must use it or whether it still pleases me."

"We don't have to like each other?"

"Hardly. In fact, I'd expect that any kind of real friendship would . . . would get in the way," Victor said, trying to appear relaxed and witty, not wanting to let her realize how important this moment was. If he could persuade her to this abstract and mathematical heartlessness, why, then, he could lead her almost anywhere and make her do almost anything at all.

Her dark eyes regarded him thoughtfully; he noticed that her eyebrows had not been plucked. It was difficult for him to tell how she was taking it. "Shall we order?" he invited, picking up his menu.

She picked up hers and considered the offerings. Had she accepted what he'd said?

He only wished Irene had been willing to come along to witness this. "The tripe is especially fine, if you like tripe," he told her.

"I put myself in your hands," she said, and then with a small, rather naughty smile added, "for lunch, anyway."

She ate well, which was a good sign. It was Victor's conviction that, while sex was a mystery, there were, nevertheless, reasonable clues to which perceptive investigators learned to pay attention. Prime among these was the evidence of appetite. Women who pick at their food do so, generally, out of vanity or, even worse, out of a distaste for physicality. Good eaters, on the other hand, enjoy the pleasures of the body, respond to stimuli, give themselves up a little, as Emily did, even closing her eyes to savor the intricate spiciness of the tripe. Yes, indeed, he could see her with the same heavy-lidded transport in altered circumstances. She masticated slowly and delightfully.

"Have you ever been to Hawaii?" he asked.

"Hawaii? No, why?"

"I thought we might consider our honeymoon. Where would you like to go? I thought someplace quiet, with ocean and orchids."

"I have no idea how serious you are about this," she said. "I keep thinking it's a joke, and then I keep wondering that maybe it isn't."

"And which would you like it to be?"

"I don't know. I mean. . . I thought I did. But . . . It's a terrible idea. But not such a terrible idea after all."

"I don't think it's such a terrible idea. It's . . . a *mariage de convenance*. The Europeans have been doing this sort of thing for years. It's not a bad system. Often, it works better than our love matches. There's so much less room for misunderstanding."

"But why would you want to marry me? I mean, it's very flattering, but . . . You don't know anything about me."

"No, nor do I want to know very much about you."

"But you want to marry me?"

"For a while. Why not? If you become tiresome, we'll end it. That's simple enough, isn't it?"

"And if I want to end it?"

"It ends," Victor assured her. "No strings either way. Except for the money, of course."

"Are you rich?" she asked, cocking her head to one side. Quite fetching.

"What difference does that make?" Victor countered. "I'm obviously not penniless. I couldn't be making such a proposal if I were. But beyond that, the question isn't what *I'm* worth, but what you are."

"It always costs you more at a doctor's if you're rich," she said.

"Yes, but not at a shop. I'm shopping, you see. The price at Bloomingdale's or Bonwit's doesn't go down for me and up for the Rockefellers. Or up for me and down for you. The only question is supply and demand. And value. What do you suppose you're worth?"

"What would I have to do?" she asked, with just a trace of a leer. She was bargaining with him! Casually, perhaps, and at least part in fun, but she was negotiating.

"No windows. No housework at all, as a matter of fact."

"That's a relief. Could I continue with my career?"

"I don't know. I'd have to think about that. Let's assume not. It isn't a long term arrangement, anyway. You'll be doing plenty of acting in the marriage. All kinds of performing, as far as that goes." He allowed himself more than a trace of a leer back to her, to see how she took it.

"I assumed that," she said. She thought for a moment. "Will you expect me to be faithful to you?"

"I'll expect you not to deceive me. If you want to have a fling—with Larry, say, or with anyone else—it would only be with my . . ." He was about to say knowledge, but the grammatical possibilities were better than he'd expected. ". . . permission."

"And how do I get permission?"

"Oh, I'll think of something, I'm sure."

"And of course, you won't be faithful to me. Because you're paying."

"Exactly."

"I don't know whether it sounds like a marriage or a war," she said.

"A good many marriages are wars, aren't they? Ours will be waged at least according to the Geneva Convention—or whatever convention we agree on, beforehand. It'll be rather more sporting than most."

"What kind of money are we talking about, anyway?" she asked.

It was a tricky moment, Victor realized. He could name a figure and open the bargaining, but he knew that to do that would be risky. Too high, and he'd have set up an expectation he couldn't possibly meet; too low, and he might discourage her or drive her away. "Why don't you suggest a figure," he invited.

"I haven't the vaguest idea," she said. "I have no experience in this kind of thing."

"Nor have I. Who does? We all hide such truths from ourselves most of the time. The present situation requires. . . how shall I say? A moral boldness. What would be interesting to you?"

"I don't know what to say. Ten thousand dollars?"

"A year?"

"A month?"

"Well, of course, that'd be extremely interesting. But not to me. Even if I could afford it, I wouldn't be interested. I'd have the feeling I was being taken. So, it wouldn't work out."

"I can see that," she said.

The waiter offered dessert. Victor offered Emily dessert. She said that she'd just have some coffee. Victor approved. It was gratifying that she was watching her figure. For him? No, of course not. For herself. But for his benefit, nonetheless—assuming that this deal went down. "Two coffees," he said, pleased with himself.

"But a thousand a month would be only twelve thousand dollars for a whole year. That wouldn't be enough."

"Twenty-five thousand a year, then?" Victor offered.

"Fifty?"

"Thirty."

"Thirty-six," she said. "Three thousand a month."

"Perhaps. It's a lot of money," he said. He was pleased that she bargained well. She would be challenging, like one of those spunky trout that fights all the way. It was not an impossible figure.

He looked across the table. She was leaning slightly forward, attentive, even eager. She was evidently pleased with herself and hopeful that he would agree. He was sure he had won. "What interests me as I turn it over in my mind," he said, "is that if we set a figure that's just a little on the high side, then that puts an obligation on you. To earn it. To keep me willing to pay it. At thirty-six thousand dollars a year, the temptation would be fairly strong, I'd expect, for me to terminate the arrangement sooner rather than later. You might come out with less, you realize, than at a lower figure."

"I'm willing to take that risk. It'd be part of the fun. I couldn't set too low a value on myself. You'd be bored. And so would I. There'd be no incentive for me to . . . to please."

"Yes, that's true, too. An intricate piece of business, isn't it?"

"I should hope so," she said. She took a sip of coffee and he thought she used it to hide a grin. He could see her eyes sparkling over the rim of the cup.

Excellent. Splendid. But he still wanted to claim the victory in some authoritative way, make it clear —not only to her but to himself as well—who was in control of whom, and enjoy the triumph. "As I said," he said, "I might be persuaded."

"Oh? How?"

From the way she said it, sliding each word upward an interval of a fourth, he knew that she knew it was a challenge.

"A demonstration might be persuasive," he told her.

"No, no. No free samples."

He was both pained and pleased by the adolescent vulgarity of her phrase. "The word I used was 'demonstration', remember?" He had been thinking of Irene and her ben-wah balls. And of the arrangement here, in the restaurant, with the long tablecloth and their corner table. It was not impossible. "Why don't I order a brandy? I can sip it slowly and watch, while you masturbate."

"Here?"

"Why not?"

"You're crazy."

"Perhaps. You can always refuse. Get up and leave. Forget the whole thing."

"But . . . That's sick!"

"Not really. Mildly kinky, but that's all."

"If I won't do it, then the whole deal is off?"

"I'd have my doubts about it. You're asking a lot of money. I'm entitled to ask for a lot in return. Obedience, for instance."

"I don't know," she said. She was rather pale. Had he gone too far? He didn't think so. And after all, wasn't that the point—to go too far? If Irene could do it, as a demonstration, to help him decide what his own feelings were, then she could do as much. Here, in a public place . . .

"I'll order the brandy," he said. "You think about it. If I finish the brandy and you've been unable to comply with my request, we'll say goodbye." He signaled for the waiter and put the contest into motion.

The waiter brought the coffee and a snifter of brandy. Victor took a sip, a very small sip, and put the snifter down.

"What do you get out of this?" Emily asked.

"I get to watch. To know. And to see what power I have."

"Is that exciting?"

"Oh, yes."

She shook her head. She had not yet removed her hands from the table. But she was thinking about it. Had to be thinking about it. He took another sip. And a sip of coffee. She took a sip of her coffee and then dropped one of her hands down into her lap. It was a gesture that appeared thoughtless, inadvertent. But as he'd told her, he knew. And it took some effort for him to restrain the muscles around his mouth that wanted to form a grin. But he had not yet won.

"I can't!" she said.

"Yes, you can," he said, firm but pleasant, and he took a small sip of brandy. The amber liquid was reduced now by about a quarter from its original level.

Yes, she was leaning back, slouching. But so many young people these days had deplorable posture, Victor thought. He saw the telltale motion of the muscle of her upper arm. He studied her face, trying to read the emotions through her impassive mask as she discovered that it was possible, that it was even easy. Her eyelids drooped a little. Her lips opened. The tip of her tongue flicked at the top of their cupids bow. Her color began to return to her face. The muscles in her arm moved a little more perceptibly, their rhythm accelerating.

He looked around the room. None of the other patrons of the restaurant seemed to be paying any attention. Or, no. A lean, lone man with a beard had averted his eyes. Victor looked at Emily, watching her as she brought herself further along.

She moved her left hand as if to touch her right shoulder, but Victor could see that the object of the move was to enable her to squeeze her left breast with her forearm. Victor looked back toward the man with the beard. Yes, he'd seen. He was staring.

Emily had not perceived him. Victor sat very still so as not to communicate his excitement. He could feel the weight of the man's gaze. On Emily, but on himself, too. On his neck that was tingling with warmth. He turned once more and frankly, boldly, met the man's stare.

He turned back to watch as Emily succeeded, drawing in her breath twice, sharply.

"Bravo!" he said. "A sip of brandy? I saved the last of it for you."

"Yes, thanks. I could use it."

She took the snifter and drained it. He took the glass back, took her hand, kissed her fingertips, catching a faint tang of her sex. "Suppose we meet tomorrow at my lawyer's office to work out the details. The three thousand a month will be acceptable."

Out of the corner of his eye, Victor saw the man with the beard paying his check, signing a credit card-charge slip. The man stood up, glanced at Victor, grinned, and left the restaurant.

"Do you know him?" Emily asked.

"I don't think so, no."

"What time at your lawyer's?" she asked.

"Why don't you give me a call in the morning. I'll have spoken to him by then."

"You'd better give me your phone number."

He gave her his card.

It was going to happen. It was happening.

Not because of his management or his shrewdness, or not only because of those things. What had done the trick, he realized, was the demonstration. She had earned the marriage, had won it as a prize. And having striven for it, she would accept it.

And she'd enjoyed it.

He took another sip of his coffee, waiting for his enormous erection to subside so that he could call for the check and leave the restaurant.

FIVE

He called Irene. It wasn't just to let her know the good news, but really to exploit the moment. He still had his doubts about Emily's ability to withstand the onslaughts of that hot-headed young man. Larry. He had been offended by the very lightness and heartless gaiety that Victor so much enjoyed. Of course, he had been offended. Young, serious, an earnest puritan, he had been offended, Victor knew, by the assault not on Emily's virtue but on his own sense of his self-importance. His response was unpredictable. For all Victor knew, the young man might decide to marry Emily, not because he was really ready to do so, or even because he wanted to, but just to keep her from considering Victor's proposal.

Impossible to guess the odds. Still, she had said she would do it. And until he heard differently, he could at least maintain the wonderful feeling of power, the giddy sensation of ownership of another life. And it was to gloat a little, to savor the richness of it, that he called Irene.

She invited him to come over for tea. She was, she said, curious about the financial end of it, the exact details of the arrangement. She suggested that he come by around four.

He appeared a few minutes ahead of time, so eager was he to talk about it, to get her reaction—support, amusement, or even disapproval. It didn't very much matter. Any kind of reaction would be an acknowledgement of the fact of what had happened. In the event, she was rather calm about it. "It's the most reasonable thing in the world," she said. "Of course it is. When we are young, women I mean, we are attractive but rather indifferent to the pleasures of the bed. It's a fact of nature. And the intelligent, realistic woman contrives an exchange by which she gives her favors, as they used to be called, and receives in return . . . presents, money, security. All of which she is likely to need, later on, when she is less attractive and more interested."

"That's not how she sees it, however," Victor explained. "As far as she is concerned, it's only a way to getting together a nest egg for her eventual marriage to her young man."

"Who disapproves, I take it?"

"Of course."

"And you're worried about his approval?"

"I'm worried that he may talk her out of it. That he may even marry her, in order to keep her out of my clutches."

"How unpleasant for you," she said. "To have

to endure suspense at your time of life is annoying. Tea?"

"Yes, thank you."

There was a tea already laid out, a silver service that was a little too rococo for Victor's taste, and tiny Sèvres cups that were translucent when held up to the light. "Just sugar, wasn't it?" she asked.

"That's right. One lump." He was pleased that she remembered. He had the uneasy feeling that her solicitous attention was more than mere good manners. What was she after? But she handed him the tiny cup with the strong dark tea and she smiled with a kind of confident indulgence to make him doubt his doubt. She was playing Lady Melbourne to his Byron, coaching from the sidelines, as good players who were graceful enough or lucky enough eventually got to do.

"They win in the end, you know," she said. "The young always win. Which is as good a reason as any for us to despise them."

"We were young, too, once," he said.

"And wasted our best chances. Didn't know what wealth we had. Threw it away."

"As they do now. So, it evens out, doesn't it?"

"Does it? I'd trade places with her. As you'd trade places with him."

"Would I? I doubt it. He's such a dreary fellow. And he has the most obscene red hair."

"I adore red hair on men. Not on their heads, necessarily. But . . . on men. It makes them look inflamed."

"It's only an appearance."

"Appearances count. Women understand that better than men, somehow."

He nodded agreement. It was very good tea. He took another sip and considered the plate of paper-thin butter cookies.

"Go ahead, indulge," she said.

"The cookies, you mean?"

"Yes, but by metonymy . . . the rest of it. I suppose that when we are young, the world seems messy, unpleasant. As we grow older, the alternative becomes clearer. And in the face of the void, we embrace the world. More and more ardently."

"Then you approve?"

"You need my approval?"

"I don't need it, but I do welcome it."

"You have it," she said.

"Thank you," he said. He glanced over at the rocking chair. He had her approval, but was less sure of his own. What a splendid woman she was! Richer, mellower, more generous than the girl, she was like a grand cru wine that had aged to perfection, with a subtlety and a depth that ought to have attracted him far more than Emily's raw Beaujolais bite. And what they had been through together!

He thought back to the time they had been in Palm Beach, rather late in the season, and had been bored. Restless. And a little antagonistic toward each other, for each was convinced that the other had grown tiresome and indifferent. All that sunshine and fresh air had become wearisome. They had invented an adventure, a challenge. They booked rooms on a cruise ship out of Port Everglades to the islands, one of the less splendid ships, and one of the shorter cruises. A five-day spin around the Carribean. On the first night out, each would indicate to the other an appropriate sexual target.

The devising of the adventure had been as much fun as the adventure itself. They had developed elaborate rules, so that each reserved up to three vetoes, lest the other select a target too repellent or too difficult. Of the four nights out, they had agreed that the first would be spent together, scouting the territory and making the selections for the other's attention. Then there were to be three contests, one on each night. And the winner of the greatest number was to pay for both of them. A nice sporting arrangement.

Victor had assumed that Irene would win, and she had won, easily. He had had, nevertheless, the satisfaction of picking out her bed-mates. And then, on the following night, pointing her at a new male, while the old nosed after her like a lovelorn hound, eager for more and entirely unaware that his success the night before and his present failure were both the whim of a stranger who sat, like a god, on a barstool, smiling over his rum punch.

He had pointed Irene at a pink-faced, rather chubby Kiwanian from Omaha, with whom she had scored easily. She had set him at a high school librarian from Cape Cod. He had bought the librarian a drink, then another five, and they had talked about books. Late in the evening, with no hope whatever of success, considering what a prim little dear she was, and having decided that he could have exercised one of his vetoes, he invited her to his cabin. "I thought you'd never ask," she had replied, and they had fucked each other's brains out. She had been insatiable, blowing him up and then polishing him off four times before they fell asleep. She saved her money all year for this five day cruise, she had said. He'd understood why.

The next day at lunch, he had pointed Irene at an automobile salesman from Yonkers. She had pointed him at a widow from Sacramento, a little long in the tooth, perhaps, but not at all repulsive. Irene had succeeded within an hour. Victor had failed, miserably. She liked to drink, eat, dance, and flirt—but that was all. He had danced with her until three in the morning, making his moves, and having her laugh them off. And then she had disappeared. For her beauty sleep. Victor had gone to his cabin alone, had imagined Irene banging the automobile salesman on all cylinders. . . Had thought of going to look for the librarian, but . . . at three thirty in the morning? He'd gone to sleep, quite sorry for himself.

And of course, he'd been wrong. The automobile salesman had been damned near impotent, so that Irene had had to blow him until the muscles of her cheeks and tongue were aching, not so much for the sake of the poor limp salesman as for his, for Victor's sake, and for the sake of their bargain. She'd managed to get him started, not hard yet, but with a little heft, and had been working him up toward intromission when he'd come, leaving her untouched and unsatisfied, and with a wheaten taste in her mouth.

Very funny. Victor had listened to her account and had complimented her on the victory, for she had all but won the bet. They had agreed to try a new game. All afternoon, on the afterdeck, they had sat together, plotting like novelists or playwrights, trying to find the right kind of entertaining outrageousness. She had been the one to suggest, at last, that she retire to her cabin after . . . say, nine o'clock. And that he should then cruise the ship, looking not for a woman for himself, but a man for her.

"What?"

"Why not?"

"What do I tell him?"

"Say it's a bet. Say it's a peculiarity of your traveling companion, that she likes novelty and anonymity."

"I suppose," he had replied. "And you'll just wait there in your cabin?"

"Yes. Imagining. I'm sure that will be the best part of the evening. The anticipation. The uncertainty. The realization that at any moment, there will be a knock on the door and . . . and someone will come in to fuck me."

And, indeed, she had been right. The anticipation, not only in the room, alone, but all that afternoon and evening, had been delicious. And they had been occupied themselves, for the cocktail hour, in his cabin, celebrating in advance.

She refilled his cup. "You seem rather pensive."

"I was remembering our cruise," he told her.

"Oh, that. Yes," she said, waving her hand in an airy gesture. "I'm not sure I'm up to that kind of thing any more."

"You're not? Then what was all that talk about embracing the world?"

"There are all kinds of embraces," she reminded him.

He told her about the lunch. Even if she vouldn't—or couldn't—participate actively, she ould still listen. He described Larry's clumsiness, is own cleverness, Emily's responses to both, and he results. "What finally happened is that we got lown to actual bargaining. We settled on three housand a month."

"That's rather expensive, isn't it? You could get hundred-dollar-a-night call girl every night for hat."

"I could. If that were the point. But it isn't just he sex. It's the power. At the end of the lunch, I ad her demonstrate her pliability. I got the idea rom you."

"You had her bring herself off?"

"While I sat there having a brandy. It was lovely."

"Still, are you sure you can afford her at those ates?"

"I'm sure I can't. But that's built into the ar- angement. It's up to her to keep me fascinated. Vhen I get bored, the relationship ends. Like hat." He executed a fillip with his fingers.

"I see. But the young man is a difficulty?"

"I don't know. He could be. He's . . . terribly arnest. Attractive in his way. He looks like a hortstop."

"How do shortstops look?"

"All wiry and energetic."

"Would you like for me to talk to him?"

"No, I don't think so. It's up to her, really."

"But what if she decides to marry you? What hen? In six months, or even less, you'll tire of her r you'll feel that you've had your money's orth."

"That's her problem. And his."

"You don't think I could help?"

"No."

"They're living together?"

"Oh, yes. That's what bothers him most, I think. He has this proprietary feeling, and I'm offending it by poaching. I guess I am."

"It's a dangerous game, you realize."

"There's a certain amoung of danger in any game."

"Well, good luck to you."

"Thanks," he said. He took a butter cookie.

After he'd left, she considered what he had told her. It was touching, this enthusiasm of his. But she had the feeling that he could get himself into rather more trouble than he seemed to realize—and that it was in some small measure her fault. If only she had called him a week earlier! She had waited just a little longer than she should have, and he'd gone gaga over this young girl. It would serve him right, of course, if she simply let him screw it all up. But he was a friend and she felt . . . kindly? Or jealous? Oh, perhaps a little of each. He had declined her offer of help. Of course. But . . .

It was an extremely unlikely situation. And she was curious about it. But even more important, she had figured out what to say to this young man—that she was interested in Victor, and that therefore she was as much opposed to this liaison as he was. They were natural allies.

Victor had refused to give her the phone number. And she had been unwilling to press him. Still, he'd said the girl was living with the young man. And the girl's telephone number was available. Ormsby would have it.

She called Ormsby, having devised a story which, in the event, she didn't need. Ormsby was out. His secretary was in. Would he be so kind as to give the name and telephone number of the girl who had sung at the backer's audition . . . ?

No problem.

Not surprisingly, Larry was furious. He had been humiliated and betrayed at the restaurant, and he was not disposed to listen to reasons, arguments, or anything but apologies and declarations of regret and adoration. Which he felt he deserved. That he was powerless to extort such declarations from Emily only infuriated him further. She came sweeping into the apartment hours later, all gaiety and smiles, to announce with some smugness that she'd been offered thirty-six thousand dollars to marry Mr. Edmunds for one year.

"And?"

"And? I'm thinking about it. What do you think I should do?"

"I don't know. I know what you should have done. You should have left the restaurant with me. You should have slapped his face. You should have done anything at all but sit there and gobble it up like so much tripe. . ."

"That's funny. That's what we had. It was very good."

"I don't know what to do. I thought of calling your mother in Ohio. . ."

"Oh? To tell her what? That a man has proposed to me? She'd be delighted. She didn't ever approve of our living together. She doesn't really approve of you. She'd be tickled pink!"

"That's why I didn't call. But . . . Jesus!"

"I don't see anything wrong with it."

"That's what gets me! That's what really gets me. I don't know. Maybe you should go ahead. Maybe we're through. I thought I knew you . . ."

"And I thought I knew you."

And so on. The words broke in waves on the rocks of their stubborn pride. The tide went out for a while, as they subsided into a quiet resentment, but came in again to splash and batter. He accused her of being a whore. She accused him of being a hypocrite. He accused Edmunds of being a pervert. She accused Larry of being just as perverted as anyone, but unwilling to admit it. The reference was to his fondness for hand-jobs in public places —through the convenient slits in his London Fog pockets.

There was no particular logic to the cross-currents of reproach and abuse. Indeed, during one of the bitterest moments he proposed, as she had expected all along that he would do. She asked him what they would live on.

"What we're living on now."

"Then why didn't we get married a year ago? You're admitting that the whole thing has been a lack of confidence or trust or love or whatever. That all your talk about a sound financial position has been . . . just so much bullshit."

"Maybe. Maybe it was. Maybe I see things better now."

"Well, maybe I see things better now, too. Better than you do."

"Will you marry me? Tomorrow?"

"Let me think about it."

"What's to think about?"

"I don't know. What is there ever to think about? Where would we go for our honeymoon. Victor has offered Hawaii."

"Oh, fuck him!"

"I very well may."

And again, they raged. It was at the peak of this turbulence that the telephone rang. Emily went to answer it. Larry, suddenly convinced that it was Victor Edmunds, intercepted her, grabbed the instrument, and snapped, "Hello?"

"Is this Larry Andrews?" a female voice asked.

"Yes. Who's this?"

It was Irene, of course. She explained that she was a friend of Victor Edmunds. . .

"I've got nothing to say to him. Or to any friend of his."

He very nearly hung up on her, but she persuaded him to listen for a moment more. There were things for them to discuss. She was against the marriage. She was sure that he, too, was opposed to it.

"Yes. I am."

"I see. Can you talk?" she asked.

"Not really, no," he said, not looking at Emily and proud of himself for his restraint.

"I think, then, that we ought to meet. As soon as possible."

"All right," he said.

"This evening?"

He agreed to meet her in an hour. At her apartment. She gave him the address.

"I'll be there," he promised.

He hung up. Emily asked who it was.

"None of your business. I'm going out."

"At this hour? What about dinner?"

"What about dinner? You're hungry, eat. I'm not hungry."

"And you won't tell me where you're going?"

"What do you care. Maybe I'm going out to get laid!"

"Have fun," she said.

SIX

They did not immediately hit it off.

Larry had not yet taken the seat Irene had offered, had hardly passed through the archway into the living room, when he blurted out, "Your friend, Mr. Edmunds, is a real creep."

"My friend, Victor, is a man of considerable charm and attainments. From what I understand, your friend, Miss Howland, is not beyond criticism. Nevertheless, we are both distressed by the prospect of their marriage—although our reasons are likely to be quite different. I do wish you were a little more . . . intelligent. Don't just stand there like a lunk—which is what Victor called you. Sit down. A drink? I think we could use one."

He sat. "Yes," he said. "Thank you, I'd like a drink."

"That's better. Scotch?"

"Please."

"You know," she said, going to the sideboard where an assortment of bottles stood on a large silver tray, "you handled that luncheon rather badly."

"I was angry."

"I can understand that. I'm . . . rather displeased, myself. Still, it is at moments of displeasure that one needs one's wits. Any fool can respond properly when he's happy. Soda?"

"Just ice, thank you."

"Good for you. You've talked to Emily since the lunch?"

"All afternoon."

"And what is she likely to do?"

"I have no idea. She can't possibly be serious about this. It's . . . it's just crazy."

"People do crazy things all the time. You didn't forbid her to do it, did you?"

"Yes, I did."

"Wonderful. The worst possible thing to do. You've made it a matter of principle, don't you see? Her preferences would have been—let us assume—to remain with you. But you've made it a question of independence. Of honor. You're driving her into his arms."

"What was I supposed to do? Approve?"

"Not necessarily. You could have been amused, perhaps. Or supportive. 'Anything you like, my dear, and I'll still love you.' Why couldn't you have said that?" She handed him a tumbler half-full of whiskey.

"I don't know. It didn't occur to me. I was angry. And frightened a little."

"I see," she said. She saw that he was attractive in a raw way. He had a rich baritone voice, and his speech patterns were interestingly overlaid, a veneer of Harvard over something far more modest that occasionally showed itself like the sinews under smooth skin in a moment of stress. He was perceptive enough, if a little clumsy. But he had good hands, which excused a lot. They were powerful looking, with the bones of the wrists protruding well, and large broad fingers. Irene knew that the correlation between the size and shape of the fingers and of the cock was not always absolutely reliable, but it was promising.

The thought had been in the back of her mind, as a mathematical possibility, a way of getting even with Victor, but that had been before. Now that he was here in the flesh, she thought about it again, more concretely. Did she want to take him on for a while? "Perhaps it isn't altogether your fault," she said, seating herself on a nearby chair. "Young men simply don't have these skills. I don't know why, but you aren't taught the first thing about handling women. Young women, on the other hand, are taught a great deal about how to deal with men. Or seem, somehow, to learn it."

"What should I do then?"

"I'm trying to think. You left angry?"

"I'm afraid so."

"Well, that may not be so bad. It shows that you care at any rate. In the wrong way, no doubt. Oppressively. Suffocatingly. But you care. Which is what she wants to know."

"I do care. She's a wonderful girl!"

"My guess is that she's a perfectly ordinary little girl. But she's young. And so are you. It amounts to the same thing, I imagine."

"What same thing?"

"Wonderfulness," Irene said, raising her eyes to the ceiling. "Perhaps if you were to go back and say that you've changed your mind. . ."

"She wouldn't believe me."

"Be convincing."

"How?"

"You always tell the truth? You rely on absolute sincerity all the time? How very tiresome!"

"It works."

"It has worked so far for you. And not very well, lately, it would appear."

"That's not my fault. It's hers."

"Ah, I see. *Now* you're making it a matter of principle. Splendid. You'll throw her out, which is what you want least in the world to do. And she'll go, which may not be what she wants to do. All for principle!"

"All right. I'm willing to say anything. But she won't believe it. It isn't my style."

"Then make it bigger. Be even more aggressive," she said. She stopped, thought for a while, looked at him appraisingly, and suggested, "You could say you came over here to talk this problem over with me, which is true, and that . . . we decided it was a fine idea. Fine for them, and fine for us, too. That will put the shoe on the other foot."

"What shoe? What foot? I don't quite see it."

"You're being either very dense or very rude, young man. You might tell her that you and I are going to be married, too. The same arrangement as Victor proposed to her. The same terms, exactly. And that will mean that at the end of the year, you'll have twice as much for your nest egg."

"Us? Get married? But I . . . We don't know each other at all!"

"And they do?"

"No, but. . ."

"But?"

"She just wouldn't believe it."

"You believed it readily enough, when she told you she was thinking of marrying Victor."

"That's different. He's an older man. Older men and younger women get married all the time."

"And so do older women and younger men. We fit together better, anyway."

"Fit? How do you mean?"

"Sexually, of course. You were at your sexual peak some years ago, when you were in your late teens. I'm at mine, right now. You are still more active than you will ever be again. There is a nice symmetry to it . . ."

She broke off. He had begun to see what she was getting at. He was slow, but he got there. She could see him staring at her, not at her argument but at her body, frankly appraising it, as one looks at bijoux in a jeweler's case. She could feel his eyes upon her. He shifted in his chair and took a bit of whiskey. She could feel her nipples coming erect.

"You see?" she prompted.

He blushed. "But what if . . . what if she approves? What if she goes ahead?"

"We don't know what she'll say, do we? My guess is that if there isn't any silly squabble going on between the two of you about self-determination and other such distracting questions, she may come to her senses. She may decide to refuse Victor after all. Which is what we both want. Tell me, have you never been unfaithful to her?"

"You mean, since we've been living together?"

"Whenever. Haven't you?"

"Well, once or twice. I don't think she ever knew."

"So it's possible. She'll believe you."

"Why are you doing all this? I still don't quite get it."

"I've told you. Victor is a friend of mine. A dear friend. I hate to see him making an ass of himself."

"Why is he making an ass of himself? I have the feeling he's making an ass of everyone else."

"It all depends on one's point of view, I suppose. I thought you were opposed to the marriage."

"I was. I am."

"Then be so good as to believe that I am also opposed to it. And the enemy of your enemy is your friend, as the Arabs say."

"Do they say that?"

"I'm not sure. I've never met an Arab. They are said to say such things. What difference does it make?"

"None, I guess."

"I think I'll have one myself," Irene said. She went to get herself a drink.

"Maybe I should just call him up. Or go see him. Threaten to beat the shit out of him. . ."

"He'd have you arrested for assault."

"Not actually do it," Larry hastened to add.

"That's assault. If you actually did it, that would be battery. Don't you do crossword puzzles?"

"No."

"No wonder you know so little."

He laughed. It was the first evidence he had given of being civilized.

"You think this will really work?"

"I don't know. I've never met the young lady. But I'll tell you this, no matter what happens, this way you'll be able to retain a minimal dignity, which is something. If she goes ahead and they actually get married, you'll be better fixed to welcome her back, if that's what you want to do."

"It's crazy. I don't know what I'd do."

"Then you don't want to close out any options, do you?"

"I guess not," he admitted. He drained his drink, looked around for a coaster, and put his empty glass down on it. That was the second encouraging demonstration. At least, she thought, he's housebroken. One could no longer be sure even of that much.

If she was successful . . . But then, she was playing a double game in which success was twice as difficult to measure as it would ordinarily have been. Figure that her advice backfired—as it was intended to do—and that the marriage took place. Victor would then be grateful to her. More important, there would be a renewal of their old intimacy of conspiratorial companionship, which might well outlast the brief marriage to the young snit. Or, on the other hand, if her suggestion actually worked and Larry was able to use it to prevent the marriage? If she worked it right, Victor would still be grateful for her efforts, even though they had failed.

Larry had been thinking, too. "If they get married, would we . . . have to get married, too?"

"We? We don't *have* to do anything," she said.

"Good. I don't think it would work."

"Work? You still don't understand, do you? Victor doesn't expect the marriage to work. It is intended to fail. It's like one of those Tinguely sculptures. It's supposed to destroy itself. He is bored, that's all. He is looking to be amused. And he must find something appealing about her. Her youth, I expect. That could be prettiness, or innocence, or, for all I know, her clumsiness."

"Now, wait a minute!"

"I've never met the girl. I'm not endorsing any of this. I'm only speculating on what Victor may be thinking."

"I guess."

"You have to guess what she's thinking and address yourself to that. Clearly, what you've been doing and saying so far has not been perfectly calculated."

"I hate calculation. I don't see that there should be any need for it between people who love each other."

"Indeed? Then call it attentiveness. Or consideration. You are selfish and lazy if you won't try to do that much for someone you care about. What arrogance!"

"Maybe. It's . . . complicated."

"Yes, it is. And it deserves our best attention, don't you think?"

He nodded.

"All right, then. You go back to her and you tell her that you approve of whatever she does. And let her know that we're considering the same kind of marriage. That's not stretching the truth very far. 'Considering' covers a lot of ground. See what she says. . . or, no, more than that, how she reacts. She may not come out and say what she thinks. You have to learn to read what people think."

"I'll try."

"Call me tomorrow and let me know how it went."

"I will. And . . . thank you."

"Don't. Don't suppose I've done any of this for you. Because I haven't. I have my own agenda."

She had thus given him fair warning. Which of course, she knew he would ignore.

She called Victor almost immediately. He was surprised. Annoyed that she had ignored his refusal of her offer of help. But still, he was pleased that she had maneuvered Larry around so that he might stop voicing such strenuous objections to Emily. He had to admit a grudging admiration for Irene's shrewdness.

"If that's what you want, it's not so difficult to arrange," she said. "I just wish you were . . . Oh, Victor! Aren't you wasting your time? And what have we got left but time?"

"But that's the point," he answered. "You know that, and I know it. But they don't, those two. And what I'm buying from them is time. I feel quite the con-man. Knowing makes all the difference."

"I suppose," she said. "Now, mind you, I can guess what he'll do and say. I can't speak about her. I've never seen her. I've no idea how his approval will affect her."

"I think it's just what she dreads hearing. Which means," he said, "that she'll believe it. Rely on it."

"And what will I tell him then?"

"Tell him anything you like. Whatever amuses you."

"I haven't decided what that ought to be," she said.

"Something will occur to you, I have no doubt."

She said goodbye and hung up. She thought about Larry, about his hands, particularly. Had she been lying to him or to herself? Would she be amused?

For a week, perhaps. He looked as though he could get a job in Rockefeller Plaza. As a fountain.

Larry walked. Inasmuch as he was not suicidal, he did not cross Central Park but went south, crossed to the west side at Central Park South, and then turned north along Broadway. It took him the better part of an hour, but he used the time to think, to consider what he wanted and what he should do. There were hookers to turn down—politely, for they could turn nasty and attack, as he had read from time to time in the newspapers. There were panhandlers. There were queers cruising at Seventy-ninth, and vague, blank stares of druggies waiting to score. A siren wailed. A few blocks later, a burglar alarm rang its long angry bleat into the night. Larry saw three young blacks running. Away from the siren? From the alarm? More likely, to or from some other nasty business.

In an odd way, the seaminess and the threats of the city reassured him. At least, there was a kind of perspective. What did it matter what he did? How seriously could he rely on a closed reasonable world of causes and effects? By the time he got to the apartment, if he was not calm he was at least jangled into a diffuse uncritical state that is the city-dweller's substitute for tranquility.

"Well?" Emily asked, when he came into the bedroom. "How was it?" She was lying on the bed, wearing one of his large rugby shirts as a nightgown and sewing, repairing a buttonhole that she had been meaning to get to for some time now.

"How was what?"

"You said you were going out to get laid, remember?" It was a joke. She was smiling. Teasing him.

"I didn't. I went to talk to a friend of Victor Edmunds, actually."

"What?"

"She was the one who'd called. We had a good talk."

"What about?"

"About . . . the proposal," Larry said. "I was wrong. It's . . . it's up to you, really. It's your decision. I see that now."

"What did she say to you?"

"That's not important. Or, I don't know. . . Maybe it is. She said I'd been handling it all wrong."

"That's certainly true. But how did she convince you?" Emily asked. "Your mind isn't easy to change."

"She suggested the same kind of arrangement. For us. I mean, for her and me. If you marry Edmunds, that is. I could marry her. We'd have twice as much money at the end of the year. We could go off to Europe. Or Mexico. Someplace pleasant and cheap. A Greek island, maybe. I could write. We could buy ourselves a lot of time."

"And you agreed?"

"No. I. . . I said it was up to you. If you go ahead with this, then I'll consider it. That's what I told her. But if you don't, I certainly won't."

"And what do you want to do?"

"What do *you* want to do?"

And around and around.

It was too easy, Emily thought. It was a trick, a

ploy. Or, if he was really giving in, then he didn't want to marry her. Which meant, she realized, that she knew what she wanted. She should marry Victor. She wanted Larry to pine, to realize how much he adored her and how much he needed her. And to be not only willing but eager to take her back afterwards. And grateful. Yes, and Victor, too, would become her devoted servant so that, later on, he would be a friend. Not jealous of Larry, but still affectionate toward her. And carefully hoarding his memories of their short months together under the palm trees of Hawaii. . .

"What's she like?" she asked Larry. "What's this friend of Victor's like?"

"A tough old bitch," Larry said. "Not bad looking in a museum-y kind of way. But . . . tough."

"You find her attractive?"

"She must be forty years old!"

"And Marlene Dietrich is seventy. Is she attractive?"

"I guess. Not a knock-out, but okay."

"You don't really want to marry her, do you?"

"It'd be easier than robbing banks. Where else am I going to get money?"

"Robbing banks might be easier. For you. You're too proud."

"What do you mean?"

"You wouldn't like it."

"You're jealous?"

"No, I'm just telling you what's obvious. You'd hate it. You wouldn't last a month."

"You want to bet?"

"It *is* a bet. The whole ting is a bet. It's set up that way. I don't know whether I can win or not. But I know you can't."

"I don't know what you're talking about."

"At the restaurant," she said, "after you left, and after we'd eaten lunch, when we were having coffee . . ."

"Yes?"

She told him how they had been bargaining and how Victor had challenged her to masturbate, right there in the restaurant. And that she had. She'd done it. "But *you* couldn't do a thing like that! You'd get angry. You'd . . . I don't know what you'd do."

"I don't believe you," he told her.

"That's up to you. It happened. If you don't want to believe it . . . that's your business."

"It doesn't make any sense. Why would you have done a thing like that?"

"To amuse him. To amuse myself. To get what I wanted. We were haggling over money."

"It doesn't figure."

"Yes, it does. It's a power. I had it. I used it."

"He had it. He used it."

"No, all he had was money."

"Money is power," Larry insisted. "You use it to get people to do what you want."

"I had something he wanted, and I'm getting money from him. Who had the power?"

"Did you really? Do it, I mean?"

"Yes."

"Right there in the restaurant?"

"It was a corner table. There was a tablecloth that came way down. Nobody could see me."

"But . . . what did he get out of it?"

"He got to watch me. It was a trip. What do you get out of hearing about it?"

"What do I get? Nothing. What do you mean?"

"You've got a hard on. I can see it."

"Do I? I guess I do."

"So, who has the power?" she asked.

He took a step toward the bed.

"No," she said. "Sit down. Over there."

"What the hell is the point?" he asked.

She pulled the rugby shirt up to her navel and spread her legs. "He couldn't really see . . . only my face. . .he had to imagine it." She was touching herself lightly, making a series of circles that brushed her labia, opening them slightly. "Did she give you a short-arms inspection? Make you show it to her?"

"No, nothing like that."

"She kiss you? Touch you?"

She shook his head.

"She let you touch her?"

He shook his head, no.

"What was she wearing?" Emily asked. She put her finger in her mouth to wet it with spit and then touched her clit with it.

"Some kind of . . . I don't know. It was a robe, or a housecoat. Chinese, with embroidery on it."

"But you could see her legs?"

"Oh, every now and then?"

"How high up?"

"Only to the knees. . . What the hell are you doing?"

"You like it?"

"It's driving me nuts!"

"Lover's nuts?"

"In a few minutes, I wouldn't be at all surprised . . ."

"You want to fuck me?"

He nodded.

"Then tell me the truth. You really didn't go to see her did you?"

"Yes, I did."

"But she didn't really say anything about getting married, did she?" She was sticking her finger into her cunt now, and showing Larry what he was missing with each stroke.

"She did. I swear!"

The telephone rang. "I'll get it," Emily said. "You stay there."

She picked up the phone. It was Victor. He wanted to know if she could meet him at nine in the morning at his lawyer's.

"Nine is fine," she said, holding the phone with one hand and playing with herself with the other.

She listened to Larry's breathing, to the faint sucking sounds of her cunt and her finger . . .

"Are you there?" Victor asked.

"Yes, I'm here."

"You've had a long, lovely, langorous evening, balling each other goodbye?"

"Oh, yes. What else?"

"Enjoy!" he said. And hung up. She heard the dial tone hum into the receiver.

"You want me to fuck him while we talk on the phone? You're kidding!" she said. "No, I don't think he'd do that." And then to Larry, she asked, "Would you do that?"

"Are you out of your mind?" he asked. He came to the bed, grabbed the phone, heard the dial tone, and slammed the phone down on its cradle.

"What was the point of that?" he demanded.

"It turned you on, didn't it?"

"It turned me off!"

She reached out toward him, grabbed his belt

with one hand and with the other felt his tumescent penis. "Some turn off!"

"Let go of me! Are you going to meet him? At nine in the morning?"

She nodded.

"You're going through with it?"

"And you?"

"Yes, damn you!"

He pulled his green velour shirt over his head and unbuckled his trousers. He kicked his shoes off, dropped his pants, and stepped out of them. "You know what you're doing?" Larry asked. "You're risking everything we have together."

She gazed up at his reddened cock and the coppery pubic hair that made it seem even redder and angrier. "If we can't risk it, then it's no good, is it?"

"That's bullshit," he said.

He was angry, hurt, confused, and a better fuck than he'd been in six months.

SEVEN

Gaity and a giddy feeling of adventure. Of breaking new ground. Bright sunlight streamed in through the floor-to-ceiling plate-glass window, and below, the city gleamed. "Masters of all we survey," Victor said, looking down. "There's just a hint of megalomania in your view here."

"It's good for business," George Kern said. "Coffee?"

"Please," Emily said.

"Yes, thanks," Victor said, turning away from the high window and taking a seat at the massive mahogany conference table.

Kern pushed a button on the intercom and ordered coffee for three. Then, to Victor and Emily, he explained, "I've been doing some reading on this since last night, when Victor called me. And it's rather interesting. The business of marriage contracts is very old. Older, actually, than the present practice of what I suppose we ought to call love-marriages. What makes this a novelty is the face that the divorce laws have changed."

"Yes, yes, we understand all that. I thought it all up, remember?" Victor observed.

Kern's girl brought in a tray with coffee and modish Dansk stoneware cups and saucers. Brewed coffee and actual cream. She served them all and retired. The got down to business.

Three thousand a month. Food, clothing, transportation, medical and dental care—all to be paid by the husband. Phone calls? Credit? Charge accounts? "We exclude all that?" Kern asked. "Otherwise, under the law, the husband is responsible for the debts of the wife."

"Exclude it. What I give her, I give. Whatever else she wants, she can pay for."

"That's not very friendly, is it?" Emily asked.

"None of this is friendly. It's a business arrangement. What's to prevent you from buying Larry half a dozen Dunhill suits?"

"Do they make suits? I thought they sold cigars."

"That's another Dunhill. Or a car. You could buy him a car. . . You can, if you want to, but you pay for it."

"Who is Larry?" Kern asked.

"Her fiancé," Victor explained, pleased with himself.

Kern's eyebrows shot up and then lowered. He didn't say a word.

Emily, perhaps sensing Victor's satisfaction and seeing in it an opportunity, asked, "What about time off? Do I get any time to myself?"

"In a marriage? What kind of time off?"

"Time to be alone."

"Alone, perhaps. With Larry? I shouldn't think so."

"That would be adultery," Kern pointed out. "But then, it doesn't matter. You are agreeing, as I understand it, to divorce on demand from either party."

"What are you saying, George?" Victor asked.

"That both of you are on your own. Or each of you is. Whatever you can stand, and whatever she can stand . . . those are the rules. The only rules. You can even set out these limitations on spending, and all that kind of financial detail; but it only means what you want it to mean. You want to give her a present? Nothing stops you. If she feels on balance that you're not being fair or generous, she can walk out at any time. Nothing stops her."

"Still, we can set our expectations down. . ."

"Oh, yes. You can do that. And the waivers of claims for alimony and . . ."

"And?" Victor asked.

"Child support? What about children?"

"I've had a vasectomy. There will be no children. Or, if there are, they won't be mine."

"That's clear enough. And a waiver on any claims on your estate?"

"Essential, yes."

"I agree to that. I know what that's about. He doesn't want to set it up so it's profitable for me to kill him. Isn't that swell?" Emily asked.

"Yes, that's swell," Kern said, dryly. Victor was amused to find that Emily was oblivious to Kern's humor.

"Any other job has a vacation, though," Emily said, bringing them back to the subject. "I don't think it's an unreasonable request."

"All right. Two weeks with pay. At the end of the first year."

"Prorated? So that at the end of six months, I'd have one week?"

"No. If it lasts a year, you get two weeks," Victor said.

"All right," she decided. "But what about the actual payments?"

"The first day of each month, for the month before?" Victor proposed.

"Fine."

"We'd better call it 'an allowance' in the document. That way, we avoid problems with taxes. It isn't actually income if a husband gives money to a wife ordinarily. We wouldn't want to lose that advantage."

"That's fine," Emily said. Victor agreed.

"All right, then. Have we left anything out?"

"Not that I can think of," Victor said.

"Do you understand that you're waiving these rights?" Kern asked Emily.

"Oh, yes."

"And other rights as well, just by getting married. You can't bring an action for . . . for rape, for example. Or kidnapping. Or indecent assault. Not against a husband."

"I understand." A faint shadow crossed her face. "If I hate it, I can always leave, can't I?" she asked.

"Oh, yes. We can put in language to that effect."

"How long will it take to draw this up?" Victor asked.

"When are you thinking of getting married? It takes three days in New York to get the blood test and the license. Or, I suppose, you could go down to Maryland. You can get married there on demand. Elkton, or wherever. The first town you get to over the Delaware line."

"Can you have the papers ready today?"

"Oh, I guess so. Late this afternoon?"

"Today?" Emily asked.

"Why not?"

"I don't know. I . . . I thought I'd have a few days yet."

"You don't want to go through with it?"

She thought for a moment.

"What if . . . what if it only lasts a week?"

"Suppose we prorate the month to a daily rate. Would that suit you?" Victor suggested.

"A daily rate?" she asked.

"Payments to end on the day you leave. Or the day I throw you out," Victor said. "I don't want to have to pay you for all the time it takes to get through the court system for the divorce."

"All right. That's fair."

"We can spend the afternoon shopping. And at the travel agent. You want to go to Hawaii, don't you?"

"Don't push her so hard," Kern warned. "It's up to you. Shall I draw up the papers?"

She nodded. "Yes," she said. "Go ahead."

"If you can be back here around . . . say, five? I can have them ready for signature."

"We'll see you at five. Come on," Victor said. "Let's go to Tiffany's."

"Tiffany's? Wow!"

"They have the cheapest gold bands of any place in New York," Victor explained.

If she was disappointed, she did a fine job of hiding it. Pride, Victor supposed. It was fine with him.

Pride was a tricky thing. It could cut both ways.

"It should be interesting," he said to Kern.

"I have no doubt. I wish you both luck," Kern said.

"Thanks for the coffee," Emily said.

Luck? What had luck to do with it? If there was any luck to it, Victor thought, it was in having thought of the experiment in the first place. But the terms of the investigation were increasingly clear. How far could he push her and how much would she tolerate? Where was the line that showed the demarcation between greed and revulsion? Or better yet, by what strategies and repeated assaults could he contrive to move that line? Ideally, she would be a moral Galatea of absolute corruption by the time he was through with her. And she'd be considerably better off than she was at the moment he'd discovered her.

She wanted to go back to her apartment to collect a few things. He persuaded her that that could all wait until tomorrow. They had things to do, shopping, lunch, the signing of the papers, and then a long drive to Maryland. They'd be back in New York by midday tomorrow. She could pick up what she needed then. He didn't want to give her the chance to change her mind, or Larry the occasion for a terrible scene.

"All right," she agreed. "I guess so. I can pick up a toothbrush, I guess."

Hygiene! How touching! But he said nothing. He took her, instead, to Tiffany's, where they found a wedding band for her. "The cheapest wedding band in the store," Victor asked for, and there was one at $49.00 plus tax, a thin, gold circlet.

"For the young lady?" the saleswoman asked.

Victor nodded.

"Good, then we can get the fit right."

Emily held out her hand. The saleswoman tried a series of sizer-rings on her fourth finger, found the right ring, and then produced one in gold from the case. She put into a little box. Victor paid for it, accepted the box, tucked it into his pocket, and led Emily out to Fifty-seventh Street.

"She had no idea whether you were my father or the groom or the groom's father or what," Emily said when they were out on the street.

"I know," Victor said.

"I was going to make some reference that would explain it, but . . . I thought I'd leave that to you."

"Quite right," he said, careful not to show his pleasure. She might begin to presume . . .

She didn't ask where they were going. She just followed along as they crossed Madison and Park. He turned north on Lexington and led her to Bloomingdale's. To the lingerie department.

"May I help you?" a rather severe saleswoman inquired.

"I'd like to see some negligees," Victor said. "In her size." He glanced to his left. No reaction. No show of embarrassment. A touch of defiance? Yes, all very well. "Something sexy," Victor said.

"Yes, of course," the saleswoman said. "This way, please?" She'd seen such couples often enough before, Victor was certain.

The designers of undergarments seemed to have anticipated his requirements exactly. There were half a dozen nightgown and negligee combinations among which to pick, any of them suitable for a high-class Storeyville whore, or a Westport matron's fantasies. He picked a filmy black negligee and held it up.

"This one, I think."

"Would you like the gown that goes with it?" the saleswoman inquired.

"The gown? No. Whatever for?" he replied, glancing at Emily who was grinning, enjoying herself. Good for her! He paid with his charge-a-plate that actually had been Margo's.

"Thank you," she said as they left the department.

"Why? It's for me as much as for you."

"Still, I get to wear it."

"Get to? Have to!"

"All right, but I still think it's pretty," she said. "Is that okay?"

"That's permitted."

He took her to lunch at the Côte Basque. She was quiet, but that was understandable. She knew how to eat, at least, and Victor thought that was a good sign. She'd been socialized if not actually civilized. And she enjoyed her food.

"Having second thoughts?" he asked over coffee.

"No, not really. I'm still busy with first thoughts, trying to . . . you know, understand that it's happening."

"Try not to say, 'you know'."

"Sorry."

"There's nothing wrong with pausing to think. Filling up the pauses with meaningless static is . . . unattractive."

"Noted."

"Good."

"Are we really going to Hawaii?"

"Why not? A trip would do me good. When we get back from today's jaunt, I'll look into it. It may take a couple of days to arrange."

"And we'll be in New York for those couple of days?"

"Yes. Why?"

"I ought to call my agent and tell him . . . not to accept jobs for me."

"That's better. The pause can be attractive, actually."

"Thank you. And I ought to call my parents."

"In Shaker Heights?" Victor asked. "There'll be plenty of time for all that. And you'll need clothes for Hawaii, I'd imagine."

"Yes, I'd imagine, too," she said, pleased.

Victor was pleased, himself. How easy it would be! And how much fun!

After lunch, they went up to Victor's apartment. Emily was impressed, pleased by its surprising mixture of heavy Victorian pieces and light Japonaiserie in the living room. There was an English dining room. The bedrooms were contemporary, with Bertoia chairs and ottomans in wire-sculptured chrome. There were greens and golds in the public rooms, light blues and white in the bedroom. The silver was Buccelatti, the crystal Baccarat, the china Lenox—all the things she had seen in display cases and vitrines. Even the bathroom was sumptuous, with a planter full of tropical plants with huge leaves, and steam-bath controls outside the enclosed tub.

Victor was in the bedroom. He'd pulled out a small suitcase and was packing a change of underwear and his toilet kit.

"I'll need a toothbrush," Emily said, "and probably some underwear. And make-up."

"We'll buy it. Here," he said. He handed her ten dollars. "There's a drugstore downstairs, a couple of doors east. Go get what you need."

"Underwear?" she asked.

"You won't need it," he said. "Not any more."

She stood there, trying to decide whether to argue. She decided not to. She went out.

He fixed himself a vermouth and soda and stretched out on the bed to sip and relax. He was delighted to discover that he had an erection, just from thinking about the girl and what they would be doing during the next twenty-four hours.

At four-thirty, they were back in Kern's office to sign the agreement in quadruplicate. One copy was for Victor, and one for the files in Kern's office. The other two were for Emily. Kern suggested that she should get a safe-deposit box and store at least one of the copies in it.

"May I leave it here with you for a day or two? When we get back from Maryland, I'll arrange all that."

"Yes, of course," Kern said.

They initialed each page and signed on the last, passing the documents back and forth.

"Is that it?" Victor asked.

"That's it," Kern said. "I hope it works out."

"No, it won't. That's what these papers are all about. I doubt if she'll ever get that end-of-the-year bonus."

"The way you talk, you make it sound like a dare," Kern said.

"Of course. That's what it is," Victor said. To

Emily, he said, "Well, let's be going. We have a long drive ahead of us."

They went back to Victor's apartment.

"Go into the bathroom," he said, "and take off your underwear."

"What?" she asked.

"You heard me."

"But why?"

"Because I told you to. Just your underwear. You can get dressed again. But with nothing underneath."

"What about . . . what about my pantyhose?"

"No. No pantyhose. Just the dress, and your shoes and that little bracelet you're wearing."

She hesitated. He watched her making up her mind. Finally, as he had hoped she would—known she would—she went into the bathroom. A couple of minutes later, she emerged, holding her filmy white brassiere, her panties, and her pantyhose in a small wad in her left hand.

Victor held his hand out. She gave him the wad. He dropped the bra and the panties into his wastebasket. He took the pantyhose and cut them with a scissors, making them into a pair of stockings. "You can put these on," he told her.

"But they won't stay up."

"Here." He handed her a pair of those cheap elastic garters from the dime store, the ones that looked like upholstered rubber bands.

"Those are supposed to be bad for your circulation."

"Once won't hurt you," he told her.

She sat down on the edge of the bed, took her shoes off, and put on the stockings. She rolled the garters up. The feel of the stockings sheathing her legs and the elastic around her lower thighs only emphasized the feeling of nakedness where she would normally have been covered by underpants and now was not. She was flushed. Her eyes were on the floor.

Victor looked at her, considering his handiwork. He noticed that her breasts looked softer under the printed jersey. He could see the points of her nipples. She raised her eyes to meet his, but she said nothing.

"Shall we go, Emily?"

The car, a small MG roadster, was in a garage underneath the apartment house. Victor put his bag into the tiny luggage compartment, then came around and got behind the wheel. Emily lowered herself gingerly into the passenger seat.

"Here," he said. "I have a present for you."

"Thank you. What is it?"

"Open it."

There was a small oblong box, wrapped in black tissue paper. She tore off the wrapping and opened the box. There were two cream-colored plastic balls, each a little over an inch in diameter. The balls were connected by a woven cord. A longer similar cord dangled from one of the balls.

"What is it?"

Victor explained that it was a set of ben-wah balls. "You've heard of them? You know what they are?"

She hadn't heard. She didn't know. He explained. "You insert them into your vagina. Or one of them. The other ought to be just outside, nestling like a little egg is the nest of your labia. There are little balls inside those larger balls. They roll around and stimulate you. They'll keep you excited."

"What does it do for you?" Emily asked.

"It'll do for me," Victor told her. "I'll know it's there. And so will you."

EIGHT

It took her a while to get up the nerve to try it. She had thought to wait until the darkness of the Lincoln tunnel, but after a couple of blocks Victor had told her, "Put them in!"

The feel of the stockings, and the sensation of where they stopped, etched clearly in her mind by the intake of air from the vent under the dash so that a breeze continually playing with her pudenda had been enough to make her feel sexy. The balls in her hand made an erratic rolling noise as the balls inside the balls wobbled and spun around. On Fifty-seventh Street, she decided to do it. She had to raise her hips some, and hike up her skirt. She was already wet. Victor paid no attention to her, even when he stopped for a light.

When they stopped, Emily looked around. High above her, there was a bus, in the window of which she could see the face of an elderly woman with a straw hat. The woman in the hat was able to see, Emily realized, understanding suddenly the expression on the woman's rage-contorted face. The light changed—mercifully—and the MG roared away from the lumbering bus.

When they emerged into the Jersey meadows with the stink of the Secaucus pig farms and the blight of oil refineries and paint factories, Victor looked over at Emily. It was easy for her to defy him, disappoint him.

"Well?"

"Not much," she said. "Almost nothing."

"Oh?"

She didn't answer. He didn't push it.

A long ride, though, and the curious rattling down there, an impertinent insistence on the obvious fact that she had a cunt. A current of air where none usually played. A nagging jiggle of breasts that were customarily restrained (bralessness being appropriate only for women who are nearly flat anyway). She waited, figuring that there might be some cumulative impact. But nothing. Just the occasional rattle of the smaller balls within the larger ones. And the very slight pressure. And the air. And the jiggle.

Half an hour later, she had all but forgotten that she was wearing them. Not quite. It was impossible to forget altogether. Like a sore finger, or a tender place on the inside of one's cheek, it was there. Like a mantra, it became meaningless with the first few hundred repetitions, and then, leached of significance began to reacquire some ghost of importance, in some odd abstract way. Somewhere past New Brunswick, it began to feel natural to be exposed to the air; to jiggle slightly. It began to be comforting to know that she had a cunt, that it was of such interest to Victor that he was willing to marry her for it, that she could exploit its power, a power of which she had hitherto never been wholly aware.

"We don't have to get married, you know," she said.

"But we do! Otherwise, it would be tawdry and banal."

"I'm willing to go with you to Hawaii. Just like that," she said, surprised that it was true and that she'd admitted its truth.

"I know."

"Then why?"

"It amuses me," he said.

"I'm not worth what you're paying me."

"I know. It's a principle of business that if you overpay someone, you own them. After all, where else can your overpaid person go?"

"And you want to own me?"

"For a while," he said. "Just for a while. That's all we have, anyway, isn't it?"

"What's all we have?"

"A while."

She nodded. She supposed it was a reference to his wife. His late wife. Victor had mentioned her once. Emily had been interested to learn that he could feel, could mourn, could love and be wounded like anyone else. He was not a monster, however hard he tried to seem like one. And if she could get through to that part of him . . . she could win. Whatever game they were playing, she could win it. And it was a game. It always was. The thing that made this game different from the one she had been playing with Larry was that this time the rules seemed a lot clearer.

"I should have called Larry," she said, having thought of him. "Just to let him know."

"We can stop, if you like."

"You don't mind?"

"Mind? Why should I mind? I'd rather enjoy it. You won't mind if I listen, will you?"

"It won't be a very long conversation, I'm afraid."

"I expect not," Victor said. He was smiling. "I'll stop at the next Ho-Jo's."

Larry would be angry, she supposed. The anger would cover the chagrin, the loss of her company. Or of her cunt. For with the balls still there, rolling around, making their erratic buzzing feeling, she found herself agreeing with Victor—or with what she had to assume Victor was thinking. And wanting to triumph a little over Larry, to even the score, getting back at him for his failure to appreciate her, to risk everything for her. He should have married her when he had the chance! And he deserved to be told, briefly, over the telephone, that she was on her way to Maryland to marry someone else. That buzzing, tingling sensation she felt would no longer be for him. Or not for a long, long time.

Would he follow her? Would he come flying to Maryland to try to find them? Abscond with his cab, and come speeding down with his big crowbar? No. And therefore, good riddance!

She was excited, she realized, not only from the prospect of the phone call but now, after all those miles, by the ben-wah balls. Or maybe just by the motion of the sports car. The motion of automobiles had sometimes affected her that way. It was probably the same thing, only exaggerated a little by the exotic appliance. Nevertheless, she brushed her breast and discovered that her nipples were engorged and erect. Well, then, it could be her secret. No need to let Victor know. She didn't want him to think she was too easy. Let him work a little. He'd appreciate it more . . .

Which, of course, was what she should have done with Larry. She had made fatal strategic errors, from the very beginning, all in the name of sincerity and honesty and openness. And see where those things had got them! Better a little calculation, which was the very least that their love deserved. Or their hopes.

Victor moved into the right lane and slowed down. "Another mile, and we can stop. You can make your call. You want coffee?"

"If you're having some."

"I could use one."

"All right," she said.

A minute later, he turned off the main roadway and onto the apron of the rest-stop. "Nothing at all? They're not working?" he asked as he turned off the engine.

"Oh, yes. They're working."

"Good," he said. But he didn't inquire further.

They went inside where a rag-bag of humanity was milling about, waiting to be seated in the restaurant or buying candy and souvenirs. Souvenirs! Of the New Jersey Turnpike!

"You have change?" Victor asked.

"I don't know how much I'll need."

"A dime. And a credit card. You'll get the dime back." He handed her both. There was a bank of phone booths along one wall. She found one vacant, entered it, sat down, and placed the call. Victor lounged just outside, leaning against the door frame. The operator came on the line.

"Just a minute," Victor interrupted.

Emily covered the mouthpiece. "What?"

"Spread your legs."

She stared at him for a moment, then slowly parted her legs. He reached under her skirt and twitched the string. "Remember," he said.

The operator was yammering in her ear. Confused, disoriented, Emily gave the credit card number, waited, and heard the ring on the other end. A second. She was trembling. Victor had turned away so that his back was toward her.

In the middle of the third ring, he answered. "Hello?"

"It's Emily," she said.

"Where the hell are you?"

"I don't know. In New Jersey somewhere."

"What the hell are you doing in New Jersey?"

"I'm on my way to Maryland. We're getting married."

"You're crazy."

"Maybe. I don't think so."

"I'm telling you. You're crazy."

"I'm still going to Maryland."

"Don't."

"Just like that? You're too late."

"Okay. I'm sorry. I . . . I think you're out of you're fucking mind, but . . . I guess, good luck. If you want to get in touch with me, you know how to find me."

"Goodbye, Larry."

"Goodbye, Emily."

She hung up the telephone.

"It wasn't such a triumph, after all, was it?" Victor commented.

"No, it wasn't. How could you tell? Could you hear?"

"I didn't have to. I see your face. He was sweet and noble, wasn't he?"

She nodded.

"Don't let it worry you. Don't even take it seriously. It was play acting, most likely. Posturing. He said what he wanted to hear himself say."

"How do you know that?"

"You're here, aren't you? If it had been real, you'd never have come."

"Is that so? I'd have to think about it."

"Forget thinking. The string is real. Those little balls are real. What you feel. What we're doing. That's real."

She closed her eyes as if to blot him out, or as if to hide, herself. Who was this man? Light banter one moment, or icy detachment, but then abrupt assaults that reduced her to a quivering responsive jelly. Was it as simple as he said? Or was Larry right about her being crazy? Victor's intuitiveness was both comforting and scary. But more scary than comforting. Because it could be a weapon.

"Coffee?" he offered.

"Please."

They were back on the road in twenty minutes, and an hour later were in Delaware. Emily was curiously tranquil, having found at the center of her feelings a kind of indifference which might have been the end result of her perplexity, a kind of giving up; or on the other hand, might have been the effect of the car and the ben-wah balls. The prospect of her marriage to this stranger beside her had seemed only mildly bizarre and rather amusing. The worst that could happen, she had supposed, was that she'd hate him physically, loathe his touching her. She didn't expect any such revulsion, but one never knew. She had masturbated for him, but they hadn't ever kissed. She had wanted to masturbate again. But when she had lifted her skirt, he'd spoken sharply, "No!"

Her indifference that had been her great protection was imperilled. The ache in her cunt, the flush of humiliation were both dangerous for her, and useful for him. She told herself that she could not let him know. The fiction of her indifference had to be maintained. He glanced over at her. She had the uncomfortable feeling that he had read her mind.

"There it is," he announced.

"There what is?"

"The Maryland line. The next exit will be the one we take."

"Good."

"Tired of the ride?"

"No, not really. I was enjoying it. But I'm looking forward to the rest."

"It may not be so restful."

"I meant, the rest of the evening. I'm curious about how it will go."

"Of course. So am I. New flesh is always appealing. I expect we'll be fine for the first couple of weeks. After that? Who knows?"

It was a disconcerting declaration. Wet with desire, she suddenly felt exposed, threatened. She had earlier added him up—at least he wasn't fat or bald. Weathered around the face, maybe, but that wasn't at all bad. It was now crucial to her self-esteem to make him want her the way he had made her want him.

The exit announced itself. He turned off the highway. Within a thousand yards, they came to a wedding chapel with a justice of the peace offering twenty-four hour service. And across the road, the Country Squire Motor Lodge. Beyond the motel, there was a Kentucky Fried Chicken stand, and beyond that a liquor store.

"All the comforts," Victor observed with a wave of his hand. "Which shall we do first? Get married? Have dinner? Or check into the motel?"

"Up to you," she said.

"An odd set of choices. I say . . . let's get married first."

"All right."

"The chapel is on the right hand side of the road. It's easier to turn off. And safer."

"Do you think they planned it that way?"

"I do hope so. In the name of public morality and decency, I do hope so."

"You're a wicked man."

"No, but I try. One must do one's best."

He turned off the road and onto the apron of the wedding chapel.

"Shall we?" he invited.

"Why not?"

In New York, Larry was, as the saying goes, beside himself. Or his rage was there, along with his depression, so that he alternated between bursts of activity—expenditures of nervous energy in which he flung pillows and paced the cluttered room—and moments of abrupt collapse in which he fell, like a pillow himself, to abject immobility. At one point, he went to the refrigerator to get ice cubes for a slug of gin, but as he stood there with the door open he froze, stricken with the poignance of the leftovers in their plastic containers or their bowls with neat plastic-wrap covers. The remains of the curry. The egg salad. The goddamned *choucroute garni* in the casserole, ready to be warmed up. He despised himself for being such a sucker as to care, but at the same time, he felt their forceful reproach. She had performed, however imperfectly, all those domestic chores that he understood only now as little acts of love. He should have married her! Not for the *choucroute* but for the care that had gone into it, the ungrudging labor of love. His eyes brimmed. He blinked hard, so that they overflowed. He wiped his cheeks with an abrupt fist, reached into the freezer compartment for the handful of ice cubes, and turned to get a glass from the dishrack.

How would he cope? No, he rejected that question as petty and selfish. And then he rejected the rejection. It wasn't the washed glass in his hand, or the *choucroute* in the fridge, but the work and the care she had put into them that he missed and mourned. How could she? How could she go off with that awful old goat, that smooth, slimy son of a bitch? He'd handled it wrong, had made some terrible mistake . . . had been instructed to do so! Of course! He'd been crazy to listen to that old bitch—who had been lying to him the whole time. She hadn't been on his side at all, but on Victor's, cooperating with him, pandering for him. Jesus! What a fool he'd been to be taken in that way, to be absolutely suckered.

He picked up the telephone to call her and let her know—not so much what he thought of her as that he'd wised up, that he realized what game she'd been playing. He sat there for a minute, trying to decide whether to place the call, and if he did, what he would say. But to hell with it! It didn't make any difference. He pulled his wallet out of his pants pocket, rummaged through it looking for the slip of paper on which he'd written down her number, found a laundry ticket he'd forgotten about, then found her number. He dialed. All this and the goddamned shirts, too! He tried to read the blurred date that was stamped on the yellow ticket. After thirty days, they threw the stuff away. Or burned it. Or whatever.

"Hello?" Irene's voice asked, "Yes?"

"It's Larry Andrews," he announced. "I've just heard from Emily. She's with your friend. They're getting married."

"I know they were talking about it. We were talking about it. Or, do you mean they are actually doing it?"

"She called me from someplace in New Jersey. They were on their way to Maryland. They're probably there by now. Maybe even married."

"I'm sorry to hear it."

"Are you?"

"Yes, of course. I just said so. I'm sorry for Victor. And for you. For everyone. It's a foolish business."

"It's worse than that. It's terrible. Awful."

"But not fatal. People do survive marriages."

"*They* will. I don't know whether I will or not."

"Don't be melodramatic. It only confuses things. My guess is that it won't last a month."

"And then what?"

"That's up to you, isn't it?" she suggested.

"If it had been up to me, I'd have done it differently. I'd have objected. I'd have raised hell. . ."

"I don't think it would have made any difference. They would still. . . Oh, I see. You blame me?"

"I guess I do, a little."

"I may have been wrong. We can't tell that. The question is what to do now. You've eaten?"

"What?"

"Dinner?"

"No. I hadn't even thought about it."

"If you like, you may come over here. I'll fix you some eggs. We can talk. If you trust me, that is."

"I don't know. I don't see what harm you can do me now," he said, after a moment's thought.

"Maybe even some good," she told him. "If only by listening."

"Okay," he said. "I'll be over in half an hour."

He hung up, surprised at what had happened. It was not at all what he had intended.

The ceremony had been extremely brief. Victor had chosen the simplest and cheapest performance, declining the Polaroid photographs, the rendition of any one of the selection of four possible pieces on the Hammond electric organ, or even the specially embossed marriage certificate with the eighteen-carat gold tooling on the leatherette case. "The bare bones," he had specified, and the justice of the peace had shrugged and complied. The fee was ten dollars.

They'd gone from the wedding chapel to the motel to register and to inquire about restaurants other than the visible Colonel's. They were told that Armando's was a mile or so down the road and that there were good steaks there. "By all means then, it's Armando's," Victor said. "Do you want to freshen up first?"

She did. They went to their room, a standard, utterly predictable room with the curious long unit that combined lowboy, luggage rack, desk, and television stand on one long wall and a pair of double beds on the opposite wall. The draperies, bedspreads, chair cushions, and carpet were all in harmonizing browns and beiges, selected so as not to show dirt. There was a dismally cheerful lithograph of a pot with dahlias in it over the desk section of the all-purpose unit. Victor tried the mattresses of the beds and sat down on the edge of the one nearer the door to wait for Emily to come out of the bathroom.

To think. He hadn't ever really expected that the thing would go this far. And while his general scheme had been amusing enough and even coherent in its way, there were great gaps in it, he now discovered, areas where the details were unclear. More important, there was a surprisingly old-fashioned feeling of disapproval. Not of himself, for he had done no more than to make the indecent suggestion, but of her for having acted upon it. What kind of terrible girl was she? And did she not deserve whatever punishments he could devise?

But what? He had planned an elaborate joke, but now he had to wonder whether the joke would be on her and the world or, by some nasty twist, turn out to be on him. It was essential that he retain the upper hand, keep control, keep to the scheme he'd dreamed up. The financial details were all agreed upon, but that was only the framework, the part that had to do with the official participation of the state in the marriage. The other part of the transaction was the sexual aspect, and there was no protection here, no way of insuring his mastery.

"Ta da!"

He looked up. She had come out of the bathroom. She was naked. He stared at her.

"I thought you ought to have a look at what you've bought. Like it?" she asked, saucily. She clasped her hands behind her head, stuck her chest out in front and her ass out behind. She struck the pose of some Gaston Lachaise woman, or a Giacommetti woman mocking one. Then she turned slowly, backlit by the glow from the bathroom and more appealing than she knew. (Or did she know? Or, better, were her instincts so keen that she could manage such effects without knowing, stupidly cunning and unthinkingly right?)

"Very nice," he said. And it was. She was. Somewhat fuller in the bosom than he had expected from her appearance in clothing, but exactly the pale pink nipples he had expected. He thought back to those unruly buttons the first time he'd seen her. A narrow waist, prominent hip bones, a cute, apple-shaped butt. Good long legs. But her neck and shoulders were perhaps her best feature, a marvel of exquisite modeling. "Very nice indeed."

She did a plié, or maybe it was supposed to be a curtsey.

"Smoother than water, whiter than milk, sweeter than honey," he said.

"What?"

"You. It's from Sappho."

"Oh. You want me to get dressed? Or do you want to get undressed?" She approached; she stood before him. Was it a demand or an offer? He didn't much care. He reached out to touch her—breasts, belly, flare of hips, curve of buttocks.

"Pull the string," she said.

The string? Oh, yes. There it was, not six inches

from his eyes, peeping out of her bush like a fuse. From the ben-wah balls. He pulled. The balls slid out of her with a barely perceptible plopping noise. He let them fall to the floor. He drew her to him to give her a first matrimonial kiss—not counting the merely ceremonial peck in the chambers of the J.P. This was spontaneous and, of course, lower. He stood up. He yanked the bedspread down. He threw his jacket on the floor and took off his pants. Still in his shirt and tie and his shoes and socks, he fell upon her.

Quick, sharp, rough, hot, sweet. She cried out. Coming? So soon? From the stimulation of the ben-wah balls? Another gasp from her. Faked? Real? His was real.

It couldn't have taken more than a minute and a half.

"Armando's?" she asked. "Or the Colonel? I'll go out for it, if you want chicken," she offered.

"No, let's go first class," he said. "Steaks."

He needed a little time to recover. And to think. There were dangers to this he had not expected. He hadn't counted on her being so good.

NINE

"And you? You're not a whore?" she asked.

"No, of course not. What do you mean?"

"You tell me you drive a taxi. You do that for love? Of course not. You do it for money. Which is whoring, isn't it? For money, and promiscuously. What else would you call it? Out on the streets like that?"

"You're just being clever. It doesn't mean anything," Larry insisted sulkily.

They were in her kitchen. He had a large tumbler of gin in front of him, having decided to keep going with the beverage with which he had made such a fair start back in his own apartment. Irene was at the stove, making an omelette and from time to time snatching a sip of white wine.

"Am I?" she asked. "I mean, more than you? Legally, you see, it isn't whoring at all. It's marriage, which is supposed to be the opposite case.

You're talking morality, which is always fuzzy and nearly always nonsense. There is something morally questionable about your driving a taxi, isn't there?"

"It's honest work."

"I don't mean taxi driving. I mean your doing it. Assuming you're as talented as you think you are, you ought to be spending your time better."

"That's absurd," he said, but she knew that a part of him agreed with her. Whether he thought he was talented or not, he'd been at Harvard, and therefore he believed that the world owed him not just a living but a decorous, graceful, pleasant living. It was supposed to come with the degree.

"If you prefer to think of it that way," she said, "I can't stop you. But it seems to me that it's a *mariage de convenance*, for which there is a long tradition in Europe and in this country too."

"Yeah, yeah."

"What an unattractive expression. You like your omelette *baveuse*?"

"What?"

"Runny?"

"Oh, yes. Thank you."

"Then it's done." She turned it out of the iron pan and onto a large oval serving plate. She brought the plate over to the small round bistro table, sat down, served out the omelette onto their two plates, and began to eat.

"Terrific," he said.

"Yes, isn't it?" After a few forkfuls, she asked, "What do you intend to do then?"

"About what? The marriage? What can I do?"

"Right now? Very little. But eventually. When it collapses, as it will in time. Even with the best of motives, half the marriages that are performed these days are unperformed within a couple of years. One must learn patience."

"Patience isn't the problem. I don't know that I'd want her back."

"That's a question for you to decide sooner or later. Not necessarily now."

"I guess."

"I shall be waiting for Victor, of course."

"It doesn't bother you? That he's married Emily?" Larry asked. He was eating his omelette and washing it down with small sips of gin.

"Not very much, no. One must learn to put up with other people's quirks and tricks. It's amusing, in its way. And not entirely without its benefits for me. He's just gone through a difficult time, losing his wife. If he'd come to me directly from her, there would be all kinds of difficulty—guilt, unflattering comparisons. But to come to me after a time with Emily . . . It will be easier."

"Is that another insult?"

"Not at all. But she is very young, isn't she?"

"So am I."

"Yes, you are," she said, smiling. "But don't be so defensive about it. It isn't a fault, you know."

"It's a pain in the ass, sometimes."

"There are other pains in other places that you have to look forward to."

"Yeah. Yes."

"Thank you," she said, acknowledging the correction. "My guess is that they'll be going to Hawaii. In fact, I think he's promised her the trip."

"Terrific!" Larry said, glumly.

"It's pleasant enough for a few weeks. It gets tiresome. But what doesn't?"

"I wouldn't know."

"If you wanted her back, it's not impossible that the first little rift might appear in Hawaii. The geology there is all uncertain anyway, with those volcanos popping off every so often."

"What have volcanos to do with anything?"

"Nothing perhaps. Or everything. It's like California, where life is all so very impromptu. I've always thought it was Saint Andrew's fault."

"Oh, the San Andreas fault?"

She nodded. "What's the point of making plans and commitments if everything can fall into the ocean at any time?"

"An interesting idea."

"Which is polite for *crazy*?"

"I don't know. It doesn't seem especially relevant."

"Nevertheless, the question is whether you think it's a good idea to go to Hawaii. You could be there to pick up the pieces."

"Oh, sure. Do you know how much it costs to fly to Hawaii? And you can't hitchhike!"

"I know."

"I can't afford it."

"But I can."

"You'd send me?"

"Certainly not."

"I don't get it," he said, his fork hovering just above the last morsel of egg left on his plate.

"I might consider taking you to Hawaii."

"We'd go together?"

"Your mastery of the common verbs in English is impressive. Yes."

"I still don't get it."

"Both of us are temporarily at liberty. We have some waiting to do. We could wait together, couldn't we?"

"You mean, get married?"

"No. It isn't necessary to be quite so earnest about frivolity as Victor has been. And, in any event, I can't afford it."

He looked down at his now empty plate, visibly disappointed.

"I didn't mean that I couldn't afford you. But marriage . . . is still set up to favor males. You could go to some benighted state like . . . oh, I don't know, South Carolina or Nebraska. You'd find the right one if you were so disposed. You'd establish residence there and then sue me for divorce. California, for instance, has a terrible rule about joint property. My suggestion is much more modest and, I think, sane. That we just go to Hawaii together."

"And what do I have to do?" Larry asked.

"I should think that would be obvious."

"You're kidding!"

"Not at all," she said. "Don't be shocked. It's too tedious. You think that only men can make indecent suggestions? I'm older than you are, and I have more money than you do. Therefore, I have the authority and the power. If that's too much for your fragile male ego, just let me know and you may withdraw. But you'll lose a nice trip to Hawaii. And the chance of getting Emily back."

"I was . . . just thinking," he said. "About Emily. If I were to go with you, that'd . . . change things. With Emily and me, I mean. I'd have less reason to object to what she'd done."

"Yes, that's true. So your chances would be better, wouldn't they. You'd get rid of all that dreary priggishness that might otherwise prevent you from taking her back when the opportunity arises. As, of course, it will."

"And she'd hardly have any reason to object, would she?"

"How touching! You need permission?"

"Whether I need it or not, I'd guess I have it."

"So?" she asked.

"I guess."

Hardly ardent, but he would have opportunities to make up for it. "As a matter of fact, the offer is conditional."

"On what?"

"On your being any good. As a lover."

"What do you want? An audition?"

"Why not?"

"Now?"

"Why not?"

He picked up his gin and took a sizeable swallow. He put it down. He looked at her. Nothing made any sense. Emily was off in Maryland with Victor. He was here with Irene. They were all going to Hawaii? Why not? She was old enough to be his mother. Or one of his mother's friends. On the other hand, she wasn't bad looking, had kept her figure, and . . . was available. What was that dumb song? "If you can't be near the one you love, then love the one you're near." Something like that. "Why not?" he echoed.

She led him into the bedroom. She sat down on the edge of the bed. "All right," she said. "Let's have a look at you."

"What you see is what you get," he answered, not quite understanding what she'd meant.

"Strip," she said, making it perfectly clear, as if addressing a not terribly bright child.

He began to unbutton his shirt. Why the hell not? Let her watch. She was eager enough. He could practically feel the weight of her gaze. Eager for it? Jesus! He leaned against the wall to take off his loafers and his socks. Then he undid the big brass buckle from his jeans. "Maybe I ought to have a little music?" he suggested.

"Maybe next time, if you like. Not now. We don't need it."

"No, I guess we don't," he said. She was perfectly right. The weirdness of the situation was a turn-on. He was hard as a rock. But that's what she wanted. And that's what she'd get. He unzipped. He dropped his jeans and his shorts. "Ta da!" It was one of Emily's pet phrases.

"Cut the crap," she said. "Come closer."

He took a couple of steps toward her.

"Closer. Next to me."

He took three more steps.

"Now," she said, "don't come." She took him into her mouth.

It took him only a few moments to figure out what the game was. She wanted to see what kind of a performer he was, or, in short, how long he could last. "It's not how long you make it; it's how you make it long," the old filthy jingle went—for some cigarette or other. Other jingles. Anything to distract his attention. "*Autem, enim, igitur, demum, verum, quoque,* also vocatives stand postpositive." Which was good to know if you were translating into Latin. But, Jesus it was hard to keep his mind on anything other than what she was doing with such enthusiasm and adeptness to his cock. A naughty tongue, she had.

"All right," she said, "lie down."

He lay down on the bed. She didn't undress but only lifted the skirts of her hostess gown and climbed on top of him, lowering herself onto his cock. She didn't move much. She didn't have to. She had some fantastic muscles in her cunt with which she was able to squeeze him with sharp hard clenchings. Larry doubted that he could endure very many of them for very long. The terms of her offer, the trip to Hawaii, the rest of it was all forgotten. In this room, at this moment, the competition, the terms of which he had never really agreed to, seemed a matter of enormous importance, critical for his self-esteem. It was weird, looking up at her, seeing her dressed, as if she were at some party . . . But if that was her whim, it was okay with him. He had himself to look out for, his own satisfaction. Or both, maybe, because it was only by pleasing her that he could satisfy himself, taking her dare and surviving.

There was no reason not to help himself, then, or to help her along, which amounted to the same thing. He reached up to hold her breasts, cupping them through the navy silk of her gown. It was . . . it was like taking a liberty, even though his cock was deep inside her. He reached down under her skirts to where they were joined and manipulated her clit. It took a moment or two, but he began to perceive a change in her rhythm, an acceleration in her jouncings. "All right, you bitch, get it over with," he thought to himself. "Come on, damn it, come!" He worked harder with his fingers, and now he was answering her moves with thrusts of his own. And at last, he got what he wanted, producing in her the shudder and the closed eyes. And the groan. It was over.

But it wasn't over. "Don't come," she said. "I'll let you know when you can come."

"Thanks, thanks a lot. You're quite a sport."

"You're not so bad yourself. I want to see just how good you are, though."

"And what do I get out of it?"

"You mean, how much?" she asked. "I hadn't really thought about it."

"It's something to think about," he said.

"Oh, yes. It is. I don't much care for the way they've got it worked out. It's like a taxi meter. The time just clicks away and it doesn't make any difference whether they're going anywhere or just waiting in traffic."

"What have you got in mind?"

"How about twenty-five dollars a pop?"

"A pop?"

"An orgasm."

"Whose?"

"Anybody's. That was twenty five dollars you just earned."

"A hundred."

"Too expensive. Forty."

"Fifty."

"All right. Fifty."

"And living expenses?"

"I don't see why you can't earn them. I'm easy enough."

"The plane fare! I can't fuck my way to Hawaii!"

"All right. You can have travel expenses. And if you move in here, I'll pay for food and booze. You can earn your own clothes, though, can't you?"

"I guess."

"Here, I'll make it easy for you. I'll let you earn yourself another quick fifty." She got off him and lay down on the bed, her legs spread wide. "Eat yourself another pair of shoes, lover."

After a curiously formal dinner at Armando's and a short ride back to the motel, Emily was feeling cautiously optimistic. He wasn't a monster, could be managed just like any other man. "Well," she asked, "what have you in mind for me now?" as they closed the door behind them.

"Bed. Sleep. I'm tired. It was a long drive."

"Do we use one bed or two?"

"We can start with one," he decided. "If I feel like moving, I'll move."

"Fair enough."

"Fair has nothing to do with it. It's what I choose. The conditions of the relationship make anything fair, as long as you're willing to put up with it. For the money."

All right, she thought. It was early days yet. Sooner or later, he would admit to himself that he was fascinated with her. As he had to be. What other explanation made any sense? How else to account for what they'd done?

He began to undress, in no hurry this time, but not stalling either. He folded his trousers and draped them carefully over the rod of the hanger, then picked his jacket from the back of the chair to drape it over the hanger's shoulderpiece. Little rituals of self. She undressed, less deliberately, and got into bed. He went into the bathroom to brush his teeth. Like a good little boy, she thought. He was not so formidable, after all.

At last, he came out of the bathroom, joined her in bed, and turned out the light. There was a plastic mattress cover that crackled like a flurry of dry leaves when either of them moved.

She lay there, waiting. Of course he would make love to her again. Long and slow and langorous and . . . epic. Huge. Not like the time before, which had been sweet but sharp and quick. But hours and hours. . .

But he wasn't. He didn't. He just lay there beside her, not even touching her. He wasn't going to make love to her! She felt . . . discarded. Cheap. As if she were selling something and the customer had changed his mind and left the shop.

But what did she care? Why did she care? So long as he was satisfied, she supposed she should be content. She'd got through the first night. And if he wasn't as ardent as she'd expected, then there would be fewer demands he'd make on her. Of course, it also meant that she'd have less control over him, less leverage in their negotiations with one another. But she would make out all right. She was confident in herself, had to be.

For the money, and for the pride in getting the money—which were undeniable proofs of her worth. Not just her body's worth, either, but that of her cunning and her spirit.

So far, it was a good game. In the morning, they

would go back to New York. And she would see how much she could get him to spend on her wardrobe for Hawaii.

She turned on her side, facing away from him. She lay there, waiting for sleep. Just as she was about to drift off, she felt—or thought she felt—him turn, curl around her, and nestle.

She was doing just fine.

TEN

There had been other great nights she could compare it with. There had been, for example, that time in Acapulco when she had been with the two beach boys all night, had been battered into surfeited insensibility by their competitive attentions, all to see which of them would get the extra fifty dollars for winning the competition for which she had been not only judge and spectator but playing field as well. Or that night in Oran in the boys' bordello where she had had five of them at once, just to see what it felt like to have a cock in her cunt, another in her ass, one in her mouth, and one in each hand, just to play with. But both of those had been nights of private fantasies embodied by faceless actors of the exploitable classes. This time, there had been a different kind of game, one in which Larry's personality, his tastes, his sexuality, his character itself had been toys for her to play with. The object at first had been simply to get him to obey her, to let her use his body as she wanted, to follow her instructions and cater to her whims. What he didn't know, couldn't be allowed to know—because it would have ruined the fun of the experiment—was that she was playing him to get him to turn on her, to get him to such a state of mindless lust that he would risk losing everything she had promised, all the money and the trip and her help in the pursuit of girl of his, all because he was crazed by desire—for her. For Irene! Not for Emily, but for her.

It had taken some time, but Irene had had the patience to wait. And there had been plenty of rewards and distractions during the long build-up of the pressure that she was so exquisitely orchestrating. She had come any number of times, the first few times hard and sharp, and then with quieter but no less pleasurable aftershocks. But the question had been how long could she extend his performance and to what tension and pressure could she bring him before he snapped. And then what would happen? How would he behave?

She was not disappointed. He endured obediently for hours, seemed to sink into a semi-conscious, almost dazed state, so that several times she wondered whether he had not dozed off, still hard, still in her. A twitch, or a slight movement, however, produced a satisfactory groan and an answering motion. She got him to the place where he was in physical pain, his testicles tender and swollen. She got him to the place where a quick lick of her tongue could produce a quivering like that of a tuning fork. She even achieved that perfect moment of equipoise where he produced a single oozed pearl of semen, the droplet before the eruption—and held him there. It occurred to her that she might one day play a different game, using his youth and virility to see what it could do and what it could endure in rather a different fashion. One day, she thought, she would have to try it, tie him up, keep him at this perfect peak of excitement, and see how long he could go with how little attention. A touch, a caress, a lick every couple of minutes, or every five. . . she could drive him crazy. But this kind of craziness was extremely pleasant. Inasmuch as he was not tied down, there was always the question of whether he would turn on her, throw off the constraints of her authority, and, with selfless, mindless, savage fury, fuck her, returning to her the nearly curdled burden of his long agony.

To keep the balance, then, she talked of Hawaii, of a trip to Europe, of sports cars and gambling in pleasant provincial casinos, of the books and records she could buy him, of theater and opera tickets . . . All the things he had craved for so long, and that she could offer him . . . and that he would be putting at risk by disobedience. She was playing his selfishness and his greed against his lust, to see what kind of young man he was, how he was built, what he could stand. For a while, she doubted him. But by three in the morning, having been kept at an intolerable level of excitement for nearly six hours, he broke free, lost himself, groaned, threw her down, not on the bed but on the floor, and went at her like a pneumatic drill, gasping in his need for release, and then abruptly exploding.

She had won. Almost immediately, he fell asleep. She left him there on the floor, but with a coverlet over him. She climbed into bed, delighted with him, delighted with herself, victorious. Even if what she had in mind didn't work, it would be diverting enough. She put her hand between her legs to feel the dampness and the heat, smiled in contentment, and fell asleep, herself.

She woke several times during the night, once in utter blackness, then in the dull wistful gray of predawn, and again in the livelier light of morning. She looked down at the sleeping figure on the floor, observing him, feeling considerable satisfaction with herself, and yet experiencing too a slight pang of . . . pity? Sympathy? Call it simply fellow-feeling. Young as he was, innocent as he was, eager to grow up and to become wise, he was so poignantly eager. She knew what he did not, could not possibly now know: that it didn't matter, that the hopes and aspirations were generally better than the attainments for which he longed. He was like a big puppy, sleeping on the floor, an attractive lithe animal. He would soon enough turn into a man, a human being, and then would discover what it was too late to do anything about—that the metamorphosis was not an improvement. She turned away from him, lay on the cool pillow on the other side of the bed, and thought about her own youth, her girlhood, her young-womanhood. Long gone! And good riddance, too, to most of it. And yet, she mourned her own ghost, the memory of what she once had been. She floated away into another short deep slumber.

At a little before nine, she got up and went to the kitchen to make coffee. She put up the coffee, drank a glass of tomato juice with a few drops of lemon and a twist of pepper, and then, while she was waiting for the coffee water to boil, she dialed

Victor's number. No answer. Good. She flipped open the little notebook under the phone to find the florist's number, ordered half a dozen roses, dictated a brief note to go with them ("Congratulations! Call me when you have a chance. Love, Irene"), and went back to the stove to pour the water through and make coffee. As it was dripping, she went to the front door to get the *Times,* partly out of habit, but partly for the reassurance that it was just another rather ordinary day. Besides, reading the paper would be a way of keeping her mind off the pressing questions that would otherwise arise: how to deal with Victor, how to use Emily, and how to use Larry to accomplish what she wanted. All of those tantalizing problems would have to wait until she had a little hard information. What would Victor's mood be? Defiant? A little chagrined? Would he understand how foolish he'd been? Or, understanding that, would he be even more stubborn and resolute, refusing to admit he'd been wrong? There was no way to tell. She would simply have to wait.

She poured herself a cup of coffee, spread the paper out on the kitchen table, and immersed herself in the reports of floods, strikes, coups, currency fluctuation, and the advertisements for dresses from Bonwit's and Saks.

When she'd finished her coffee, she poured a second cup and took it into the bedroom to see whether Larry was stirring. He was still on the floor, wrapped up in the coverlet. With a bare foot, she picked up the edge of the coverlet, holding a corner of it between her first and second toe. Not at all surprisingly, he had a morning erection. She looked down at him, enjoying the artistic tension between his repose and his tumescence. He looked quite boyish, defenseless, unaware of the power at his loins. She put her coffee cup down on the nightstand and knelt down to study him as if he were a sculpture. The delicacy of his eyelids! The modeling of his shoulders! He was almost girlishly pretty, except for that great red hard on. She leaned over him to suck him awake and into action.

The light of day in Maryland showed the motel room in all its blunt tackiness. Victor awoke early, felt at first disoriented, then vaguely uncomfortable, then apprehensive. Had he made a terrible mistake? But, no, the girl lying asleep beside him was the one attractive thing in the room. It was the room that was intolerable. He got out of bed, took a shower, and then woke her to tell her he wanted to get back to New York.

She yawned, stretched, smiled, said, "Good morning," and got out of bed.

In ten minutes, they were on the road. They stopped for breakfast somewhere outside of Wilmington, and then pushed on to arrive in Manhattan a little after ten. Victor was surprised to learn from the doorman that there was a package that had arrived for him. He hadn't expected anything, hadn't ordered anything. And then it turned out to be a long box from a florist. From whom? Upstairs, in the apartment, he opened it and looked at the card. From Irene. Congratulations. But how did she know . . . ? Of course, from Larry.

Emily was pleased by the roses, or at least made a convincing show of being pleased. She took them off to find a vase and to put them in water. "You want coffee?" she called from the kitchen.

"Yes, please," he called. And he picked up the telephone to call Irene. To thank her, but also to find out what she wanted. There had to be some hook in it, somewhere. 'Call me when you have a chance,' he thought, was as close to an order as she was likely to give.

"Irene? Victor. Thank you for the flowers. They're lovely."

"Congratulations. I hear you've gone and done it."

"Yes, last night."

"You had a pleasant time, I trust?"

"Oh, yes. Quite."

"So did I. Her young man came over to complain that my advice hadn't helped. We contrived to console each other. It was very pleasant."

"How nice for you," he said, wondering why she was telling him this.

"So, I wanted to thank you for that. It was a spin-off, I think they call it, of your little adventure."

"Possibly so, but I take no credit for it."

"Of course not. Still, I can see some possible problems. . . or, anyway, aspects of the situation that you ought to know about."

"Oh?"

"I think we should meet."

"I'm sure you do. We can't talk on the telephone?"

"Not really. Besides, I have another present for you."

"Besides the roses?"

"Yes, something rather naughtier."

"Well, we're leaving in a day or two for our honeymoon, but I suppose I can manage a drink this afternoon."

"Splendid. The Plaza?"

"Oh, all right. At four?"

"As close to four as I can make it."

"I'll look for you."

"That was him, wasn't it?"

"Yes."

"What have you got to say to him?"

"That's my business, isn't it?"

"Yes, but it's mine, too. I'm involved too."

"Yes, you are. But I don't have to tell you everything. I don't have to tell you anything."

"No, I guess you don't."

"Of course, I can choose to tell you whatever I please."

He nodded.

Now that she had his submission, she could reward him, like the trainer giving the tidbit to the puppy who has done its trick. "I'm meeting Victor at four this afternoon. At the Plaza."

"That's interesting," he said, not even daring to ask the obvious questions: why? what for?

"Almost certainly, Emily will be at home, in his apartment. If you like, you might pay a call on her."

"Why are you telling me this?"

"I thought you'd want to know. It's fun to do favors for people sometimes, when they're pleasing. And you've been pleasing so far."

"And that's all? It's just a favor to me?"

"Not exactly," she admitted. "It's partly a favor, and partly a chance for you to find out how she's feeling, what's on her mind . . . This is of interest to both of us, for different reasons. Or maybe for the same reason. We want to know when the marriage will collapse."

"Or whether."

"Oh, it will. There's no question of that. But how long will it take?"

He looked at her with great attention, as if he supposed she could tell him the answer—if only she felt like it.

"I have no idea. I'll be finding out the same sorts of things from Victor."

He nodded, concealing imperfectly his disappointment.

"Don't bully her! No reproaches and no complaints. You understand?"

"I'll try."

"Never mind trying. Just do what I tell you. Let her know you still love her. That you care, no matter what she does. You might try to seduce her. . ."

"But not too hard?"

"You don't want to rape her, no. But you can make the offer. She may even accept."

"And you'll be seducing Victor?"

"No, I won't have to. There are other ways to accomplish the same thing."

"What other ways?"

"They're not relevant to your situation, believe me. Except that you must be sympathetic, affectionate, but not fawning, and if you can manage it, fun. Pleasant company. She'll be expecting you to be horrid. Disappoint her expectation and be amiable, and you'll have great success. She'll be pleased, but she'll also be a little bit puzzled. Therefore, insecure. You don't want to be too well understood."

"Wasn't it Verlaine who said that?"

"Very good! Yes."

"More coffee?" he offered.

"I'll get it. I think you should get dressed. It wouldn't be a bad idea for you to go down to Saks and get yourself something presentable to wear."

"To impress her?"

"Partly. But also to let her know that what you're telling her about us is true."

"I should tell her about us?"

"Well, of course! Otherwise, you'd appear to be reproaching her, wouldn't you. And you don't want to do that. Let her reproach herself. It's so much more efficient."

He bounded out of bed and went off to shower. She poured herself another half-cup of coffee and lay there thinking that, so far it was going well enough. If Victor was as manageable as young Larry, she'd have nothing at all to worry about. It would almost be too easy and therefore boring.

She picked up the telephone to make an appointment with her hairdresser so that, at four, she would look absolutely delicious.

He knew he had to be wary, but however suspicious he tried to remain, it still seemed as though her advice was sound. How else should he try to talk to Emily? Whatever Irene's motives were, he had to admit that she'd been dealing with him honestly and fairly at least some of the time. There had been no counterfeiting of her sexual involvement. Or her generosity, either. She'd given him her Saks card, explained that they'd probably call her to confirm it, but told him that she'd be home until noon. She'd advised him to get something expensive, just a little more stylish and flamboyant than what he ordinarily wore—when he dressed in something more imposing than blue jeans and work boots. And that, too, seemed exactly right, with regard to the impression he wanted to make on Emily. And generous of her, too. He supposed that she could put a limit on his spending when they telephoned her. But she had encouraged him to spend . . . He could get himself something in buttery cashmere! Or he could get some really great shirts. And shoes . . . He could not help remembering her the night before, and her ordering him to eat himself another pair of shoes. Well, he'd earned them. He could wear them. Some sumptuous cordovans, perhaps. Or supple Bally loafers? It hardly mattered. The important thing was the novelty of treating his body as something other, an external object, something between a toy and a weapon. To deck it in finery and to celebrate it was, in a way, to join Irene, or at least to see it through her eyes. How odd that Emily had never made him feel quite that way about it. Had that been her fault? Or her virtue? A mark of her sincerity? Or of her hypocrisy?

Irene had been absolutely correct, though, about one thing. Emily would be expecting him to snarl. She would be unsettled indeed if he was affectionate, supporting, and if he strutted just a little. Oh, yes! And he was looking forward to it.

He left the bus and crossed the street to Saks. With Irene's card in his pocket as his passport, he entered the store as if he were entering the land of milk and honey.

She was unsettled by his appearance. In both senses. By the way he looked, and also—at first, even more—by the mere fact of his having appeared, having shown up. The doorman called up to announce him, and she'd almost told him not to admit Larry. What good could possibly come of it? On the other hand, the cowardice of sending him away would be as difficult to admit as his tirades would be uncomfortable to listen to. She figured she owed him at least that much. So, yes, she decided. "Tell him to come up."

And in the long minute that it took him to get to the elevator bank and to ascend to their floor, she tried to rehearse her excuses, her justifications, her defenses against what she had no doubt would be an attack. But when she opened the door, he was smiling. And looking extremely sharp in a tan blazer—camel's hair? cashmere? vicuña?—she had never seen before. And a maroon voile shirt, tan slacks, and chocolate Bally loafers.

"Hi, there. I thought I'd come by to offer my best wishes. All around."

"Victor's not here," she said, "but come in."

"Thanks. I . . . I hope you don't mind my coming over. But I wanted to let you know that . . . that it's okay. That there are no hard feelings. That nothing's changed."

"That's nice of you."

"No, not really. Just less awful than I'd been before. You had to put up with a lot."

"You're looking different," she said.

"So are you."

She was wearing a front-and-back wrap skirt of merino wool flannel, a collarless blouse in tissue faille, and a bronzine challis shawl. And she'd had her hair styled so that it swept starkly to the side with little fringes that came down to emphasize her forehead.

"You like it?" she asked.

"I'm not sure. I guess so." He looked around the living room at the rosewood Victorian love seat, the Japanese screen, the green and gold sumptuousness. "It's all a little intimidating, isn't it?"

"I don't know. It's fun. Don't you think? You like it too. I mean, look at you!"

"This stuff?" He indicated his new costume and explained, "It's a present. I figured that if you were doing all this—for us, I think you said it was—then I could contribute, too."

"I don't get it."

"You wanted to get married for a few months. To get some bread. For us, right?"

"That was the idea."

"Well, I've got the same kind of deal. With Irene Tarashoff. She's a friend of Victor's, actually. Anyway, I'm with her."

"You got married?" she asked. "But how could you?"

"No, I didn't get married. But it's a funny question, coming from you, isn't it?"

"I meant, where did you find the time? We had to go to Maryland."

"Oh. Anyway, we didn't. But I'm living there, more or less. Kept. Like you. It's not bad."

"What about the apartment?"

"Ours? I'll hold onto it. We may wind up there yet."

"I've got some stuff there I'll need."

"Any time. Take whatever you want."

"Is that what you want, still? For us to wind up there?"

"There, or somewhere nicer. But together. No, I haven't given up on that. Have you?"

"No," she said. "You want coffee? A drink?"

"No, nothing. I'm glad you haven't given up on us."

"I forced you into this, didn't I?"

"I don't think so. Anyway, it's not so bad. It's not . . . fatal, anyway. It's just a question of time. And patience."

"You're not jealous?"

"Are you?"

"A little," she admitted.

"Yeah."

"We may go away."

"I know. I heard."

"From her?"

He nodded.

"But it won't be for very long. A couple of weeks. Maybe a month. God, I need a drink, even if you don't."

"All right. I'll have one with you."

There was an English campaign tray with bottles and glasses and an ice bucket, but there was no ice in the bucket. Emily took two glasses into the kitchen to get ice from the freezer, brought them back, and handed one to Larry. "Help yourself," she said, inviting him to anything he wanted from the tray.

He poured himself a couple of fingers of scotch. She held out her glass and he poured her the same. "You leaving soon?"

"The apartment, you mean? Or on the trip."

"The trip."

"I don't know. A day or two, I think."

"You know where you're going?"

"Hawaii."

"It should be nice. All I know about it is from the television program. Aloha!" The last word had been a kind of toast, with the glass raised. Sarcastic? Angry? She couldn't be sure.

"I'm sorry. . ." she began.

"Don't be. You want to go to Hawaii? Go. When you get back, I'll be here."

"I meant to say I'm sorry we didn't have a chance to . . . to talk a little. To get things straight. Even to say goodbye properly."

"I don't know that talking would have done a whole lot of good. I wasn't listening anyway. And what way is the right way to say goodbye?"

She looked down at her glass.

"We can still do that. Say goodbye, I mean. Unless you take this marriage much more seriously than I think you do."

"I don't know how long he'll be gone," she said.

"You afraid of him?"

"I don't know."

"He'll be gone for a while yet," Larry said, looking at his watch. "I'd say we had a half-hour anyway, to count on."

"How do you know?"

"He's having tea with Irene. Downtown, at the Plaza."

"You want to?" she asked, after a beat.

"Sure," he said, with no pause at all.

He embraced her. He cupped her breast with his hand. "No underwear?" he asked.

It was a silly thing, a joke. But he'd noticed it, and he asked her. He had not at all expected her answer. "No, no underwear. He . . . he doesn't let me wear any."

It was racy. Provocative. And paradoxically, it was all the more provocative because it had not been done for him. It was Victor's idea. Emily was, at least for the moment, Victor's. That proposition, which he would have rejected absolutely until his discovery, now seemed plausible. Tenable. In which case, he, Larry, was poaching—was expected to poach, Irene having set things up for them.

It felt dirty. And wonderful for being dirty. And for being hurried and furtive. But then, there was a sharp thrust of intromission, and all circumstances and considerations fell away.

For the moment.

ELEVEN

Four desperado musicians sawed away at their instruments in a series of Viennese waltzes. Victor couldn't understand why Irene liked the place or what there was to compensate for that assault of indifferent music indifferently performed.

"But that's just what I like about it," she explained. "The illusion of being on shipboard. Where else can one find that particular note played that particular way?"

"You actually like it?"

"Oh, yes. Just as you seem actually to like your young lady. Your bride."

"So far, it's working out."

"I'm glad for you. I truly am."

"I find that 'honestly,' 'truly,' and 'sincerely' are adverbs that are more frequently attached to falsehoods than any others I can think of."

"A little work," she suggested, "and that could

turn into a second-rate epigram."

"Thank you."

"Tea? Or a drink?"

"Tea, I think."

"Good. Me too. And those terrible little cakes."

"Are they terrible?" he asked.

"No, they're quite good. Fattening, of course. Terribly."

"I see," he said, grinning. Good old Irene. It was pleasant to see her and to exchange their own brand of banter. He was almost tempted to believe that her purpose—'truly'—had been to congratulate him. It was not impossible, if only as a way of her being predictably unpredictable. He caught a waiter's eye and ordered tea and cakes.

"So, tell me all about it," she said, as soon as the waiter went off to get them their tea. "I'm dying to hear."

"All the lurid details?"

"No, I can imagine them well enough. But your feelings. Your reactions. No doubts at all?"

"Not really. There was a moment, early this morning, when I was depressed. But it was just a moment. I think it had more to do with the motel room than anything else."

"A motel room? How very piquant!"

"I liked the idea well enough last night. It's all set up, you know. Matrimony is the big industry of this little town. Thruway exit, actually. Marriage is to Elkton what cigarettes are to those towns in North Carolina, or chiropractors are to New Hampshire. A quirk of legislation and highway design. It had its appeal. Or I thought it did. But they had those awful plastic mattress covers . . ."

"What a tender little man! It's a version of the

story of the princess and the pea, isn't it?"

"I don't think they're worried about pee."

"Don't be horrid!" she warned, stern around the mouth but smiling around the eyes. "Ah, the tea!"

They were served. Still, they had to wait for the tea to steep. Irene nibbled one of the little glazed cakes. "Otherwise, no regrets? No doubts?"

"No, none. What can I possibly have to doubt? I have no great expectations, after all."

"Still, it's better to manage these things gracefully. For one's own aesthetic satisfaction."

"I have in no way misled her. I have nothing to reproach myself for."

"So far, no."

"Now or ever."

"What about her young man?"

"Him? A dolt. Oh, but I forgot. You and he are an item now?"

"An item. Or a footnote to yours."

"You work awfully quickly, don't you?"

"On occasion. He called me when he heard from Emily. He came over to complain. We found better things to do."

"How nice for you. Not that I'm interested much . . ."

"But you should be. It's your responsibility."

"That you and he are doing the number? Why?"

"No, not for that. But for her, afterwards, when you become bored or restless or indifferent. As you know perfectly well you will. What happens to her then? Will he take her back?"

"I don't much care. I'd say it's up to him. And up to her. She may not want him back. After me?"

"Modesty is not your worst sin."

"False modesty? No."

"He's not so bad, you know," she said. "Just young. Innocent."

"Innocent is a nice word for doltish."

"Another apothegm?"

"If it is, it's nonetheless true."

"Perhaps. Tea?"

"Please."

She poured. They sipped. He tasted one of the cakes. They were, as she had promised, quite good.

"Having taken his part, you feel obliged to take his part? Is that it?"

"Not at all. As a matter of fact, I was thinking of you. There will come a time when you'll appreciate it."

"That you and he are getting it on?"

"That's not the point. That I'm bringing him along, helping him to grow up. She may need him when you're through with her."

"It's possible."

"I don't claim anything more," she said. "More tea?"

"Please."

"Oh, and I have a present for you," she said, filling his cup.

"More than your news of young Larry?"

"Oh, yes. An object. A toy. I know how you like toys. This is even better than those ben-wah balls."

"Oh, that kind of toy."

"Here," she said, handing him a small package. He opened it, tearing off the gold wrapping paper and opening the cardboard box. There was a small black plastic oblong solid. It looked like a remote control switch for a television set. "What is it?" he asked.

"You see the little switch?"

"I see it."

"Throw the switch."

He did so. Nothing happened.

"So?"

"It feels fine," she said.

"What does?"

"It does. It's a remote control whizzer."

"Terrific! What does it do?"

"It's like the ben-wah balls, only it's electronic. And the remote control switch is what you have in your hand. It's like a gizmo that opens garage doors and turns your television channels. You'd better turn it off."

He turned it off. He turned it on again, watching her face. Off again. On. "You're not kidding, are you?"

She shook her head. Her eyes closed. Her lower lip stretched down and away from her teeth. She sighed. He turned it off.

"That's fantastic!"

"Give it back. That was just a demonstration. The other package is for you. It has both parts. And the instructions."

"Where does it come from?"

"Denmark, I think."

"How very clever."

"Yes, isn't it. It will save you so much effort. And the power is what you're really after anyway, isn't it?"

"Power? I don't know. I'd say the amusement. But that may be just another word for it. There's complicity, certainly, in this piece of machinery. The woman has to agree to it in the first place."

"Oh, yes, that's true. You think she will?"

"I think so."

"Perhaps you'd like to come to dinner then?"

"She and I?" Victor asked.

"It might be amusing," Irene suggested. "A goodbye party, before you go off to Hawaii?"

"Will her young man be there?"

"Why not?"

"I can think of a number of reasons."

"You're not jealous, surely? Besides, there is an equivalent piece of applied engineering for men. An electronic cockring with a vibrator. And a remote control switch. I might have him in the equivalent posture. We could let them say a last goodbye to each other . . ."

"What a mawkish idea. Still, with this little . . . what do you call it?"

"The whizzer?"

"How droll. With the whizzer, or whizzers, it might be interesting," he admitted. And then, after a moment of reflection, he asked, "What do you mean by a 'last goodbye'? Or was that just a turn of phrase."

"I think they're saying goodbye now," she told him.

"You set this up? You set them up! And me!"

"Yes, I did. Do you mind?"

"I resent the meddling, I think."

"The word is unpleasant. I wanted to find out how you think of her. And of your marriage. You expect love? Or fidelity? If you do, you'd better come to your senses. You can't just walk in and reinvent lives that way to suit yourself."

"What would you call your own behavior? Isn't that a little reinvention? And I'm sure it suits you, although I can't see what benefit there is in it for you."

"You're very cynical. I can see a good deal of benefit in it for you. To keep the thing light. As a test of its lightness. Start to take this seriously, and there will be damage. All around."

"You're becoming a moralist in your young middle age. I never would have expected it of you," he said.

"A realist, rather. Have another one of those cakes. If you don't eat it, I probably will. And you can afford the calories better than I can."

"I can afford the calories?"

"Well, you have to keep up your strength. As a bridegroom?" She lowered her head and gave him a coy look that was only half mocking. "What about my dinner party then?"

"Oh, why not. The harm's already done."

"I don't think I've done you any harm."

"I don't know. It's too early to say. Perhaps you haven't."

"I meant well."

"I'm sure. But for whom?"

"For you, darling!"

"Silly of me even to have asked," he said. "But this dinner party . . . had better be soon. I'd been planning on leaving the day after tomorrow."

"Tomorow night then?"

"If you can manage. Or will there just be the four of us?"

"Oh, no. I'll do it properly. It wants to be eight at least. Otherwise, it could degenerate into an orgy. And you wouldn't approve of that, would you?"

"Not quite yet, no."

"Ah, but in some weeks or months?"

"Who knows? Do you want more tea? Or are you keeping me here for a set time to give their farewell a graceful and unhurried decorousness?"

"What a suspicious little mind!" she chided. "But I think we could probably go another pot of tea, yes."

"You're not worried that there won't be any left for Mama?" he asked, feigning solicitousness.

"Oh no, no fear. He's young and fresh."

"You make him sound like some sort of vegetable," Victor observed dryly. Still, he waved to the waiter for more tea.

The question now arose for Victor as to whether to ask Emily about Larry's visit. But it was no good. He'd worked himself (or been worked by Irene's machinations) into a no-win situation. He'd resent it if Emily lied and he'd resent it if Emily told the truth. In which case?

In which case, he had to admit that he cared. It was infuriating to have to admit that he had violated his own rules, for he cared about the arrangement, but he cared about Emily, too. Her bovine passivity had been deceptive. She was foxier than she had at first appeared, with the shrewdness of a fox. . .

By no means could he let her know that he had been hurt. Offended, perhaps. Even annoyed. But not hurt. He had to go back to his original equation: knowledge plus indifference equals power. And if the indifference had to be feigned, he supposed he could manage that imposture. After all, she had broken one of the first rules, and had fucked someone without his permission. That tiresome, that banal young man. . .

Was that the point? Was Victor jealous? What an awful thought! He didn't want to think of himself as quite that far gone in what was, evidently, something of an infatuation. Still, it had been Irene's idea . . . But, on the other hand, he didn't trust Irene. Emily's infidelity had been Irene's accomplishment, too.

Keep cool, he told himself. And he allowed himself to entertain the idea that she might have done nothing more than talk.

Horseshit. Whoreshit! Did he believe that? Not for a minute.

The cab turned onto Victor's street. The traffic was blocked. "That's okay," Victor said. "I'll get out here. It's just a few doors down from the corner here."

He paid, tipped well, and sauntered toward the entrance to his building.

He seemed cheerful enough, although quiet. Tired? She didn't know his habits and rhythms enough to be able to judge. She had washed the highball glasses and had put them away, and even had had a chance to take a shower between the time Larry had left and Victor's arrival. And to put on her new slinky Scaasi with the plunging neckline for dinner.

He fixed himself a drink, sat down at the small kidney-shaped desk to examine his mail, offered her a drink if she wanted one, and busied himself with opening envelopes. He had a long silver letter opener that he used almost ceremonially. She poured herself a small whiskey.

"Have a good afternoon?" he asked, not bothering to look up.

"Oh, yes. And you?"

"Very pleasant, thank you."

"Good," she said, amazed that that was all there was to it. She picked up a *New Yorker* and glanced at the cartoons.

"I saw Irene today," he said.

"Oh?"

"She invited us to dinner."

"That's nice."

"I accepted."

"Fine," Emily said.

"Larry will be there."

"Oh?"

"You don't mind, do you?"

"No, I don't mind."

"They're seeing each other, you know."

"Yes, I know."

"He told you?"

"Yes."

"He was here?"

"Yes."

Of course, he'd known all along. She decided if he asked her, she'd tell him the truth. Bad manners to answer his bad manners in asking.

But he didn't ask. Instead, he asked, "How do you feel about Chinese food?"

"Love it."

"Good. So do I."

She wasn't sure who'd won.

Neither was he. Therefore, after dinner, when they were back at the apartment, he showed her the whizzer, had her put it on, and, wearing it, watch television. He kept the switch in the pocket of his bathrobe, every now and then giving her a jolt. It was more aggressive than the ben-wah balls. Or she had less control. With the ben-wah balls, she could sit very still and stop their vibration. With this, there was a tingle right behind her clit and up into her vagina . . .

"Do you like it?" he asked.

"Not very much."

"Does it turn you on?"

"The machine? Or the idea of it?"

"Either."

"The idea of it turns me off. The machine . . . turns me on."

"You mean, it could make you come?"

"Yes, probably."

"Good. You'll wear it to dinner tomorrow."

"Oh."

"It amuses me."

"Evidently."

"You won't be alone."

"Oh?" she asked. "Irene will have one, too?"

"No, but Larry will. It's a slightly different device, but it works the same way."

"I think it's sick."

"Think whatever you like. Just so long as you do it."

"I'll do it."

"Good," he said. "Tomorrow, we'll do that shopping. And the day after tomorrow, we'll fly to Hawaii."

"All right."

"You haven't changed your mind?" he asked. "About coming with me to Hawaii?"

"No."

He gave her a long jolt. Then off. Then on again. She knew she could let herself go, could think of Larry, or could think of nothing, and she'd come. But she wanted to see whether it was irresistible. She paid close attention to the words of the television set. "Would Drano hurt your pipes?"

It was funny. She managed not to laugh, not even to smile.

He turned it off. "Here," he said. "You can have the switch for a while."

"What's the point?"

"You're fighting it."

She didn't contradict him.

"Play with it, yourself. I'll watch."

It wasn't quite so bad when she operated it, herself. Pretty good, in fact.

The party was fun, more fun than most of them knew. The Jorises had no idea what was going on. They were just there, loyal members of Irene's B list, eager for culture and glamor. Ormsby was there with Monique Something-or-other, mostly so Victor could show off his new wife to Ormsby—at whose apartment they had met, after all. Those four were the audience.

But even the participants were unaware of the intricacy of their own situation. Victor had his little remote control switch in his pocket, and he gave Emily little long-distance twitches with it from time to time. But he had no idea that Irene was wearing the same device, set to the same wavelength, so that he was unknowingly stimulating both women. Nor did he know that Larry was getting stimulated at exactly the same time, by means of the control device that Irene had placed on the floor under her foot, like the call button for maids in old-fashioned apartments. It wasn't perfect. Nor did Irene intend it to be. The relay could not be so obvious that Victor would figure it out. Or Emily. Or Larry, for that matter. She wanted it to be her own little secret that she might or might not impart to one or more of the participants later on

Victor apparently liked the toy. He played with it a good deal, while Ormsby tried to interest Eugene Joris in investing in the production of the Baudelaire musical, making obviously rehearsed remarks about the aesthetics of depravity. A lot he knew about depravity—or aesthetics for that matter.

Irene had to admire Emily. Either the girl had a leather cunt, or she had remarkable poise and self-control. With no practice at all—Irene had to assume this sort of situation was new to her—she managed to sit up straight, look attentive, answer questions that were put to her, and maintain something quite close to a normal appearance at a dinner table. A little bright of eye? A little distracted in her replies? Who could say, except Larry of course, that this was not her norm? And Larry was busy with the same effort of concealment, the electronic devices—the whizzer and his own nervous system—speaking to each other in a rhythm that Irene dictated, or translated from Victor's dictation. Oh, how intricate!

It was exactly like those pornographic fantasies in which slaves of whatever sex wander on hands and knees beneath the table to fasten upon the sexual organs of the guests, whose job it is not to show any reaction. Except that in this, as with everything else, the place of servants had been taken by electronic machinery. The dishwasher, the trashmasher, the garbage disposal, and the whizzer.

Ormsby said it was a shame that Joris could not hear Emily sing some of the songs, turned to Emily, and asked her to testify to their wit and their beauty.

"I don't remember them very well," she said. "Not well enough to sing. Besides, there's no piano."

"I didn't mean for you to sing them now," Ormsby corrected quickly. "But your recollection? Your impression?"

"Oh, they were very nice. Very good. Oh, yes, they were wonderful songs. . ."

"You see," Ormsby said, unaware of Emily's orgasm, or of Irene's for that matter, "it's a hell of a show."

"Yes, it must be," Larry said, glaring. At Irene. He'd figured it out. Or part of it, anyway. "Excuse me," he said. And off he went to the bathroom. To take off his little ring? Presumably.

Victor was satisfied at Emily's performance, or her threat—and there was certainly something threatening about her near incoherence, at least the threat that she could let Ormsby and the Jorises know what was happening—even whip the little gizmo out and put it on the side of her plate like a nasty piece of chewed gristle. He was either satisfied or bored, for there were no further buzzes. Larry returned to the table. Dessert was conventional and dull, even if the strawberries were especially good.

All in all, Irene was not disappointed. The fun of these things—as with so many other sports—was the narrow averting of disaster. Hang-gliding or ski-jumping couldn't be any more breathtaking. It had, to use a cute expression, come off rather well. For her, anyway. Larry, she could punish later.

Victor and Emily took their leave early. They had some packing to finish and would be flying off to Hawaii in the morning. Ormsby and Monique left with the Jorises, Ormsby looking as though he were going to make a serious pitch for Joris's money.

"Good night, good night. Thank you for coming!" She closed the door behind them.

"You're both sick," Larry said, sitting on the sofa in a graceless sprawl.

"No one's keeping you here."

"I know."

"She managed better than you."

"I thought so. I didn't mind it so much for me. But she had some damned machine too, didn't she?"

"Yes. So did I."

"You?"

"Yes. It was fun, rather. Victor thought he was goosing her. He was giving it to both of us."

"And you don't think that's sick?"

"What a little prig you are."

"Maybe."

"You must learn better."

"Must I?" he asked.

"Yes, either that or go back to your apartment and drive a cab and pretend to be a writer."

"Pretend? What do you mean?"

"What kind of writer can you be if you're afraid of life? If it disgusts you?"

"Not everything disgusts me."

"How wonderfully saintly of you!"

"Oh, for Christ's sakes!"

"No, but for your own sake. And for hers. You'd do well to change your attitude."

"For hers?"

"He's going to turn her on. He has his limitations, but he's clever and he can be likeable. He's going to discard her. Do you want to be there to pick up the pieces? Or not? And if you're going to be there, it might be useful for you to have a tolerance and a sophistication and a little basic humanity so that you can be useful to her. And those same things are likely to be important for your writing—if you have any talent. Which remains entirely to be seen."

"All right."

"All right what?" she asked.

"All right, I'll go with you. To Hawaii."

"You'll have to earn your passage."

"All right."

"Go take off your clothes. And put that cock-ring back on."

"And what are you going to do?"

"Nothing. I'm going to sit here and watch you come off like a monkey in a cage in a zoo."

"That's just great."

"You can leave if you want to."

He sat there, looking at the door to the apartment, at the door to the bedroom, back at the front door. . .

She could see the machinery working. Finally he arrived at a decision and got up. He went to the bedroom.

As, of course, she had known he would.

TWELVE

She had never been to Hawaii, but she had her expectations, mostly from motion pictures and travel posters, of a lush tropical paradise, all orchids and palm trees and white sand beaches in crescent lagoons. She was unprepared for the long stretches of arid emptiness, the expanse of volcanic rubble where astronauts, training to negotiate the surface of the moon, had practiced walking. They had flown to Honolulu and had transferred.

The terrain changed a little as they climbed the flank of the volcanic hills, and on the slopes there was some scrubby vegetation, punctuated from time to time by a cluster of buildings, tin roofed shacks mostly, to justify the map's claim for a village. More frequent than the villages, and always off to the right, down toward the water, Emily could see developments of resort condominiums, mostly in the fake Tahitian style. "Is it one of those?" she asked.

Victor shook his head. "Certainly not. What do

you take me for?"

"I don't know. I know very little about you."

"You've seen my apartment."

"But that was your wife's," Emily said.

"But I picked her, so it works out to be the same thing."

"You picked me, too."

"As a curio."

She was not insulted. Indeed, she suspected that much of his gruffness might be bluff. He had hardly alluded to her meeting with Larry, but she supposed that his decision to come at once to Hawaii could very well have been influenced by his desire to get her away from her lover, separating them by some five thousand miles. It was susceptible of flattering interpretations. At the very least, it suggested that he was much less indifferent than he wanted her to think.

At length, he slowed the car, turned off the main road, and negotiated his way down a narrower strip of pavement that was either a small secondary road or a large driveway, descending by a series of hairpin turns toward the water. There was no building in sight, or not at first. Suddenly, visible to the right, nestled under a bluff, there was an angular structure in bleached wood and glass, cantilevered against the slope and protruding with a V-shaped deck that jutted out toward the water below.

"What a nice place," she said.

"What an awful word."

"What word?"

"Nice."

"All right. Attractive," she said, refusing to be ruffled. "All by itself this way. . ."

"There's another one just like it down the hill. There are two brothers. They inherited the land. They hate each other, I'm told, so each house is as private as possible."

"But they're both the same?"

"They saved money that way. They only had to pay the architect once. They just had the builder do the same thing again."

"They're friends of yours?"

"No. The rental agent explained it to me."

"I see. Well, it's very . . . pleasant."

They lugged the suitcases up the stairs and into the house. There was a big open living room, and then a bedroom with sliding glass doors that gave access to the deck and a view of the ocean. The floors were tile and there were rustic hemp rugs here and there. Against the solid wall, there was a huge bed that took up only a small part of the room. It had old-fashioned carvings at its corners, finials in the shapes of massive pineapples in the dark wood of the headboard and the footboard. There was also a fireplace, a small captain's desk, a pair of upholstered chairs in a vivid orange, and a large brass tray that served as a coffee table.

She was warm from carrying the suitcase up the stairs from the carport. It was warm. "Is there air conditioning?" she asked.

"Yes, but I hate air conditioning. The point of the tropics is to be warm, isn't it?"

"But this warm?"

"Then strip."

It didn't have the tone of a sexual invitation. She hesitated.

"As a matter of fact, you might give me the key to your suitcase."

He was going to unpack for her? It didn't quite make sense. Still, he was standing there, his hand out, palm up, looking impatient. She rummaged in her purse and found the key. She handed it over.

"Now, take off your clothes."

"It sounds like . . . like an order."

"It is, actually."

Some kind of game? But why not? She took her clothes off, blouse, skirt, shoes. He ignored the shoes, but he took the other articles and put them into one of the suitcases. Then he locked the case and put the key in his pocket.

"What's the sense of that? What are you doing?"

"You are my captive," he told her. It was funny. But he wasn't smiling.

"All right, I'm your captive. What do you want me to do?"

"Anything you like, for the moment. But you're unlikely to leave, aren't you?"

"Whatever you say."

"Exactly."

There was no point in arguing. She'd wait and see. There were always ways out. With a towel, if need be. And he'd have to sleep sometime. She could steal the key, unlock the suitcase. . .

It was odd. Being completely naked was much more comfortable than she would have expected. She wasn't revealing herself. It was beyond that. With complete nudity, she could expect satiety and indifference. He'd get bored with it, she was sure. Meanwhile, it wasn't all that inappropriate. She needed a shower. The trip had been long and tiresome. And it was quite warm. So, after the shower, she could go out onto the deck for a sunbath. She could get a tan. All over.

Perhaps an hour later, Emily was out on the chaise, still naked, still the subject of Victor's curious whim, but in no way uncomfortable. She had smeared a lot of Bain de Soleil over herself, and she gleamed with the grease and the sweat, but she felt good. There was an intermittent breeze from the water that cut the thickness of the sun's heat just enough to make it pleasant. She heard a motor and then the motor stopped. She heard a door slam. A car? A truck? A visitor! She looked around for a towel. There was none. Had she left it inside? Had Victor come out to take it away? She got up and went to the sliding glass door that led to the bedroom. It was locked. She knew she hadn't locked it. Victor must have.

She looked around the deck. There was no way off except through the house. Down below the railing, there was a drop of fifteen feet to the rocky ground. She tried the door again. Yes, locked.

She went to the prow of the deck to see whether there was a door that opened from the kitchen. No, nothing but a pass-through, so one could serve food and drinks onto the countertop arrangement. And in the kitchen, a lean young man with black hair and oriental features was staring at her, mouth agape.

There was no place to hide. She turned away. But at the same time, she realized that the flush of her face was of anger. She'd been set up. That was why he'd locked her out here! Of course. To humiliate her. And, in a way, the delivery boy, too, although she was sure he was enjoying himself. And Victor? Where was he? Watching from the other room? To see the delivery boy's reaction and to imagine hers.

"Emily?"

She did not answer Victor's call.

"Emily? Where are you?"

Yes, of course, as if he had no idea. "You know where I am! You locked me out here!"

"Oh, did I? Sorry. Have you met John? He's our delivery man. He'll be bringing us supplies. Is there anything you want?" She turned her head. Victor was in the kitchen now, with John.

"A robe," she suggested. "I don't have any clothes on, remember?"

"Oh, don't you? I'm sure John doesn't mind."

Apparently, he did mind. Or was sufficiently embarrassed to flee. Or had the good manners to do so. He'd left the kitchen and was inside the house, on the stairs that led down to the driveway, perhaps. A moment later, there was the whine of the starter, and the sound of the engine as the truck pulled away.

Victor came out onto the deck. "What an effect!" he said, appreciating the aesthetics of it.

"What a dumb schoolboy trick!"

"It amused me. That's all that matters."

"It didn't amuse me."

"Should that trouble me? Did it trouble you to think that I might not be pleased by your goodbye fuck with your old boyfriend? We'd been perfectly clear about how the arrangement was to go. You owe me one."

"I owe you one what?"

"You'll lay someone I'll pick out."

"You think so?"

"I'm sure of it."

"We'll see," she said.

"Oh, yes. We'll certainly see. Or I will. You'll be

here . . . blindfolded, I think. And waiting, while I go cruising the bars of Kailua to pick up . . . a tourist, or a soldier. There's an army base around here somewhere. Anyone who strikes my fancy. And I'll bring him home and you'll fuck him."

She froze. Was he out of his mind? It was . . . awful. Horrid and awful. She was surprised at herself. It had been a fantasy with her, which she'd shared with classmates in college, other girls who had acknowledged the same kinds of fantasies, to screw some absolute stranger. But . . . not this way. No, certainly not! But if she showed the distaste she felt, that might be dangerous. He might go ahead and actually do it. Just as he might go ahead if she tried to feign eagerness. No, the only thing was to . . . to play it cool. To assume that it was just to test her, to play with her and see how she'd react.

It wasn't lust, she told herself. It was . . . a game. And if the game drew upon some fantasy in him, then the way to deal with it was to try to tame it, to direct it.

"It's a tacky idea," she said. Contempt, perhaps, was the only way to begin.

"Good."

"Good?"

"At least, you're being honest. I could see you thinking. Your mind is as naked as you are. It was like watching the machinery of a pinball machine, with the bells ringing and the lights flashing. You were wondering what to say, how to deal with me. You were trying to decide whether to lie and say you liked the idea. I'm glad you didn't. I'd have known it was a lie, and I'd have had to punish you for that, too."

"Punish me?"

"Perhaps. Would you like some white wine? I'm going to have some."

While he was in the kitchen, looking for the glasses and getting the wine, she took slow deep breaths to calm herself. It would do no good to get jangled. She needed to be calm and reasonable so that she could figure out what to do. He liked head-trips? Fine, that was okay with her. Just so long as they stayed mostly in his head. The thing to do, she figured, was to fuck him. Quickly. Relieve some of that pressure. They'd made love in Maryland, in the motel, and then in New York. After that kinky dinner party with the remote control vibrators, they'd come back to his apartment and screwed a couple of times. And he'd been normal enough then. He'd wanted her the way she had wanted him to. He had something of a pot, like the nudes in Gothic paintings. His cock, insignificant in repose, was capable of amazing extension, not just in length but in girth. When he was detumescent, the only hint of his size was from his balls, which were quite large, larger than any Emily had ever seen. All that juice in them . . . She knew that after as little as three or four days, with Larry, there was the peculiar goaty smell. Maybe it made them crazy.

So, to keep him sane, and to keep him . . . grateful, and adoring, she would have to keep him active, sexually. For her own sake. When she saw him return with two glasses of white wine on the rocks, then, she was amiable. "I'm sorry I got upset," she said.

"That's all right. You can get upset. I don't mind. I even enjoy it."

"He was bug-eyed, wasn't he?"

Victor nodded.

"It was a funny thing to do."

"I liked it."

"I bet he's jerking off in his truck. You think?"

"I don't know. I haven't given it much thought."

"Did it excite you?"

"It diverted me. 'Excite' is perhaps too strong a word."

"About a four on the peter-meter?"

"Maybe a two."

"Let me see. You're very overdressed. After all, I'm wearing nothing."

He was wearing a pair of canary yellow Bermuda shorts, a black polo shirt and a pair of black canvas shoes.

"Is that a come-on?" he asked, taking a sip of wine perhaps to hide a smile.

"It's always a possibility, isn't it?"

"There is always that possibility. Which is why you're dressed—or undressed—as you are."

"But with both of us undressed, the possibility would be doubled, wouldn't it."

"All right, why not!" he said, kicking off his shoes. "It is, as you say, warm." He took off his polo shirt. "But would you indulge me, perhaps? I have one mildly kinky fantasy in which you could cooperate."

"What's that?" she asked.

"Will you do it?"

"Will you tell me what it is?"

"First, agree to it."

"Does it involve other people?"

"Not immediately."

"What does that mean?"

"If I explain it, I'll have to tell you what it is."

"Well . . ." She hesitated. Did she trust her scheme? It was probable, but not certain. Still, she felt that it was the likeliest way to control him. "All right," she said. "Now, what is it?"

"Let me tie you up."

"For how long?"

"How long can it last?" he asked.

An hour at the most, she supposed. She nodded.

He led her into the bedroom. He instructed her to lie on the bed from which he had removed the coverlet. The ironed sheets under her felt crisp and cool.

"Spread your arms."

He tied her to the posts of the headboard, fastening each extended wrist with a linen dishcloth. He spent a few minutes looking around the house for something stronger for her feet and returned with rubber-coated clothesline, from which he cut suitable lengths with a kitchen knife.

"Now your legs."

He looped the clothesline several times around her ankles and then tied each ankle to the bedposts at the foot of the bed.

"That ought to do," he said, to himself as much as to her. To her, he said, "Try to get loose."

She pulled, tugged, yanked. . . "No, I can't. It's secure."

"Too tight anywhere?"

"I don't think so."

He took another dishcloth, folded it, and wrapped it around her eyes. "Don't move, now.

I'm securing this with a safety pin. Don't want to stab you."

She held still while he fastened the pin.

"Can you see?"

"No."

"Anything?"

"Light and dark, through the cloth, but that's about it."

"Fine."

She waited. The sensation was not unpleasant. The restraint of her limbs restored the feeling of vulnerability that she'd had in the car. "Well?" she asked.

"Well, now we wait. Or, rather, you wait."

"What's the point?"

He didn't answer. She listened hard. She could hear nothing. She began to be afraid. What was he going to do to her?

"Okay," she said. "Okay. I'm sorry. I shouldn't have done it. I'll make it up to you."

Nothing. No response at all.

"Victor? Please! I'll do whatever you want. I promise." Even as she said it, she knew that it was absurd, that tied up this way, she had no choice, that she could refuse him nothing.

"Victor? For God's sake. Victor!"

She felt a chill. Afraid, she had broken out into a cold sweat, even though the room was warm enough. She could feel the beads of perspiration on her brow and on her upper lip. She could not wipe them away.

"Victor?"

He had either left the room or was sitting there, letting her think so.

"Creep!" she screamed.

And immediately, she realized her mistake. Either he'd heard it and had enjoyed it, or he wasn't even there.

"Creep," she whispered to herself.

Out on the deck, naked now himself, Victor sat where Emily had sat, catching the gentler rays of the late afternoon sun and holding a glass in his hand with the last of the wine in it. It was a perfectly ordinary California chablis, but it tasted just fine, the dry clarity perfectly matching the exhilaration Victor felt from within. He was quivering with delight. It was even better than an erection. It was as if all the nerves in his body were stretched taut with the excitement of the situation. He had intended to go slower, to let her accustom herself to her captivity and their isolation in this wonderfully remote house. But this was even better. Bound as she was, and blindfolded, she would learn submission. He had had to decide on the spot what to do about her sexual advance, which he had not expected or planned for. What had she wanted? Humiliated as she had been by the impromptu trick with the delivery boy, she certainly had not been expressing affection or desire. A stratagem, then? A maneuver by which she hoped to find some vulnerability in his post-coital ease, hoping that *tristesse* could be turned to remorse or pity? He doubted that she was as clever as that. But it wasn't impossible.

He had decided, then and there, to see if she would submit to being bound. His original plan had been to wait until she was asleep. Enough wine and watchfulness, and he had been sure he could outlast her. She would not have been expecting any such move, certainly. And he could have been able to tie her hands and feet so that when she awoke. . .

But this was better. He had contrived her complicity, which was all to the good. He had her body now. The more elusive and valuable quarry of her mind, her very spirit, was now before him. And he looked forward to the combat with an enthusiasm he had not known in years. The breeze on his body was sublime. His mildly accelerated heartbeat and his slowed breaths were distinctly pleasurable. The syrupy ooze of the sun's warmth on his face, his chest, and his thighs was exquisitely soothing.

Inside, afraid, tied so that she could not move, her whole world diminished to the sheet under her back and the bonds on her wrists and ankles, she was . . . open to invasion. By now, she would have gone beyond fighting to the anticipation of the penetration he had promised. And that he might withhold for a while, fanning the flame of her appetite until it was an inferno of lust. The trick by which she had thought to tame him by sex could be turned around. It was only a matter of time—hating it, but waiting for it, and betrayed by her own mind so that, in her impatience, the waiting for it would turn terror to eagerness—if only to get it over with. Or to test herself and to see whether she could survive it.

He drained the last of the wine, felt its stony chill, put down the glass, got up, and went into the bedroom. It was the fourth time he had gone into the room to look at her, to enjoy her, to enjoy his power to come and go without her having any idea that he was standing there. In his bare feet, he could be quite noiseless on the tile floor.

Lovely. Supine as she was, her breasts were

gentle cones of flesh. Her thighs were poignantly slender. She had a remarkably thick bush, through which, with her legs spread, he could see the pale pink of her labia. Was she asleep? No, she moved her head.

He padded silently into the bathroom and found his toilet kit. He took out the tube of K-Y surgical lubricating jelly, and just held it for a moment. His breathing was very fast and shallow. He unscrewed the cap and squeezed a little onto his finger. He put the cap back, put the tube down on the vanity, and returned to the bedroom. It was easy to lean over her, and just as he had promised, suddenly to introduce his lubricated finger into her vagina.

She shrieked. A short splendid gasp of rage and mortification.

He was rock hard. He threw himself on her and entered her with his cock. He lay on top of her as she writhed, struggling, and unwittingly giving him indescribable pleasure.

Like so many young men, Larry turned out to be something of a muddle. He was not stupid, Irene found, not at all. And yet, he was not smooth or sophisticated. It stood to reason, she supposed. He had come from some dismal steelmill town in Pennsylvania, and had gone to Harvard, fleeing the mean and ugly scenes of his youth, but carrying them with him, too, as one always does. She had read some of his poems and stories, and had been surprised by their delicacy and suppleness—a quality he didn't display much in his nonwriting life. A quality, then, she had to suppose, of which he was ashamed? At the very least, it was something of an ambivalent attitude.

Clearly, his attitude about Emily had been ambivalent in much the same way. He had seen her—Irene had gathered this, putting it together in a way she wasn't sure Larry had, himself—both as a beautiful woman, an object of desire, and also as a trap where, once caught, he would be risking reduction to his father's agony of meaningless labor, progeny, debts, and hopelessness, from which the only refuge was strong drink.

Irene's strategic advantage, she came to realize, was that Larry did not take her seriously, or at least did not see her as a threat. And therefore, she could reach him in ways that Emily had not been able to do, circumventing the defenses he had erected in that quarter. That, at least, had been her hope. But his lower-middle class inhibitions and his not yet abandoned respect for *machismo* dogged him and got in her way. The worm began to turn on the plane. He went to the lavatory and took off the cockring. Then, later, he told her he was going to sit by himself for a while, in the no-smoking section.

"But you smoke," she protested.

"That's not the point," he answered. "I want to sit by myself. I want to think a little."

And he'd moved away. To think—which was an activity that could gain him nothing. The point had been to assert his independence. Or to assert, at least, their mutual dependence.

More annoying, then, than the carefully moderated slight—he had done nothing to embarrass her publicly, had in no way torn the fragile social fabric—was the declaration behind the gesture, the announcement that he would have to be reckoned with. She was annoyed, and registered that, but only as a chord pattern on which to improvise what her melody might be. Tricky enough to have to deal with Victor and Emily, but now she would have to deal with Larry as well.

He had come with her, had endured a series of sexual demands and humiliations in order to get his passage to Hawaii—first class, although that extravagance was more for her own *amour propre* than for any amour of him. So, figure that he wanted Emily. Wanted her back? Or wanted to impose some humiliation on or extract some exquisite vengeance from her? Or both, needing to humiliate her in order to enable himself to stand doing what he wanted, which was taking Emily back.

Clearly, then, it would be to her advantage to keep from him for as long as possible any precise information about Emily's whereabouts. On the island, of course, but it was a big island. A bargaining chip. (And how long can one play with one chip? With a run of luck, a long time!)

Having demonstrated his independence by sitting in the no-smoking section for a while, Larry came to join her for the meal service. So there was another chip, too, although of a small denomination. His basic courtesy, she supposed, was something she could use. Merely courtesy? Or a conventionality that could be the emblem like that on the top of some chocolates, designating a soft center? Time would tell.

After the movie, he went back to sit alone and doze, or pretend to doze. She decided that she ought to take some risks. Had to, right away. If he was going to rebel or just walk away from her, it would be better for him to do it sooner, on some trivial issue, than later, when she had come to depend upon . . . not him, but her expectations of him, her assessment of his character.

So, when they deplaned at the agglomeration of imitation grass shacks that made up the Kona Airport and crossed the blacktop to the luggage claim area, Irene had already made up her mind what her first test would be.

As they stood waiting for their bags to appear, she said, "I'll go and rent a car. I've reserved one."

"All right," he said. "I'll wait for the bags, I guess."

"If you would. But I have to ask you . . . whether you will indulge my whim. Once I have the car . . . I'll drive. You'll wear a blindfold."

"What?"

"A blindfold. A handkerchief. Anything. I don't want you to know where I'm taking you."

"Why not?"

"That's my business."

"And if I refuse?"

"I take the car and my bags, and I drive away. You'll be on the island, but you'll have no way of finding her. And of course, I'll let Victor know you're here."

"He's going to find out sooner or later, anyway, isn't he?"

"If I warn him that you're here. And that you're angry. Violent, perhaps? There are all kinds of things I can tell him that would make him pack up and clear out in two hours. And you'd never find her."

"I don't even know that I want to find her."

"You want to go back to New York? I'll give you your return ticket. You can leave now."

"But if I stay, I . . . wear the blindfold?"

She nodded. He stood there for a moment, thinking about it. He looked up at the flank of Mauna Kea, the top of which was wreathed in clouds. He looked out toward the water. He shrugged. "Okay," he said finally, "whatever you say."

"Exactly," she said, and she went off to rent the car.

On line, waiting for the slow placid Hawaiian behind the counter to complete the transaction with the man in front of her, she considered his acquiescence. Sight is . . . independence. Autonomy. The opportunity to perceive for oneself. And blindness is dependence. Trust. The yielding of autonomy.

She'd made a reasonably good beginning. She could build on it.

She had no idea that, not twenty miles away, Victor had been playing the very same games.

PART TWO

THIRTEEN

She awoke to a nightmare. She was still tied up, and she was hot and sticky. She still had the suntan oil from the previous afternoon on her body. And she was slick with sweat. Under her buttocks the sheet was crinkly and rough. Crusty.

She remembered that assault. His, she assumed. He could not have found a sailor or a delivery boy so quickly. She didn't think so, anyway. Her sense of time was disturbed. She assumed that it was morning, but for all she knew it was still the middle of the night and he had left the lights on . . .

"Victor?" she called.

No answer. Had he gone? From the room? From the house? For all she knew, he had left Hawaii, consigning her to perish of thirst or hunger. She couldn't think that. What she should have done, yesterday, was now clear. She could have grabbed a kitchen knife and demanded the keys to her suitcase. She could have left the house, naked, or with a towel . . . Anything but this.

"Victor!"

"Coming! Be right there," he called. From far away. The deck? The kitchen? She heard a rattle of crockery. The kitchen then. And she smelled coffee. All right, coffee and a shower . . . He had to untie her! She had to pee, for God's sake. They'd discuss this reasonably. The fact that she had agreed to her bondage yesterday would have to count in her favor. She'd agreed to it then, and by extension, to what had happened afterwards. But this was a new day. He'd surely untie her. The thing was to conceal her anger at his having left her tied up all night.

"Good morning," he said. "I've got coffee."

"Terrific. Untie me, would you?"

"No, but I'll help you drink the coffee."

"Look," she said, "I have to go to the bathroom, okay?"

"I'll get you a bedpan."

"You'll what?"

"A bedpan."

"But I have to take a shower," she said.

"I'll give you a sponge bath."

"I'm not an invalid!"

"Oh, yes. You are. Invalid. Captive. Dependent. Toy. All those things."

"You're sick, you know that?"

"I'm up and around. You're the one in bed."

She didn't answer. She had to think. Her hunch was that she shouldn't show fear. Or even anger. Annoyance, maybe. And reasonableness. Those would get her her best chance. "Just let me go to the bathroom and have coffee, and then you can tie me up again, okay?"

"No, it isn't okay."

"Why not?"

"For one thing, you're willing to promise anything, but you don't make good on your promises. You promised that you wouldn't fuck anybody but me without my permission. And then you fucked Larry, didn't you?"

"That was different. We'd been living together."

"And we were married."

"All right, I was wrong. I'm sorry."

"Sorry?" he asked.

"What more do you want of me?"

"This. Exactly this."

"But what for?" she asked, fighting to keep her voice calm and conversational. "I'll do whatever you want."

"Yes, you will. You have no choice."

"But why force me to do what I'm willing to do?"

"I want to. I want to have you entirely dependent on me. To eat. To wash. To pee. It will be a relationship of wonderful intimacy," he said. What was especially ominous, she thought, was the deliberation with which he spoke. It was very cold and calculating.

"How do you take your coffee?" he asked.

"Black with sugar."

"Yes, I thought so."

"Will you at least take the blindfold off? You can put it back on any time."

"I'll think about it."

"It's make it easier for me to drink the coffee."

"All right, yes." He took the blindfold off. She

blinked. She wanted to rub her eyes but couldn't. She saw that he was wearing a pair of light cerise trousers and a white short-sleeved shirt. He had shaved and combed his hair.

"Which would you like first?" he asked. "The coffee or the bed pan?"

"The coffee," she said. She would put off the humiliation of the bedpan for as long as possible.

He propped her head up with a pillow and held the cup to her lips, allowing her to slurp a mouthful. And another. She realized that his compliance with her request to remove the blindfold was not an unalloyed kindness. She would be a witness to the rest of it, the bedpan, the spongebath . . . Of course, she could always close her eyes.

"Another sip?" Victor offered.

"Please," she said. She remembered a time, years ago, when she had gone to bed with a basketball player at Western Reserve but had not felt comfortable enough with him to use the toilet of his apartment—its door wouldn't close. She had risen from his waterbed, had dressed, left him, driven away, and stopped six blocks away to use the women's room of a gas station. It was silly, she realized, but she felt nevertheless that she was being punished for that excessive fastidiousness by the intricate machinery of the world's workings.

He put the cup down and left the room. He went into the bathroom and returned with the bedpan and a washcloth. He put the bedpan down on the floor, and with the washcloth he started the not unpleasant business of her sponge bath, washing her face, her neck, her arms. He made several trips back and forth, wringing out the cloth in the bathroom sink and returning with it hotter and wetter.

He was not particularly tender, but neither was he rough or ungentle. It was a bland, almost abstract proceeding. Her chest, her breasts, her abdomen. Another trip to the sink to freshen the cloth, and a careful sponging of her vulva, where he was extremely thorough. She could not suppress a *frisson* of pleasure. Then he freshened the cloth once more and did her thighs and calves.

"Better?" he asked when he was done.

She nodded.

"You want the pan now?"

"It's disgusting," she protested.

"No. It's not particularly pleasant, but it's not disgusting. One empties a cat box and hardly thinks anything of it. You give yourself too much importance. It's not such a big thing as you make it out."

"Will you at least leave the room?"

"This time? Yes."

"All right," she said at last. "Give me the bedpan."

"Say 'Please.' "

She said nothing.

"I'll leave, if you'd prefer it, and take the bedpan with me."

"Please," she managed to pronounce through clenched teeth.

"That's better. Raise yourself up a little."

With some effort, she managed to elevate her buttocks so that he could slide the bedpan under her.

"It's going to be messy if I can't sit up."

"Then it will be messy. I don't mind."

"You might even enjoy it!"

He picked up his coffee cup and went into the

kitchen. "That is not the point of this procedure," he said. "Call me when you're ready."

She lay there arched over the bedpan. He'd won. And what was worse was the prospect of his further victories. He could do with her whatever he wanted. She had very little to say about it and no way to fight it. She was just so much meat.

She allowed herself to feel now what she had so carefully fought off while he had been in the room. Tears came to her eyes and overflowed, running down the sides of her temples. And lower down the flow of urine, mostly into the bedpan but wetting the insides of her thighs and buttocks as well.

Like an animal, he thought. The trick was to make her like an animal, to bring *out* the animal in her. To break her, as one breaks a horse. Or to train her, as one trains a dog. In that way, he might discover what sort of an animal she was. He had spent a pleasant morning, tending her. He had fixed a couple of soft boiled eggs and had put them into a small Pyrex dish. He had brought them into her and had fed her, at first with a spoon, and then, more intimately, by dipping his fingers into the egg and letting her lick her nourishment from his yellowy glistening fingers. It was just the thing he might have done with a half-wild beast, engaging its dumb trust, and at the same time tempting it to bite. He thought she might, and was fully prepared to punish her for doing so, not by any violence that would engender fear, but by a simple withdrawal of his presence and his attentions. Let her lie there thirsting, hungering, sweating and stewing, and she would behave better.

But the need never arose. She was clever enough

to anticipate what the result would be of her obstreperousness. Like a baby at the breast, then, she licked and sucked his fingers, opening her mouth at their touch on her lips—for he had replaced the blindfold in order to foster that beautiful blind trust that was his object. A few days, even a week, and she would be a new creature, entirely open to him, so that he could put his fingers into her, or his cock, and have her respond instantly and gratefully, not merely despite herself, but without any baggage of self to worry about.

He took a piece of toast from the tray, put it into his own mouth, chewed it for a moment, then took out the sodden lump and put it into her mouth. She chewed and swallowed.

He hesitated. He thought he heard the sound of an automobile. A gardener? A delivery man? He supposed he ought to check. He turned on the radio so she would not be able to hear anything except the blare of the cheap music—Johnny Pineapple and the Hilo Monsters. He went out to the deck to look. Nothing. He went back into the house, down the stairs to the carport, and out to the common driveway. The only other house in the area was that of the estranged brother of the builder of his own. He must be in residence. Or must have rented it. It was none of Victor's business. Still, considering the unconventional enterprise in which he was involved, he thought he ought to go and have a discreet look.

He was barefoot, but the driveway was not very long. Below the turnoff to his own carport there was another hairpin turn, and a steep grade to the other house. He went down to the turn, looking for a vantage point from which he could see without being seen. The other house should have remained unrented. But he could easily keep the knowledge of the near neighbors from Emily. He wondered what kind of people they would turn out to be. Just in case he could not avoid a greeting, he improvised a story about . . . an invalid wife. Recovering from a spell in a mental hospital. Just in case.

He rounded the turn and took a turn.

What the hell? Irene!

What was she doing here? And with Larry? And how had she found him?

He retreated up the drive, walked back to his own house, and climbed the steps, two at a time.

They had not been in the house for more than half an hour, enough time to open the suitcases but not unpack them, and for Irene to disappear into the bathroom for a relaxing soak in the tub—with a rum and tonic on the rim, delivered from the kitchen by Larry—when the telephone rang.

"You expecting anyone?" he called.

"No. It's probably the agent checking to see that we're here and that the supplies and the booze were delivered. Answer it, would you?"

He did. It was Victor. "Welcome to Hawaii," Victor said, hardly bothering to hide the sarcasm.

"Where are you?" Larry asked. It was too abrupt. If nothing else, it revealed the important information that Larry had no idea where Victor and Emily were.

"Right here, on the telephone," Victor teased.

"Is Emily with you?"

"Is Irene with you?"

"She's here. Is Emily all right?"

"Couldn't be better," Victor replied. "And you? How was your trip?"

"Fine," Larry said, forcing himself to adopt the cheerful social tone with which Victor was punishing him.

"Is Irene there, by any chance? I mean, is she available? To talk on the phone?"

"I'll ask her," Larry said. He went to the bathroom door to tell Irene that Victor was calling.

"I'll be right there," she said, and to Larry's surprise, she came running, still wet, water dripping down from her legs to form spatters around the clear footprints she left on the tile of the bedroom floor.

"Hello there! Or should I say, 'Aloha'?" she bubbled, all girlish heartiness. Had he discovered how she'd tricked the agent into betraying Victor's whereabouts? "We just got in. How sweet of you to call so promptly!"

"What in hell are you doing here?" Victor asked.

"Wonderful. Just wonderful! And your flight?"

"That's not a responsive remark."

"I know!" she said, as if he'd adverted to the beauty of the sunsets or the majesty of the mountains—some such grand and glorious thing.

"I take it you can't talk?"

"Yes, it'd be fine to see you," she said.

"He doesn't know where I am, does he?" Victor asked, not so much to elicit the information but to check her veracity.

"Well, of course not. How about the bar at the Kona Hilton?"

"Just you and me?"

"Just the two of us, yes."

"What time?"

"I'll be leaving the house in . . . say, half an hour? And it's what? A twenty minute drive?"

"I'd guess that's right."

"I'll see you soon, then."

She made kiss-kiss noises and hung up.

"Why can't I come?" Larry asked.

"First of all, because you weren't invited. And second, I have a much better chance of finding out where they're staying if I'm alone than if you're with me."

"You don't even know where they are?"

"Don't worry about it," she told him. "I'll find out soon enough."

She went back into the bathroom to deal with her hair.

"What about dinner?"

"There should be some steaks in the refrigerator. Fix yourself one."

"I meant, will you be having dinner with him? Shall I wait for you?"

"How sweet! I really don't know. I suppose I might, if it appears to be . . . useful. But I can't tell yet. If you get hungry, eat."

"You're sure you don't want me to come with you?"

"Positive," she said. She came out of the bathroom, naked, to hunt for some underwear from the suitcase. "What you might do while I'm gone," she said, "is unpack all this."

He sighed. But he didn't refuse.

Victor was waiting at the head of the driveway. Irene stopped. Victor got in. She asked, "Where to?"

"Well, my place is out, I'm afraid."

"Mine too. The Hilton, then?"

"Why not?"

She nodded, put the car into gear, and eased onto the roadway.

"May I ask what you're doing here?"

"Vacationing. Just as you are."

"Next door? By some long coincidence?"

"Not quite. I found out where you were going to be. I thought I'd come along to . . . shall we say, pick up the pieces?"

"I'm grateful for your solicitous attention, but I'm not at all sure that there will be any need for it. I'm perfectly capable of taking care of myself."

"And of her?"

"Why should she be any concern of yours? And what is that young man doing with you?"

"Whatever I tell him to do," she said with a quick sideways glance and a naughty laugh.

"How very nice for you, I'm sure."

"Oh, it is. It is."

"Good. You aren't married, are you?"

"To him? No. That was your hobby horse. It isn't mine."

"He's just a traveling companion?"

"Yes, that's right. And he's available if you should get tired of yours," she said.

"He's available? For what? I'm heterosexual, you know."

"I remember. I meant for her. To deal with her."

So that was it. If the purpose of Larry's availability was to stand in readiness for Emily, then clearly it must be Irene's purpose to lie in wait for himself, Victor figured. "But she's not merely a traveling companion. She's my wife. Still, despite your solicitous attentions in New York."

"Are you turning solemn? Or sentimental?"

"Neither, I hope. Merely selfish. Which is normal for . . . both of us."

"Yes, it is," she agreed.

It was dusk. They traveled along the road that was at first winding and then straighter as it led up the coast to Kailua and the Kona Hilton.

He was not terribly worried. Her unexpected appearance might, at another time, have been diverting. In a way, it was flattering that she had cared enough to go to all this trouble and expense. But he needed some time still to be alone with Emily. Another week, and he would have established a perfect passivity and dependence in the girl that would be wonderful to see—and to demonstrate to Irene. And to Larry, for that matter. It would get the punk off his back for good.

But not quite yet.

They parked in the lot and walked down to the main entrance, crossed a bridge over a fish pool where great carp lolled in gaudy ease as an example to the guests. They made their way to the bar, which was built out over the sea wall. They ordered drinks, a Mai Tai for Victor and a rum and tonic for Irene.

"Now," Victor said, "I'm sure you have some explanation for this curious behavior. I can hardly say how eager I am to hear it, however improbable it may be."

"I don't mean to meddle," she began.

"Oh, no. Of course not. Nothing of the kind. You simply invite me to tea at the Plaza in order to unleash your stud. . ."

"Victor, would you answer one question for me?"

"What is that?"

"Are you in love with the girl? If the answer is yes, then your complaints are justified. And I'd owe you an apology. But I simply cannot believe it of you. You can't have gone gaga. You're too young for that. And you cannot complain about my games if you're merely playing games, yourself."

"Where does it say that if one person is playing games, or two are, then a third necessarily has the right to join in?"

"I simply assumed, inasmuch as we were old friends . . ." She waved her hand in a vague gesture of circumambient understanding.

A waitress brought the drinks they had ordered. Victor checked his wristwatch. Irene noticed his not quite furtive gesture and asked, "You haven't actually answered my question. Are you in love with her? I see you're checking the time, which is something you seldom do in my company."

"Jealous?"

"Should I be?"

"Perhaps. Not because I'm in love with her, but because she's younger. And more pliable. She can be anything I want her to be."

"You make her sound like a lump of clay, Victor."

"Yes, exactly. And to an artist, a lump of clay is more interesting than a finished piece."

"I take it I'm the finished piece—in whatever sense you mean that?"

"A very attractive piece, my dear, but . . . your urn is fairly well-wrought."

"She'll bore you, you know."

"I'll let you know when that happens. I'll call you. In New York."

"Or here."

"I'd really just as soon have it my way. In New York."

"Very well. I promise not to intrude on you at all during my stay here on the island. I'll be here two weeks. If you want me, you know the number. How did you get it, by the way? From that blabby agent?" Victor inclined his head. "If I don't hear from you, well, that's your decision. I'll abide by it. I promise."

"And you won't let young Larry know where Emily is?"

"I won't."

"If you do, it'll be the end of us. Of you and me, I mean."

"You mean this isn't the end? Right now?"

"I hope not."

"Then . . . at least, confide in me. As friends confide in friends."

He drained his drink. He looked at his watch again. He had been away for nearly an hour, and it would be twenty minutes more on the road, even if they left now. All that time, she was lying there, not only in the bed but, more important, in his imagination—bound, blindfolded, naked, waiting for him to come home, either alone or with half a dozen lust-crazed Samoans. Anything.

"You do love her, don't you?" Irene asked.

"What? No, not really. Not the way you mean."

"I saw that faraway look on your face. It's poignant, really. I feel sorry for you."

"Drop it. Please?"

"All right. You want me to finish my drink, don't you?"

"Yes, as a matter of fact."

Without a word, she picked up her glass and finished it off in three large, quick, angry gulps. She put it down. "I don't mean to keep you."

He called for the check.

In the antagonistic silence on the way back to Punalu'u, he decided that he had made a tactical error. Strategically, he had been correct, and for that matter had had little choice. She had forced his hand by arriving this way, and it had been necessary for him to warn her away. But he was uncomfortable. She was angry, had been rebuffed, and could, at her leisure, invent mischief, devising elaborate ways of exacting retribution. On her own, or with Larry, or with other dramatis personae of whom Victor as yet was unaware. It was a threat to the wonderfully heady feeling of power he had, its intimacy and its richness, his precious secret.

He glanced at Irene, who was driving. Her eyes were on the road. Her brow was ever so slightly furrowed. And he could see the muscles of her jaw working. So, he had to do something. For his own safety, it was necessary to finish her off.

She deserved it. Had asked for it, in fact. If she was offended, as he rather expected her to be, or if she was jealous, as she very well could be, she would nevertheless know how things stood. And for whatever reason—he hardly cared which reason—she would leave him and Emily in privacy.

"You're angry with me, aren't you?" he asked, simply interrogating her about a matter of fact.

"A little, yes."

"I deserve it, I suppose. But . . . it's a complicated situation. If you have a moment to spare me, perhaps I can show you what I mean. We'll stop at the house for a moment."

"At your house?"

"Yes."

She thought about it for a moment. He half hoped that she would decline his invitation. Perhaps the first stroke, back at the bar, had been mortal after all. But no. "All right," she said. "I'll stop by."

FOURTEEN

The room was elastic. Because she could not see, she was at liberty to imagine, and because her position was impossible, her mind had rejected it. She could not remember the actual room. She felt, indeed, only a remote connection to her body, was not an inhabitant of that body, but soared above it, perching on a high place that was sometimes the capital of a column, sometimes a balcony within an ogive arch. The room had expanded somehow and was very high. The bed was at the center rather than up against one wall. It was dark, of course. But she could see in the dark, could perceive whatever she chose. From high up in the vaulting, she could look down at the girl's body, at her own body, and feel for it a rather abstract sympathy. The poor dear! To be tied up that way! To have had a pillow shoved under her buttocks so that her pubis was thrust upward, vulnerable, open . . . It was only by an effort, straining at her bonds, that she could contrive to bring her thighs close enough together to close the aperture of her labia. Not defend herself but merely close the gaping of her sex.

From her lofty perch, she could look out on a barren landscape in which dark clouds scudded across a pale moon. Somewhere out there were her worshippers, winding up the hill in serpentine lines . . . That she was an object of worship seemed strangely reasonable. That her body should be an altar to be consecrated by their rough piety was natural, an inevitable thing. How had she lived so long without realizing what a sacred vessel she was?

Elsewhere, as the bubblegum rock and the commercials from the radio station demonstrated, there were people who were unaware of the wonderful, terrible events that were taking place in their midst.

She thought, of course, of Victor, whose character and intentions had become as indeterminate as the architecture of the room itself. In one way, some diminishing part of her attention remembered that she was furious with him, that his tying her up, his strenuous efforts to humiliate her, and his acting out of his fantasies were simply unacceptable, and that she had filed away somewhere her intention to resist if possible, to escape if possible, to get out of this any way she could. But there was another part of her, up in the vaulting of the chamber of her fantasy, that felt flattered by his attentions. It was grotesque, but the irresistible truth remained that she had never before taken her sexuality so seriously—had never had occasion to take it so. She would not have been able to imagine herself imagining long lines of townspeople out of some Gothic movie coming up the mountain to her forbidding room . . . to worship her upraised mount of Venus?

Her thought—but in some way his too, she realized. It would have been considerably easier for him simply to have screwed her, to have extracted his payment for the trip in much the way men back in New York extracted payment for dinners, trips to the theater, or evenings at a disco . . . That was what she supposed she had expected at the beginning, when he had made his impish proposal. But he had gone to all this trouble. So that there was either pathology—in which case he might wind up butchering her—or there was some dark and hidden recognition of her power, the woman's power she'd always had but never realized. From the imaginary height of the small stone balcony her fancy had carved some twenty feet up—above a sumptuary tapestry of a virgin and a unicorn—she could look down and allow the tiny figure of herself such possibilities.

At the same time, the tiny brain that was left in the little body rebelled. No! Bullshit! He's not thinking or feeling, or implying any such thing. He's such a pervert . . . And if there was anything clever in his method it was only the possibility of his having figured out that she might, after a time, begin to collaborate with him. She mustn't let herself do that. She must fight him mentally now, if she had any expectation of fighting him physically, later. She must not let herself be suckered into his crazy games. . .

The entire structure, the castle, the hill, the lofty vantage point crumbled at what she thought was the sound of a door closing. She could not be sure. She strained to listen through the moronic blare of the radio. Had she imagined it? She tried to discern another confirming sound. Or after a long enough period of silence, a lack of confirmation by which she could hope that she had merely imagined the door's closing. Had he gone out? She had never been able to decide. She had thought it unlikely that he would leave her tied up, helpless, to perish in a fire, perhaps . . . So, even if there were a sound, it wouldn't necessarily mean anything more than that Victor, after a nap, had got up and was going to the bathroom. Or into the kitchen. . .

She wished she could escape again from her body's bondage and perch way up on the ceiling, looking down. It was dreadful to be tied up, but it was even worse to be confined to the tied-up body, doubly bound.

Another sound. A different kind of door. The refrigerator? She had no idea how long she had been lying there. An hour? Two? More? Long enough, certainly, for her mind to have wandered. But even that freedom was gone. She struggled again, trying to pull her arms free, but the linen dishcloths were like iron. There was no way. All she could do was clench her leg muscles to bring her thighs slightly together.

She heard another sound, the clinking of ice in a glass. She felt a wave of relief. After all that, it was nothing more than Victor coming in with something for her to drink.

"Victor?"

There was no answer. But she knew he was there. He was playing games again. "Victor?" she asked a second time, not worried, or not letting any worry show. If he wanted to play, she could play too, and deny him his little victories. "I'm thirsty. Can I have some of your drink?"

She felt a hand behind her head, lifting. She opened her mouth. She felt a straw at her lips. She sucked. It was some kind of rum drink with fruit juice in it, sweet and cold.

She felt a fingertip stroking the inside of her calf and upward toward her thigh.

It took her a moment to realize that with one hand holding her head and one hand holding the glass, the fingertip on her thigh belonged to a third hand.

She gasped, gagged, coughed.

She caught her breath and tried to think. Had he done it? Had he actually gone out to bring someone back to her? Or was it some kind of elaborate trick? No, it couldn't be . . . There was no way he could be holding her head and the glass and stroking her thigh.

Worst of all, she felt herself lubricating . . .

Victor had explained to Irene his program for Emily. He had half supposed (and half hoped) that Irene might be offended, that there might be an argument, and that in the end she might tell him to get out of the car and drive away, disappearing below the hairpin turn of their common driveway. He had not expected her to be shocked by what he was doing—it was almost a point of honor with Irene never to be shocked at anything. But it had seemed possible that her sisterly feelings for Emily, however theoretical, might be aroused, and that on Emily's behalf she might resent his efforts to achieve a dumb dependence and unthinking passivity, not only sexual but spiritual as well.

They sat in the car under the house. Victor explained. Irene listened, showing so little in her reaction that Victor was puzzled . . . until she said, "It's a charming fantasy, I grant you. I don't believe you. Not for a minute."

"You want me to show you?"

"Isn't that what you'd offered?" she asked. And then, "Cold feet? Or is it all an invention, after all?"

He got out of the car. She followed him up the steps and into the living room. The door slammed behind them. He led her to the doorway of the bedroom from which Irene could see Emily on the bed, naked, bound, and blindfolded, just as Victor had said.

"A drink?" Victor offered in a whisper.

Irene nodded. Victor led the way into the kitchen. He had a pitcher of rum punch in the refrigerator. He poured a couple of glasses, dropped in a few ice cubes, and handed one to Irene. "So, you see?"

"I see. I saw, anyway. I'm not sure I understand it. Do you love her or hate her?"

"I haven't quite decided."

"This is so . . . unlike you."

"Isn't it? It's frightening, in a way. I'm surprised at myself. It's appalling and exhilarating at the same time. But it requires that I be . . . left alone. You can understand that."

"In a way, yes, of course," Irene said, lounging against the countertop, sipping her drink, and studying Victor. "You're ashamed of yourself."

"No. Or only partly. It's just that this is a delicate moment in the process. . ."

"Why the blindfold?"

"I've told her that I might recruit surrogates,

that she would have to submit to anyone I brought into the house . . . Not that I've decided actually to go through with it. But she has no way of knowing."

"Well, at least I understand why you were looking at your watch. It wasn't just rudeness."

"I was eager to get back. I was worried about her. I'm sorry."

"Accepted," she said. "I suppose I could help you."

"No, no thank you."

"You sure? I could give you a hand. Literally. I've been thinking about her . . . It would be difficult not to. Lying there in the passivity you've arranged, she has to assume that you are keeping her to yourself. If only to allay her fears, she has to dismiss what you've told her about bringing strangers back for her. . . Not that it's so terrible. I remember when we played a similar game. Of course, I wasn't tied up or blindfolded. But it was close enough."

"I remember," Victor said. "It's stayed with me, evidently."

"There was some fear. But it was very exciting. The utter abdication of control was . . . delicious."

"Yes, that's what I want."

"Why don't I give her a sip of my drink?"

It took Victor a moment to figure out what the significance of that offer was. With Irene giving Emily a sip of the rum punch, another hand, or another pair of hands, on another part of Emily's body, would produce a *frisson* of terrified delight. The power he had was a power to control those limited cues by which Emily was connected to the real world.

"If it would amuse you . . ." he agreed.

"If it would amuse you. It's a repayment, shall we say, of an old favor."

"All right, why not?"

They went back to the bedroom.

"Victor?" Emily asked.

He put his finger to his lips, enjoining silence.

"Victor?" she asked a second time. She was frightened, her muscles tensed, the bonds taut. Irene jiggled the ice cubes in her drink. "I'm thirsty," Emily said. "Can I have some of your drink?"

Irene lifted Emily's head and supported it with one hand. With her other hand, she lowered the glass and put the straws of the drink to Emily's lips. At the bottom of the bed, Victor saw an unself-conscious smile come to Irene's lips. Of pity? Envy? Something beyond either of those sentiments? Emily's position, helpless and infantile, was very close, he thought, to what we all want—a baby's security in which our wants are met and our appetites tended by more or less ghostly presences. She lay there, a great pink baby, to be tended and stroked, fed and cleaned, even aroused and gratified sexually, with nothing required of her, nothing expected except her acceptance, her acquiescence, her recognition of the desirability of this vacation from the complications of living.

Irene, sophisticated and experienced as she was, could see it better than Emily. And could smile, betraying her recognition of what it must be like . . . Except that Emily was still fighting it. He supposed that she was still fighting. He touched the inside of her calf with the pads of the fingertips of his right hand, stroking lightly and roving upward past the interesting articulation of her knee to the swelling of her slender thigh. He felt the renewed violence of her muscles as they clenched, fighting their bonds. He heard her gag and cough. Irene took away the drink and put it down.

Victor sat down on the bed. Irene looked down at Emily's supine form. She touched one of the erect nipples with a fingertip, kissed the finger, and blew the kiss to Victor. She waved goodbye.

Victor was torn. He had not yet forgotten his concern about Irene's motives—which he didn't understand—or her possible interference. And yet there had been something appealing about her participation, something that had elicited from him a response that was partly sexual and partly emotional. He could not go after her to bring her back. He wasn't sure he wanted to. Besides, Emily's strenuous bucking suggested that Irene's plan had been effective. Emily had to think that the hands at her head had been Victor's—which meant that she would also have to believe that the hands that were now high up on the insides of her thighs and stroking the crease between her leg and her groin were not his, were some stranger's . . .

So be it! He took one finger, put it into his mouth to wet it with spit, and entered her with it.

"No. Nooooooo! Victor? Victor!" she called. She called to him in a loud voice as if he were in another room. For help. To save her from the stranger.

But he was the stranger, and he did what the stranger would have done or should have done. He played with her. She was wet anyway, which was interesting. A part of her, that part of her, was already convinced. He removed his finger, tore off his trousers, and entered her hurriedly, as that stranger they were both imagining would have done. And hurriedly, lest Victor come back, the stranger fucked her.

"Oh, no! Oh, God, no! Oh, no!" came from her mouth, but from her other more reliable mouth, a series of yeses that ended in an ultimate assent.

He had been waiting for that. And he joined in it.

He lay there, breathing hard, resting, satisfied. Thinking. What had he never done? What would be the signature of that stranger? He got off her, tweaked her nipple, and turned off the radio. He picked up his pants, put them on, as surely the stranger would have to do, and left the room.

Let her lie there digesting what had happened—or what she had to think had happened.

He closed the bedroom door behind him. Let her imagine the fatuous farewells of Victor and the stranger. Even, perhaps, the payment of money—from either one of them. It worked just as well, either way.

It was a difficult decision for her. Had she not cared about Victor, it would have been easier. Indeed, there would have been no decision to make. She simply would have remained to witness, perhaps to participate . . . To pretend to be a man? Why not? How many such opportunities present themselves?

But she had a deeper instinct to listen to and to trust in. She could not rely upon Victor's mood of the moment. She had to take a longer view, and at least allow for the possibility that once the excitement had passed, he could quite conceivably look back upon his own behavior with amazement or distaste or even horror. She could not afford to associate herself too closely with his ecstasy, because to do so would be to risk being included in his revulsion.

Therefore, she decided that she'd better leave while it was still possible to do so with grace. She looked down at the girl, unnecessarily writhing, safer than she knew, better loved than she could suppose . . . Or, no, the girl seemed to be responding to the situation, despite herself. The nipples were erect, stiff as the tops of a couple of toothpaste tubes. Irene felt her own nipples tingle. She realized that if she was going to depart it had better be immediately. She touched one of Emily's nipples with her fingertip, touched the fingertip to her pursed lips, and blew Victor a kiss.

He was grinning like a little boy with a new toy.

Irene waved goodbye and left the room. She hesitated. In the living room, she had second thoughts. Perhaps Victor would come after her. What then? Should she yield? Return? Better not . . . Besides, he was not following her, apparently, had better things to do for the moment.

So, thinking of the game he was playing, realizing that she was supposed to stand for Victor in the charade they were playing for the blindfolded girl, she decided that she'd done enough. She let herself out, latching the door behind her and closing it as quietly as she could. She got into her car, started the engine, backed out into the driveway, and drove the hundred yards or so to her own carport.

She was agitated, convinced that she had done the right thing, or anyway the shrewd thing, but not comfortable about it. Angry, in fact. Why should she have to cope, do all the thinking for everyone, and even in the pursuit of pleasure function like some executive? The image of the frightened, excited girl, bound to the bed and transported upon it beyond the boundaries of her own intentions to some primitive jungle of the nerves where pure sensation quivered . . . held Irene, fascinated her. She was jealous, she realized. A silly, stupid emotion of which she disapproved on principle, and still, there it was. The combination of Victor's tender solicitude, checking his watch that way and impatient to get back to her, with the girl's nipples, rigid and aroused, was irresistible. She wanted to be aroused that way, and to have such care, such loving attention lavished upon her.

Inside, there was just Larry, whose companionship was better than nothing but not ardent, not passionate. Larry knew that she was using him, and Larry was using her, to get near Emily . . .

Well, then, by God, she would use him. Really use him. Why not? Tie him up as Victor had tied up Emily! Or not quite the same way. To punish him for his youth, his sentimentality, his smug self-confidence.

And then? Let him escape? Let him save Emily from the best time that girl was ever likely to know in her life. And appear contrite before Victor . . .

Some such rough scheme seemed as satisfying as anything she could devise. It touched some of the right bases, and then it arrived at a place close enough to where she was aiming, had been aiming from the beginning.

She took a deep breath. The faint sound of the ocean came from her right, below. It sounded like an echo of the rush of passion she knew was spending itself above, where she had left Victor and Emily. Irene felt like a rock, black and ugly, at low tide, waiting for the water to come back, cover it, make it shine, make it gleam and sparkle, make it beautiful.

"You find out anything?" Larry asked. He was sprawled on a white flokati on the floor, watching television. Some cop show.

Irene nodded.

"Well? You know where they are?"

"Yes."

"You going to tell me? What is this, some kind of game? I get twenty questions?"

"You get a lot further by getting up, by turning off the television set, by inquiring, perhaps, if I've eaten."

"Ah, shit," he said, but he got up. "Well?"

"Shit will get you shit. I'm hungry. Fix me a steak."

"I waited for you," he told her. "I'll fix us both steaks. Okay?"

She nodded.

"I'm sorry," he said.

"Don't worry about it. I'm not angry."

"Is she all right?"

"Yes, I think so."

"And you know where they are?"

"Yes."

"Well?"

"Fix the steaks. We'll talk about it after dinner."

He hesitated, trying to decide whether to push it or not.

"Make mine rare," she prompted.

Finally, he figured out what ought to be immediately obvious—that they were going to do it her way or not at all. He went off to the kitchen to broil the steaks. She followed him, went to the refrigerator, and took out a bottle of Perrier water. She poured it into a glass, watched as Larry struggled with himself once more about asking about Emily, and left him to marinate in his discomfort. She needed a good soak in a tepid tub with a little bath oil. And the cold bubbly spring water in easy reach on the rim of the tub.

In the kitchen, Larry strewed some frozen french fries onto a cookie sheet and stuck them in the oven. He had no idea whether Irene would want any potatoes. He wanted some. At the worst, there'd be some left over to be thrown away. He figured how long the potatoes would take and when the steak would have to go under the broiler. This was crazy! He was worried about Emily, and he was figuring the cooking times of food? Nuts! But what chance had he of finding Emily without Irene's help? And that woman was power mad! Stay cool, he told himself. Don't get upset. And more important, don't let her see that you're upset. This whole trip had been crazy, making sense only as a way of getting to Emily—whose trip had been ever crazier.

Irene returned to the kitchen. She was wearing a white terry cloth robe and had her hair bound in a towel wrapped as a turban. "You haven't put the steaks in?"

"I was waiting for the potatoes," he explained. "I figured that the object was to get them to come out together."

"Very good. Put some mustard on the steaks.

Just a little. It's good."

He went to the refrigerator for the mustard.

"I'll tell you where she is," Irene said, "in the morning. And I expect that you'll go to her . . ."

"Yes, probably."

"And then what?"

"I don't know. I haven't figured that out. I'll see what's coming down. How it is, and how I feel about it. It's no good deciding these things ahead of time."

"Quite right. It's no good at all. But my hunch is that either you'll make up with her and the two of you will go away together, or she'll want to stay with Victor. And you'll go away alone."

"Maybe."

"So, let's have a night of it. I deserve something, after all, having brought you here. And we could say goodbye to each other as pleasantly as possible. Does that sound reasonable?"

"Sure," he said, wondering what she was up to. His hunch was that she knew something that she wasn't telling him, something important or relevant about Emily. The worst? That Emily and Victor were getting along famously, and that, as Irene had just suggested as a possibility, Emily might not come away with him, might want to stay in Hawaii with Victor . . . What then? What could he possibly do? Come back to Irene? Was that what she had in mind, then—that he'd come back and would have to accept his position as a menial and a stud?

"Is there wine? There was supposed to be," she said.

"I don't know. Is there? I should have opened it to let it breathe."

"Ah, so you do know some of the rituals of

gracious living. But I don't believe in that one. What it breathes in the bottle in an hour it will do in the glass in five minutes." She rummaged under the cabinets, found a bottle of wine, handed it to Larry, and told him, "There must be a corkscrew somewhere."

"In a minute. It's time for me to put the steaks in."

The rhythm of dinner, its preparation and its consumption, carried them for the better part of an hour. Each of them was cautious, but for that reason each of them made an effort to be amiable. Irene made coffee while Larry cleared the table. Then, out on the deck, overlooking the ocean, they sat down to drink their coffee and talk. Larry was surprised at her candor.

"I must warn you," she said. "About Emily, I mean."

"Oh?"

"They're apparently into bondage."

"What?"

"Bondage. Being tied up."

"You mean he's tied up?"

"She is."

"Emily? He's sick!"

"Not necessarily. Both of them, perhaps, but why pick on him?"

"She agreed to this?"

"Evidently."

"Tell me! What did he say? And why would he tell you?"

"To boast, perhaps. Or to confide. Both, quite likely."

"I've got to get to her!" He actually put his cup down.

"Now? You've no idea where they are!"

"You'll tell me that."

"And if I did? You rush over there. And then what? Break in? That's burglary. Fight with Victor? That's assault. You have to remember that they're married. They are consenting adults. You have no rights at all. He could have you locked up for coming to the rescue of the maiden in distress. Or woman. She's not a maiden any more."

"What do I do, then?"

"As I suggested before, whatever you do ought to wait until morning. More coffee?"

"Thanks, yes." He picked his cup up. She poured another cup for him.

"Why would she want to do that?" he asked, after a sip.

"If you trust the person . . . it can be pleasant. Intensified. Haven't you ever read *The Joy of Sex?* That book, all by itself, helped save the clothesline industry in America. I mean, everyone has a dryer! What do you think all those people are doing with the clotheslines?"

"I don't know," he said. "I never thought about it."

"Perhaps you should have."

"What do you mean by that?"

"It seems to turn her on."

"We never needed kinky stuff like that."

"Didn't you? Perhaps she needed something . . . to be taken seriously."

"What's that got to do with being tied up?"

"If you have to ask, I can't explain it," she said, smiling, but he wasn't sure whether she was joking or not.

"You've done it?" he asked.

"Oh, yes."

"And it's . . . good?"

"It can be."

He tried to imagine Emily tied up. What on earth for? That Victor was a depraved old creep was more reasonable, or anyway more comfortable, than the idea that Emily was a willing participant.

"Would you like to see what it feels like?" Irene asked.

"Me? No!"

"Suit yourself. But my fear is that . . . that you and Emily will have differences to overcome. She may have acquired a sophistication that you could find uncomfortable. Or intolerable. In which case, your whole effort of coming after her to save her from Victor's clutches could be pointless. And that's even assuming that she wants to be saved."

"I don't believe it."

"Why not? It seems clear enough to me. Even obvious."

"That I should tie you up? Or be tied up?" he asked. "I don't see the point to it."

"But that's just the point—that you don't see it. And evidently, she does. That's a difference in more than technique, I'd imagine. It's a question of attitude, playfulness, or in another way, seriousness. One must accept one's animal nature. Or coax it out of its hiding places. But suit yourself. . ."

"What would happen? What would you actually do?" he asked after a moment's thought.

He was hooked. It was only a matter of time and patience to play him and bring him to gaff. Within the hour, she had him on the bed, his hands and feet bound not by dishcloths but by electrical extension cords. And blindfolded, with a dishcloth.

"So? So now what?" he asked.

She slapped him smartly across the face, using her open palm but with enough force to leave a red mark.

"What the hell? What's that for?"

She slapped him again.

"You'll speak when I give you permission," she said.

"I . . . I didn't figure on any of this," he said.

A third time, she hit him.

This time, he'd learned. He kept still. She went out to the kitchen to get herself a brandy, but she brought back some chocolate syrup too. She sipped the brandy. She poured the chocolate sauce over his genitals in a delicate thin stream with squiggles and scrolls.

"Wha . . ." He wanted to know what it was. But he didn't want to be slapped again.

"It's chocolate sauce," she said. "A kind of sundae on a stick. Or it will be, when there's a stick."

She looked down and watched him as his cock pulsated from limp to firm, lolling sideways, then completing its half-arc to erect. It was the stickiness on his penis and his scrotum, but more than that it was the thought in his head of what was going to happen, what it would feel like . . . She could see the ropy veins bulging purple.

It was utterly unlike her reaction to Emily in the same situation. For Emily, she had felt an empathetic connection, a mixture of sadness and desire, but that had been perhaps misleading. She could understand Victor better, now, for she enjoyed the power, enjoyed the sense of control, and was surprised to find that she could be quite mean. Not to his cock, but to his head, his face and his mouth. When he prompted her with a "Well?" she slapped him once again.

"Not a word. Not a goddamned word. I'll do it my way, at my pleasure, and in my own time. You just lie there, you hear? You're meat. Just meat. Meat doesn't talk. And it never talks back."

But that wasn't true. She didn't think of him as meat. Meat would have been easier to deal with. One just consumes it or spits it out. He was meat struggling against himself, against his own nature. He was . . . like one of those old dinosaurs, with a brain in its head and another brain in its tail. There was a brain, however rudimentary, in his cock, in its bulging glans . . . And she would communicate with it, teach it to think on its own, bring it into its power and let it think for itself. Humiliate the other brain, and encourage this one! It was beautifully simple.

But having glimpsed this vision of what it was that Victor might be experiencing, she felt for the first time a despair, for she knew as she had not known before what Victor saw in the girl, what he had stumbled upon, and, most important, how difficult it would be for her to compete. The best she could hope for was that the game would eventually play itself out, that there would come a time when, having won an absolute submission for himself from the girl, he might weary of it and of her. Until then? It would be well to do what he had asked her to do, leaving them alone. With Larry, that would not be intolerable, after all.

She stroked the rigid penis, stared at the chocolate on her fingertip, and put her finger into her mouth. Utter freedom and absolute slavery. What would amuse her to do with them?

"How would you like a little dessert?" she asked.

He didn't answer.

"You may speak. You have permission."

"What do you mean?" he asked.

"Before I have my sundae on a stick, I thought you might like some . . . chocolate pie?"

"How would I eat it?"

"I'll arrange it for you," she said. She undressed, hung up her dress in the closet and put her underwear into the hamper in the bathroom. She returned to the bedroom, poured some of the chocolate syrup onto her hand and smoothed in onto her breast. She lowered herself over Larry's face and let him lick and lap and suck the chocolate off.

It was, in itself, mildly pleasant. The excruciatingly sweet part of it was the idea that she had of . . . What was the word? Synaesthesia! The switching of senses, so that one could hear blue, or see the color of E-flat. "I could have you here for days," she murmured. "Weeks, even. And feed you only from my body. Baby food. Milk shakes. Anything I could smear on, or douche myself with. Eat and drink sex. Hunger and thirst for it! Be a slave to it . . . the way she is, with Victor."

"What? He's doing this to her?"

She slapped him as hard as she could, twice.

Teach him to blabber like that!

"Not a word. Not a fucking word!" she shouted.

She rearranged herself on the bed so that she could lick some of the chocolate off him. Not greedily. A dessert, to nibble, almost absent mindedly. She took a sip of brandy from the snifter she had left on the nightstand. And a little more chocolate.

She had all the time in the world.

FIFTEEN

For closeness, for intimacy, Victor slept in the other room. It was a paradoxical refinement he had figured out in what was for him an ecstatic rush of creation and connection. The separate bedrooms, for instance, came to him as a happy thought begotten by the discovery in the linen closet of an old-fashioned cheap alarm clock, one of those dumpy circles of metal with the twin bells on the top. The bells put him in mind of old Pavlov with his salivating dogs—from which it was only a racy half-step (samba? tango?) to an application to Emily's delicate situation. How to manage it so that, at the clanging of the alarm clock she felt a similar rush of fluids?

It had taken him only a few minutes of delicious speculation to realize that her sensorium was limited to what he allowed. If he were to sleep in the same bed, which would be uncomfortable anyway, what with the bonds and her spread limbs, she would be able to sense his movements, would know whether he was there or not there, awake or asleep. On the other hand, if he were to sleep in the bed in the other room, he would always be imminent, liable at any moment to appear . . . And the liability was what fascinated him. By absenting himself, he could be continually present as a menace, a hope, a possibility. And the clock could be the machinery by which she could be kept continually mindful of him and of her own vulnerability. By setting the clock at random times, he could apply Pavlov's principles, appearing whenever the bell sounded . . . Or, no, not every time. He wouldn't have to be a slave to it, himself, but could enslave her even more absolutely by the refinement of random reward. If she recognized the bell as a cue for his appearance, then after the first two or three reinforcements of that connection, he wouldn't even need to appear. As Pavlov did not have to present the dogs with food.

So, with the blinds drawn against the gorgeous Hawaiian sunshine, and with the lights in the bedroom always on, Emily would float in a timelessness punctuated only at the ringing of the bell, never knowing whether it was night or day, whether the interval between his appearances would be five minutes or five hours . . . His, absolutely!

Sometimes, he came into her room, bluntly fucked her, and left her. But sometimes he made love to her, gently, slowly, condescending to please. And there were occasions when he simply brought her food, or lemonade, or sponged her body, dried her, and sprinkled cologne on her, fussing over her as if she were a large doll. But sometimes he would let the clock go off and leave her alone, letting her mind do the work that he didn't have to do and that it could do even more efficiently and insidiously than he could.

She had stopped fighting him. Partly, that had been the result of the hopelessness of fighting, but he had defused some of her fear and anger, not needing them, not seeing them as useful to the purpose that he was in the process of learning, discovering it as he went along. He had realized that this exquisite arrangement could not go on forever, that eventually he would have to release the girl. And then what? Throw her away like a used tissue? Or continue to explore?

To win her confidence, to make the progress more efficient, and to take into account Irene's unexpected appearance, Victor decided that the best thing to do would be to let Emily understand that her predicament was not quite so menacing or dangerous as he had first let her imagine.

He brought her a small plate of chicken salad that he had prepared, with curry powder—just a dash—in the chicken salad and tomato wedges and cornichons symmetrically arranged. He removed her blindfold so that she could appreciate it. And he asked her how she was feeling.

"All right," she said, but rather morosely.

"You seem discontented."

"Now whatever gave you an idea like that? What would I have to complain about?"

"Yes, what? A good question!"

"Who was it that you brought in to me . . . yesterday or the day before. I have no idea what time it is. I don't even know what day it is."

"We're on vacation. On a honeymoon! What do you care what time it is?"

"You know. Why shouldn't I?"

"Have some chicken salad?" he asked, ignoring her complaint.

She opened her mouth. He put a forkful of food into it. There was a small morsel of celery that had fallen to her chin. He picked it off and put it into his own mouth.

"There was someone here. But nobody for you to worry about. It was Irene."

"I don't believe you."

"Oh, yes. I was surprised, myself."

"It couldn't have been!"

"Why not? She was the one who gave you the drink. I was at the bottom of the bed. She left. I was the one who stayed."

She thought about it. He gave her another forkful of chicken salad. She chewed—on the chicken and on the question. She swallowed. "But why would she be here?"

"I don't know," Victor answered, truthfully. And then, to let her know that he was being truthful, to prove it to her, he added, "Larry is here with her."

"Here? In the house?"

"Here in Hawaii."

"I don't get it."

"Neither do I, really. Unless we've invented a new art form, which I rather doubt . . ."

"He's here after me," she said.

"Oh?"

"I'm sure of it."

"Why?" Victor asked. "Is that what you want?"

"I've . . . thought of it. But that's not why I think he's here for me. I . . . I know him. He's hurt and angry. So he came after me. She was a convenient way for him to get here."

"He came after you to save you? Or to punish you?"

"I don't know. I don't even know that he knows."

"And what do you want?"

"Now? I'm not sure. It was better when I didn't have to think."

He turned away in order to keep her from seeing his face. He was touched. Moved. What he had wanted to happen to her, for her, for them both . . . had happened. It was amazing.

"What gets me," Emily said, "is what she's doing. That's what I can't figure."

"Irene?"

"Irene. My guess is that Larry's here because I'm here. But that doesn't explain her."

"Maybe she's here because I'm here?" It was a question, a joke, and then, by only the slightest rearrangement of the bits of glass in the kaleidescope, a certainty. Of course! How could he have failed to see it? "I suppose we should be flattered by all this attention," he said, ruefully.

"We could go somewhere else," Emily suggested. "Somewhere else on the island. Some other island. Anywhere . . ."

He didn't answer. He was thinking about it. Would that really solve anything?

"You don't have to worry about . . . about untying me. I won't run away."

"No, I know."

He had won. And, yes, he felt a kind of satisfaction. But he felt a great sadness, too. It was something he had not foreseen. If his attentions to Emily had been those of a wrangler breaking a horse, then he supposed that the secret they shared was the sadness, the regret when the fight goes out of the animal, the mourning for that spirit that had been the challenge. It just went away, trotting off into the plains, to leave behind another workhorse, of no particular interest. "I know," he said again.

"How long has it been?" Emily asked.

"Three days."

"Is that all?"

He nodded.

For Emily, it had been a weird time. She had struggled at first not only against her restraints, trying to work the knots in the dishcloths loose, but against Victor's domination, his arrogance, his megalomania . . . She had been shrewd enough to understand what he was doing and what the purpose of each gesture and strategem had been. The clock, for instance . . . He had put the clock where she could hear it, not next to his bed in the other room but on a small table in the little hall. She had been subjected, therefore, not only to the ringing of its loud bell, but to its ticking, too, each tick announcing clearly that the bell would go off one second sooner. Or half a second. . .

She knew about Pavlov, had studied his experiments in college, and resented what Victor was doing. He was treating her like a dog. A thing! He was short-circuiting her, and dealing directly with her cunt, which was a thing. He was evil! But not always cruel. He fooled her, over and over again. Sometimes he would come when the bell rang and would do pleasant even comical things . . . Give her a douche with club soda. Or put face-mask stuff on her breasts, letting it dry and then peeling it off. Or feed her. Or bring her drinks with rum in them that she would gulp down in the hope that drunkenness was a place in which to hide. Or sometimes, every now and then, he wouldn't come at all . . . She'd hear the bell, and know that it was the cue for him to come, would feel herself getting excited, and be furious with herself, hating him . . . And then be furious with her hatred, as if her willing it had held him off, and it was her own fault that he had not appeared for her.

So she lay there, suspended in the half-light that she could perceive through the blindfold. It was quiet. Victor had turned the radio off very early on, and he had replaced it with the ticking of the clock that insisted on time's passing—which was all the more outrageous because she never had any idea what time it was. What day it was. She had asked him once what time it was, but he had refused to tell her. "What difference does it make?" he had joked. Only it wasn't a joke. It was the truth. He could bring her cornflakes in the afternoon, just to confuse her. Or steak in the middle of the night. And then, five minutes later, orange juice. And an hour after that, a pot of mint tea. Or a glass of champagne and a bowl of fruit. He liked to feed her by hand, putting slices of fresh peaches into her mouth and letting her lick the juice from his fingers.

Once, he came in when the bell rang, took the blindfold off, and let her watch him as he stood over her, one foot on each side of her waist, and masturbated, and came all over her breasts and then smeared the come . . . And put the blindfold back and went away. Leaving her to feel it drying on her. And to decide whether it had been ridiculous or disgusting or . . . teasing. To admit, to have to admit, that she would have preferred it if he'd fucked her.

He was clever about making her want him. Or it. He could be wonderfully langorous, coming into the room silently, probably with bare feet, so that the first sign of his presence was the wetness of his tongue at her cunt. He liked to go down on her, liked to eat her, nibbling and licking and tonguing her until she was so wet she thought she was going to dissolve, just melt from the waist down, from the neck down, into a pool of jelly. He made her come, not just once or twice, but countless times so that she was almost hysterical, giddy, laughing. Or sometimes he would do it just the opposite way, working her up to a plateau and then keeping her there, lying still with his tongue resting lightly on her clit, and flicking it like a wicked snake every now and then to keep her up there, for hours, ages, until she was writhing with lust. Then, sometimes, he entered her and just lay there, letting her feel him inside her, and not moving at all. He made her come by sucking on her nipples. And then he started to move, long slow thrusts, that squeezed out another orgasm like the last toothpaste in the nearly empty tube. Once, he lay there on her, in her, motionless, until she fell asleep.

He was brisk, even violent sometimes, surprising her with an explosive fuck. But then he would play with her with his fingers, rewarding her with an orgasm. Or give her the whizzer and let it make her come while he kissed her mouth and fondled her breasts.

The time stretched out. She seemed to have been there on that bed, in that room, listening to the clock, hearing the sound of the ocean washing on the rocks, and getting laid forever. He was either very ardent, turned on by the situation (or by her?), or she had lost all sense of days and nights so that the time between sex shrank, not counting. At the beginning, she had tried to resist, to fight him, mentally if not physically, but even there she realized that it was hopeless, that her resistance was working against her and for him, because it was an acknowledgement of what was happening. She was thinking of him, of fucking and of him, of being eaten and of him. She was doing his work for him. As, of course, he knew, and had known, all along. She had attributed to him the omniscience that seems always to go with omnipotence. She had had to suppose that he knew the results of each of these actions . . . And she had been flattered by such intense attention.

So that, when he came in to talk to her, she had assumed it was one more ploy, one more test of will, one more calculated manipulation, the effect of which he had worked out in advance. She had assumed that he was thinking about her as much as she was thinking about him, that there was a weird kind of balance to it, so that he, as captor, was as much involved and absorbed as she, the captive. She had replied to his assertion about Irene honestly, because she had supposed any dissimulation would be found out and punished. And the news about the identity of the stranger that first night was reassuring. And Larry?

That, too, she was sure, had to be a test. And not knowing how to answer, she had said what she thought, because that was the safest thing to do.

She had surprised herself by suggesting that they

go away. That they keep up their game as long as possible, without interruptions by Larry or Irene. "You don't have to worry about . . . about untying me. I won't run away," she said.

"No, I know," he said. And then, after a long pause, "I know," again.

She wondered whether it was still a game. What did he know? The mood was funny, was different. "How long has it been?" she asked.

"Three days."

"Is that all?"

He nodded. He seemed to sag.

"Have I done anything wrong?"

"No," he said. "It's . . . It couldn't be helped." He got up and went to the foot of the bed. He untied her right ankle. Then her left. He rubbed the ankles. Then he came around to the head of the bed and untied her wrists.

"Is it all over?" she asked.

"That part of it," he said. "That's over. What's left for us . . . we'll see."

"You want me to tie you up?"

"No."

"Can I do anything?"

"Why don't you make coffee?" he asked.

She got up, got out of the bed and staggered . . . She sat down.

"Never mind," he said. "I'll do it."

"No, I want to. I just have to get my balance back."

"All right."

She stood up, slowly this time. She held onto the pineapple finial of the headboard for a moment. Then, walking slowly, she crossed the room to the doorway.

In the kitchen, she filled the kettle with water and put it on the burner. It was a simple mechanical action, not at all the kind of thing she had imagined herself doing. What was interesting was what she was not doing. She was not, for instance, running outside, as she could have done. Or grabbing a kitchen knife. Or . . . She could hardly remember her fantasies of flight or fighting. She poured the beans into the grinder, pressed the button for twenty seconds, released it, poured the ground coffee into the filter, and went from the kitchen to the bathroom. To pee. All by herself.

It wasn't until she was seated on the toilet that she remembered how she had imagined herself in some impossibly distant future, doing just this. She'd forgotten to close the door. And lock it. But it hardly made any difference now. It wasn't so important after all. There was the feel of the tiles under her soles, the plastic toilet seat, the ceramic pot she could touch with her fingertips . . . The gleaming chrome spigots and the bright yellow of the basin shimmered. She was still a little light-headed. She dabbed at herself with the toilet paper, flushed, and went back to the kitchen to pour the boiling water through the coffee grounds.

She prepared a tray, just the way Victor had done it for her. A cup and saucer, a spoon, the little sugar bowl and cream pitcher. She poured a little milk into the pitcher. A napkin. What else? A flower? There was a bush outside with bright red flowers. She could surprise him. She went down the steps to the door that led outside. She opened the door. She was still naked, of course, but she only thought about it now that she was about to venture outside the house. What the hell! There wasn't anyone around. It was dazzling outside. She went to the bush, pinched off one of the red blossoms, and brought it back to the door. . .

Amazing. She would never in a million years have been able to imagine herself this way. Now she could hardly imagine herself the way she had been. She brought the flower upstairs, looked for a little bud vase, couldn't find one, improvised with a narrow juice glass, put it on the tray . . . Yes! She poured the coffee into the cup. She brought the tray back to the bedroom. She put it down on the metal tray-table.

"Cream? Sugar?" she asked.

"Black. With sugar."

"Oh, yes. Sorry."

She stirred a spoonful of sugar into the coffee. He sat on one of the bright orange chairs. She brought him the cup. He nodded, accepted it, sipped.

Too sweet. Not the coffee, but the girl. Standing there like a fantasy creature, naked, eager, waiting on him . . . Flesh had done what flesh could do, and it was the spirit after all that was interesting. So, he had to face one of those awful moments of recognition of the obvious, like mortality and any other consequent implication of limitation and condition. He had to admit that he was, after all, and despite his own struggles, a sentimentalist. How . . . interesting! It was as if *he* had been tied to the bed and released, as if he had gone through a surrealist hell.

What should he do with her now? What should he do with himself? Her offer, that they could go somewhere else, that she would be willing to be tied up again . . . That had done it. If it was her whim, her wish, then he was no longer imposing his will upon her.

"Where did you get the flower?" he asked.

"On a bush. Outside."

She had gone outside. And had come back. Tamed. What would become of them now? He took another sip of the coffee. "It's very nice," he said.

"The flower? Or the coffee?"

"Both. Everything," he said. Nice, but awful. Unexplored. He hadn't thought this far ahead. For all his intricate cleverness, he had been stupid. It was hard to think. He was tired. "I'm tired," he said. "I think I'll take a nap."

"You want me to change the bed?" she asked.

"No, don't bother," he said. He was too tired to sit up while she stripped the bed and put new linens on. Besides, there was a rightness to his using it just the way it was. As the saying goes, he'd made his bed and ought therefore to lie in it. He thought of telling her the thought, the curious application of the old saw . . .

But he was too tired. He stretched out and fell asleep.

Larry, more aggressive, was fighting Irene with a different strategy and different results. He had rather enjoyed the beginning of his bondage. Not the very beginning, which had startled him. She'd been extremely free with slaps and insults, but he'd been more annoyed than frightened. He never supposed that she intended to do him any real harm. He didn't think she cared enough about him, or was sufficiently unhappy with her life, in a general way, to be seriously dangerous. She wanted to come on a little butch? That was okay with him. Just so long as he kept his mouth closed, or, at any rate, refrained from speech, he was in no trouble. Indeed, he was in pretty good shape. That it was her object to get him hard and keep him there, stretching him out on a rack of his own sexuality, didn't bother him. It was enjoyable. Or, more to the point, he thought it was enjoyable. He'd been conditioned, as most young men are, to suppose that an erection is a manifestation of well-being and delight. How could he object to so trivial a thing as the style of her attentions? On what flimsy grounds?

He was puzzled by the cold technique of the woman. He'd always supposed that girls—and women, too—were the emotional ones, more sentimental than men, and eager to talk about love rather than sex. But Irene didn't even show any particular liking for him. Contempt and indifference, if anything. In a technical, almost clinical way, she got him up, kept him up, and worked him higher. He was utterly hard, almost faint from being so hard, and she could keep him there just by stroking the length of his penis with a feather, producing a shudder in his leg muscles and a sharp intake of breath, but not the ejaculation he craved. He forgot all about her weird prohibition of speech, cried out, and begged her to let him come. She slapped him across the face. She slapped his testicles that were already congested with seminal fluid and made him groan in pain, but kept him there, right at the brink, just out of reach of that blessed relief of orgasm. He bucked and thrust with his hips to try to get more friction, more pressure, when she touched him. But she drew her hand away. She held her hand over his cock without actually touching it, just a fraction of an inch away so that he could feel the heat of her palm, could feel the proximity but not the actual touch . . . and that was nearly as exciting as if she had touched him, and exciting enough to keep him right where she wanted him. His cock felt like an enormous spike by which his whole body was impaled on the bed. His balls felt incredibly heavy and ached in fullness. His skin was on fire all over.

She found an elastic bandage, the kind he'd used to tape up a strained ankle at Harvard when he'd played soccer; but she used it to wrap his cock and his balls, binding them tightly, so that she could leave him alone in the room and still have him stay hard. He tried to think of nonsexy things, doing arithmetic in his head to make it go down. The pressure of the bandage was too much for him. He tried to think sexy, to make himself come off, the way he could in a dream sometimes. But try as he would, he could not stimulate himself mentally in such a way as to achieve an orgasm. She had been out on the deck, sunning herself. She came back into the bedroom, undid the bandage, and blew on him. Just a current of air! He'd never had a literal blowjob before. She just breathed on him, hot breath through her open lips, and then, pursing the lips, cool breath.

Finally, she got onto the bed, straddled him, and lowered herself onto his cock. She didn't move, but she didn't have to. He could buck and wiggle. He could bring himself off. He came, spasm after spasm, gushing up into her, feeling the constrictions in his vesicles sharp enough to be painful.

Great gouts of it! She hardly seemed to notice. She just sat there and felt him pumping his stuff up into her, with a distant smile on her face. She was smiling too, in relief, in gratitude even. But her smile continued and his faded. He had come, he had come by the bucketful, he had spurted enough up into that bitch to have it come dribbling out of her nose! But he hadn't gotten softer. His hard-on was still there. His cock was as rigid as it had been before the orgasm. She sat there, clenching the muscles in her cunt, enjoying the wet hotness of his rod in her. She moved, rocking slightly back and forth and shifting up and down. He was still rigid! He felt her come. And again. And once more. And nothing happened. He couldn't come again. He wasn't ready for that, wasn't back up there to a level of excitement that could enable it. But he didn't get soft, either. He was going to be hard forever! He was going to die with a damned hard-on. They'd have to build a special coffin to fit him in it. Or hack his cock off with an axe!

She uncunted, careful not to hurt him. And untied him. "There," she said. "What do you think now? It was the best fuck you ever had in your life, wasn't it?"

"I don't know. I'm still hard."

"I'll fix you. Roll over."

"On my stomach?"

"That's right. Do it!"

He rolled over. He looked as she stuck her finger in her cunt to lubricate it. What the hell was she doing? He had hardly framed the question, when she stuck her finger up his ass and started to massage his prostate. He exploded, coming again, astonished. Ashamed.

"Now," she said. "You still want to go to Emily?"

"Yes," he said.

She shook her head.

There was nothing to be done with him. Some people cannot even imagine their own experience—while it is actually happening to them! He was apparently one of that benighted group. "They've gone back to New York," she said. She twitched her finger, still embedded in his most private place.

"You're lying."

"No. When Victor found out we'd followed him, he took off. He left last night."

"And you kept me here?"

"Why not? I thought I ought to give you a chance to earn your return ticket. Besides, it was always possible that you might . . . prefer to stay. You want to?"

"Stay? With you?"

"Yes. It's up to you."

He thought about it for a minute. Maybe ninety seconds. The dull pressure of her obscene invasion was distracting. Pleasurable. Disorienting. Disgusting. He couldn't make the leap. He held back, was afraid. As she knew he would be. "No, I . . . I'd better go back."

She was not vain. But realistically, objectively, she knew that it was extremely unlikely that what she had asserted before was untrue. This *had* been the best fuck he'd ever known, better than anything he'd even been able to dream of. If he was going to walk away from it, then he wasn't the right young man for her. She thought of sex as an art form. And any art requires dedication—which he didn't have. Slowly, she withdrew her finger.

His anus continued to throb in an afterglow of sensation.

"I'll drive you back to the airport as soon as you're packed," she said.

"You're staying here?"

"I've paid for the house. I might as well live in it for a while. I could use the rest."

He didn't question it.

She gave him his return ticket. He packed quickly. Half an hour later, they were in the car, maneuvering up the driveway past the house in which Emily and Victor were living and, presumably, enjoying themselves. They turned onto the highway and headed for the Kona Airport.

SIXTEEN

Irene was sobered but not depressed. She had miscalculated, had misread the young man's character, attending more to her own hopes for him than to his limitations. And there were extenuating if not justifying circumstances. She had been playing a complicated game, after all, with her attention divided among several foci. She had been thinking of Victor and Emily as much as of Larry. And what she had attempted with Larry required more than the left hand. She had been beguiled by the example of Emily's bondage, and had assumed that what was sauce for the goose could be sauce for the gander.

She did not brood. She wasn't a brooder. She forced herself to venture out of the house. She drove up to explore the volcanos that were only half an hour away, to tramp the trails, and to look down into the steaming caldera of Kilauea, the very size of which reduced the scale of human intentions, frailties, errors, and even sins. It was difficult to resist the idea that fate played a greater part in human affairs than most of us like to admit most of the time. Not that Irene was a fatalist. But if she had made a mistake, then perhaps it was right for her to have done so, and perhaps it would all come round in the end. She had no idea how. Victor and Emily were obviously having a fine old time. It was unlikely to last very long—but Irene was no longer sure how brief their game would be. She had been wrong about her decision to come to Hawaii. She should have been more patient, figuring that when their delights began to pall, Victor would return to New York. And perhaps even alone. She could have waited there. . . But how can one know these things before the fact?

She went to the black sand beach where the waves and the wind had pulverized the dark lava to fine granules that looked even blacker under the pale blue of the sky and the darker blue of the ocean. She thought, considering the rhythm of the gentle breakers, that her timing had been off. She had always prided herself on her instincts, her timing . . . Her sense of the rhythms of emotions, usually reliable, had been her guide to such questions as when to break off a relationship, when to retreat, when to put herself forward. But in a more general way, it had been the foundation of her life. The fact that the problem she had set herself had been so very strange, the situation so unprecedented, allowed her some excuse, but she could hardly be pleased with herself.

Her instinct now was to withdraw. Not just slink away, but make a graceful exit. The only question was how to disguise her defeat. As far as Victor was concerned, Larry's departure would be good news.

She could take credit for it. And once she returned to New York? There, she could admit that she had been meddling—out of concern, of course. And she could wish him well. All that was clear enough. What it wanted was an occasion. A dinner tonight? She thought it unlikely that he'd be eager to accept. Or even able to accept. But why not? He could leave the girl tied up and come down to the lower house for an hour or so . . . She'd invite them both, expect only Victor, and not be surprised if he declined, himself. Still, she'd have offered.

When? Tonight? That could be too soon. Or she could call tomorrow and play it by ear. Late morning would give her time to assemble the food and wine in the unlikely event that he were to accept. And if not, not. She'd stay one more day and then . . . San Francisco, perhaps. Or Carmel. And then back to New York. Perhaps directly back to New York. There was no need to try to fool herself, after all.

If Irene's instincts—or perhaps luck—had failed her with Larry, nevertheless they were in remarkably fine tune *vis à vis* Victor.

After Victor untied Emily, it was a morning of free fall. Each of them, separately, and both of them together had to explore the implications of what had already happened, discover the possibilities that lay before them, and, most demanding of all, reinvent themselves in this new topography, this new geometry. Victor took a nap. Emily took a bath. Then she went out to the deck to lie in the sun for half an hour. Warmed by the sun, she went inside to make a pitcher of iced tea and to check on Victor to see whether he was awake.

He heard the sound of the ice tinkling in the pitcher and opened his eyes. "What time is it?" he asked, rolling over.

"I don't know," she said. "I guess you've been sleeping for a half an hour or so."

"And you? What have you been doing?"

"I took a bath. I went out onto the deck. I got thirsty out there so I came in to make some iced tea. I thought you might want some."

"Yes, thanks."

"Sugar?"

He nodded. He had not intended to fall asleep. He had, indeed, felt tired, but he had thought only to lie down for a while. If she thought he was asleep . . . she could have tried to escape, to leave. He had intended to lie there, listening to her, keeping tabs on her. But none of that had been necessary. He had known that, and his body had known it too. It had been confident enough to go to sleep. Extraordinary!

She went back to the kitchen to pour him a tall glass of iced tea and to stir in a little sugar. She brought it into the bedroom, handed it to him, and stood there while he sipped it.

"Terrific," he said. "Thank you." He took another sip. "What would you like to do today?"

"Up to you," she said.

We have available all the conventional diversions, I believe. Fishing, sailing, swimming, mountains. . ."

"Whatever you like."

"Or we could just stay here. Would you like that?"

"Whatever you say."

"You're allowed to express an opinion. To have a preference."

"But do I have to?" she asked.

"No, you don't have to."

"Then I won't," she said. "You wanted to do the thinking. You wanted to make the decisions. You wanted to . . . I don't know . . . have the power. Have it! I kind of liked it, not having to think."

He considered that for a moment, sipped his iced tea, and tried to decide how she had meant that. Was there a side to it? Was she putting him on? It would be easy enough to find out, he thought. "All right," he said. "Fine. You can strip the bed to begin with." He got up from the bed, crossed the room, and sat down in one of the bright orange chairs to watch her. It was rather pleasant to observe her as she worked, to watch how her breasts wiggled as she struggled with the king-sized sheet's fitted corners, and to note her lack of self-consciousness. Touching. And funny, too. He wondered how she would look in one of those little white aprons that was a part of the conventional costume for chambermaids in French bedroom farces. Not the whole costume, of course. Just the apron. Or, on second thought, that would cover too much. The right touch would be one of a purely symbolic nature, covering as little flesh as possible. A bow tie? A dog collar!

"When you're finished with that," he said, "you might scrub the kitchen floor."

No response. Nothing. Had she heard him? He wondered for a moment whether he had spoken the instruction aloud or merely thought it in a kind of mental tryout. But he was unwilling to risk the dilution of authority that would be the consequence of his repeating himself. He watched as she carried the bundle of dirty linen into the bathroom and then returned with fresh sheets and pillow slips from the linen closet. By the time he had finished his glass of tea, she had just about finished making the bed. It was with particular satisfaction that he watched her go into the kitchen and listened to her rummaging about in the broom closet for a bucket and cleaning supplies. He heard the noise of water running and resounding in the bucket.

With a studied indifference, he sauntered through the kitchen on his way out to the deck and, yes, there she was, down on her hands and knees, scrubbing the floor with an old-fashioned scrub brush. It was at this moment that the telephone rang.

"Answer it," he told her.

She was facing away from him. She turned her head, looking back at him, so that her face made a third circle, to the right of and a little bit beyond the two orbs of her buttocks. Resisting? Imploring? Victor looked away. The telephone continued to ring. Emily got to her feet, tiptoed daintily over the wet floor, reached the countertop on which she could lean, and stretched to get the telephone from the wall. "Hello?"

A pause.

"Yes. Fine, thank you."

A pause.

"Oh, I'd better let you speak to Victor." She covered the mouthpiece of the telephone with her palm. "It's Irene," she said. "She's inviting us to dinner."

"All right," Victor said. "I'll talk to her."

She brought him the phone. It had one of those extra-long cords. She handed it to him. She went back to her scrubbing.

"Hello?" Victor said. "Irene?"

"Yes, it's me. I hope you don't mind my calling."

"Not at all."

"I wanted to let you know that you were right, after all. I shouldn't have come. The whole idea was ill-conceived. You'll forgive me?"

"Of course," he said, wondering what she was getting toward.

"Larry's already gone. I'll be leaving in a day or two. I thought, before I left, we might get together. Would you come for dinner?"

"Dinner?" he asked, seizing on the last of these pieces of information. Larry had gone? Presumably their relationship had come to an end, although that didn't necessarily follow. She might simply have *sent* him home, planning to follow shortly.

"Just the three of us," he heard her say. It sounded natural enough. Almost impromptu. But why had she come to Hawaii? Nobody flies six thousand miles to offer a dinner invitation, get on a plane again, and fly back. "Or the two of us, if Emily's tied up," she said. "Although she did answer the phone, didn't she? I must confess I'm terribly curious. . ."

Was that the motive? It was plausible. The important question was what he wanted. The prospect of an excursion outside of the house was intriguing. He could use this invitation as a first step . . . taking her down the hill with a dog collar. A leash, even! Irene would have no possible ground for complaint, having already visited, already knowing about the nature of his games with Emily, and having specified that there would be no one else at dinner. Why not?

"Why not?" he repeated, aloud. "When were you thinking of having this dinner?"

"Whenever suits," she said, as if it were no great thing. "Tonight? Tomorrow night?"

"Tonight would be fine," he said, looking at Emily and watching as the brush stopped, as if stuck for a moment, and then started again.

"Sevenish?"

"Perfect," he said. "Can I bring anything?"

"No, no. I'll be going into town anyway. I can manage."

"Well, thank you. I'm looking forward to it."

"You'll bring Emily?"

"Of course."

"Good," she said. "See you around seven, then."

Victor hung up the telephone himself. "We're invited to dinner," he told Emily.

She stopped scrubbing. She didn't say anything.

"I accepted."

She nodded.

He supposed he ought to mention Larry's departure. But she didn't ask. She wasn't saying anything. Out of submission or in some kind of passive aggression? He couldn't be sure. He tried to recall the words of the telephone conversation, remembering what he'd said and what clues she might have picked up from what she'd been able to hear. Nothing! Then let her think he was still there! If she asked, he'd tell her the truth. But if she didn't ask . . . it wasn't up to him to impose the information on her if she wasn't interested enough to ask. Besides, the vision that had begun to form in his mind was clarifying itself. And for her to be uncertain about Larry's whereabouts would add a certain charm to the picture, a kind of dramatic backlighting.

He left her to finish the floor. He changed his clothes, took the car keys, told Emily he was going out, got no answer at all, and left for a little drive into Naalehu, a small town where he was able to pick up a large dog collar and a cheap leash made out of chain links with a swivel clasp at one end and a leather loop-handle at the other. The clerk dropped them into a brown paper bag and handed them to Victor.

Back at the house, he presented his purchases. She showed no particular surprise, but no displeasure either. "Put it on," he said.

"Don't you want to put it on for me?"

"All right. It'd be more fitting, wouldn't it? Come!" he commanded, mostly as a joke. But she took it straight. She came to him and got down on her hands and knees. He bent over her and fastened the collar around her neck. He snapped on the leash. He patted her head, stroked her neck, patted her rump, and realized that he was aroused. He licked his fingers, smeared the spittle on her vulva, then opened his fly and mounted her, dog fashion. He humped away at her rapidly, not at all interested in her response, not caring whether she had an orgasm . . . preferring, somehow, that she not. In a quick, sharp, satisfying spasm, he came. He uncoupled. He zipped his fly. He went into the kichen for a glass of pineapple juice. And to admire the spotlessly clean floor.

He dressed casually for dinner. White slacks, a

blue blazer, and a powder-blue shirt open at the collar. That was about right, he thought. Emily had showered and set her hair with a blow-drier, as he'd told her to do. When she'd got her hair the way she wanted it, she turned to him for approval.

"Fine," he said. "Now, make-up. What have you got that's dark?"

She rummaged in her make-up kit. He came over to the dressing table and rummaged with her. He chose a blood-red lipstick. Mascara. A dark blue eye shadow. Rouge. "Do yourself up, semi-tarty. Bold. Dramatic."

She nodded. It took her another ten minutes. He watched as she worked, making the eyes huge, almost Egyptian. And putting on a bright slash of a mouth.

"Yes," he told her. "That's very good. Now, put this on." He handed her the negligee they had bought at Bloomie's. It was black, filmy, transparent. It came to just above her knees, but did not at all hide what it covered. She was more naked in it than without it. And the dog collar was just the right surrealist note to grace it. He snapped on the leash. He looked at their image in the mirror of the bathroom. Quite bizarre.

"I'll need a purse," she said. "For my make-up. If we're going to eat, I'll have to fix my lipstick at least. . ."

"I'll take it," he said. He slipped the lipstick into his pocket. He led her out of the bathroom and out of the house.

She was surprised when they did not get into the car. And worried. She was barefooted after all. He led her down the drive to the lower house. It wasn't until they were within thirty feet of the front door that she held back. "Will Larry be there?" she asked at last.

"Do you care?"

"I don't know. I guess I do."

"Which way? Do you want him there or not there?"

"Both, really."

"Then why worry about it?"

She nodded. She took a step, slackening the leash. She followed him up the steps. He rang the doorbell. They waited. He could see that her eyes were closed. And she was breathing in slow heaving sighs. He could see the rise and fall of her breasts under the gauzy black fabric. His own breathing was rather rapid and shallow.

Irene opened the door. "Welcome," she said, did a take as she saw Emily, recovered, and yet could not help exclaiming, "How very piquant!"

"Thank you," Victor said, cheerfully, accepting it as a compliment.

"You're looking . . . well," Irene said to Emily.

"Thank you."

"I think this demands a drink," Irene decided.

"Gin and tonic for me," Victor said. "Emily?"

"The same, thank you."

"Simple enough," Irene said. There was a bar at one end of the living room. She busied herself with the making of the drinks. "How have you been getting on?" she asked. "Or is that a silly question?"

"As you see," Victor said. "Splendidly. I'm sorry things didn't work out with you and Larry." He looked at Emily to see her reaction. It was difficult to read, but he thought she relaxed some. It figured, anyway.

"It was a long shot, I suppose," Irene said. She

brought the drinks. "I'm glad to see you two have done better. Congratulations!" She raised her glass in a toast to them. And drank.

"That's generous of you," Victor said. "To your generosity." He drank to her. Emily just drank, several long pulls.

"You want to tell me about it? Or leave me to guess?" Victor asked.

"Oh, there's not very much to tell. He was headstrong. He refused to be tied up. Sauce for the gander and all that. I decided to try it here. He wouldn't be part of it. He just wouldn't get into the spirit. Insecure, perhaps . . . Or stubborn. Or maybe he just didn't like me enough."

"That's unlikely," Victor said, gallantly. He could afford to be gallant, sitting on the sofa holding Emily's leash loosely in one hand.

"He wouldn't have liked it," Emily said.

"Why not?" Victor asked. "You've managed. Wonderfully well. . ."

"I don't know. He . . . just wouldn't. Unless he thought she loved him. And even then. . ."

"You think I love you?"

"In your way, yes."

"She's right, you know," Irene said. "I think that's what impressed me . . . and what excited me, that night, when I saw you two together."

"That I love her?" Victor asked, skeptically.

"As she says. In your way. You wouldn't have gone to this trouble if you didn't, would you?"

"I don't know. I'd have to think about it."

"Let me get some nibbles. I have them all ready," Irene said. She went out to the kitchen.

"It's all right if I talk, isn't it?" Emily asked.

"Of course," Victor said, hardly thinking about

it. He was thinking about what she'd said before. And what Irene had endorsed. It was a weird question to come up at this stage of the proceedings. *Love* her? Love *her*? It was as if their roles—even their costumes—had been reversed, and he were the one who was virtually naked.

Irene returned with a platter of raw carrot sticks, cauliflower buds, and celery stalks around a bowl of some kind of dip. She held it out in front of Victor. He took a carrot stick, dipped it, and put it into Emily's mouth. Cheerfully obscene, she sucked the dip off the carrot stick, ran her tongue over her upper lip, and then bit the carrot.

"And you, dear? Do you love him?" Irene asked.

"I haven't thought about it," Emily answered. " 'Love?' I've been in love before. It wasn't anything like this. This is something else."

"Passion?" Irene suggested.

Emily thought about it for a moment. She nodded.

"How wonderful," Irene said. "But Victor, where do you go from here?"

"I don't know. We're making it up as we go along."

"Another round?" Irene offered. "I know I could use one."

Dinner was mahimahi, or dolphin, broiled with lemon butter, and then a large fruit salad. Dessert was a baked Alaska that Irene had prepared. It was a surprise. She'd taken it from the freezer and put it in the oven, had set the oven, and returned to the table. When the alarm bell of the oven sounded, Emily gasped, startled.

"What a bundle of nerves!" Irene observed. "I'd

have thought you'd be wonderfully relaxed."

"It's the bell that did it," Victor said. "I've been playing with bells, just as Pavlov did. . ." He broke off. "Tell her, Emily."

Emily looked at Victor, then at Irene, and then at her plate.

"Tell her!" Victor insisted.

"He would set the clock. It was an alarm clock. He'd set it to go off. I could hear it ticking. Then the bell would ring. He'd come in. . ."

"Wonderful! How wicked," Irene exclaimed. "But I'd better get the dessert. For which the bell tolls."

She returned with the baked Alaska, sliced it in thirds, and served it. "So!" she said. "I understand about the way you jumped when the oven bell went off . . . but not entirely. Were you just startled? Or were you excited?"

"Both," Emily said.

"Remarkable," Irene said. "A shame to waste it. You want to go into the bedroom?"

"But that's the beauty of it," Victor explained. "It's a matter of random reward. Sometimes I'd let the alarm go off and just do nothing. She never knew what was going to happen to her. Did you?"

Emily shook her head, no.

"Still, the offer stands. I owe you that much. From the old cruise, remember?"

"Tell her about it," Victor suggested to Irene. What he had in mind was evening out the balance of confession. After all, Emily had complied so obediently when he'd ordered her to explain about the bell. He wanted to show her that he wasn't picking on her, or at least not viciously. Besides, it seemed fair to make Irene pay a little.

But Irene showed no discomfort at all. She was amused, amusing and rather sisterly about it, telling Emily how it was on the ship. "And probably the best part of it was what was going on in our heads—as you've been discovering," she said. She brought a spoonful of baked Alaska to her mouth, swallowed, and continued, with the enthusiasm of a golfer or a tennis player describing a particularly good day. "I would lie there in the stateroom, trying to imagine what sort of man Victor would bring me, trying to see it through his eyes, and knowing that he'd be looking at all those men through my eyes. And then, when he actually brought someone, at least half of the fun of it was thinking of Victor outside, imagining him imagining me . . . But then the head is so much more various than the body. It needs the body, but it has so many more possibilities. In the last analysis, it's all done with mirrors. Don't you think?"

Emily nodded but didn't answer. Victor replied for her, as he realized she wanted him to do. "I think that's probably true. It certainly sounds plausible." He stopped. He was thinking about that time in the restaurant when he had noticed the man who had seen what Emily was doing as she masturbated. All done with mirrors? Quite possibly so.

"Of course it's plausible," Irene insisted. "It's obvious. I suppose that that was partly what I had in mind when I offered the use of my bedroom." She looked at Emily, then at Victor, then at Emily again. "One is never entirely altruistic in these things. Indeed, one ought not be. No?"

Victor considered what she'd said. It was as close to a direct offer as she was likely to come. Or that's what it appeared to be. "Tell me," he asked, "which of us are you propositioning? Her or me?"

"I'm not sure I was propositioning anyone," Irene said, but not angrily. She was smiling. "Which would you prefer?" she asked.

He could not blame Irene. After all, with whatever motive, he had dressed Emily up in that outlandish way. To demonstrate his domination, to boast to Irene, to show off the girl . . . And to let Emily know, too, how proud he was of her. But she was provocative. They'd been his instructions, his whims, that she'd been obeying, so he'd been provocative. Irene had responded, or had been provocative on her own, perhaps having been disappointed by Larry. They'd drunk enough, the gin and tonics before dinner and the Moselle with dinner. And there hadn't been all that much resistance or inhibition to overcome, anyway. The turning point came, he supposed, when he followed up on Irene's question, asking Emily if she'd ever had a lesbian experience. Emily blushed. Shook her head, no. And said . . . nothing. No objections. No thinking. Still passive, still willing to let him have the direction and control, indeed eager for him to have the responsibility that went along with that control.

"Why don't you start with her, then?" Victor offered Irene, as if he were suggesting a brandy.

Irene said, "Thank you, I will." She took a last spoonful of her excellent dessert, got up from her chair, and went around to Emily's side. Emily's leash lay coiled in her lap. Irene picked up the handle of the leash, held it for a moment, then changed her mind. She undid the clasp that fastened the leash to the collar and dropped the leash on the floor. She extended a hand.

Emily looked at Victor. Victor nodded. Emily took Irene's hand and allowed herself to be led off to the bedroom. Victor remained where he was, more to please himself than out of consideration for Emily. He was perfectly well aware that the first few minutes would be the most trying, that there might be a moment of panic—that she might dislike it, or more threatening, that she like it too much. But he was considering what Irene had said about mirrors. Better, in a way, to imagine it, to think of Irene playing his role. Or Emily, for surely she was playing his role, too, acting as his surrogate. Because, as they had agreed, or at least asserted without denial, he loved her in his way. Yes, he supposed he did.

He reached for one of the rather clumsy water goblets and took a sip of ice water. In her own apartment, Irene would not have tolerated such glassware. But away from home, one puts up with what there is, making do . . . As, perhaps, Irene was doing with him and with Emily. Did that account for her behavior? He had no particular reason to distrust her. Still, he had an uneasy feeling about her involvement.

The easiest explanation was that she'd been turned on, which admitted of no explanations and needed none. Sure enough of herself to be able to surrender herself to an impulse, when she felt an impulse, she had pursued them, fascinated by the girl in the same odd way he had been, himself. And he still didn't understand what it was about Emily that had so entranced him. Perhaps that lack of understanding was at the very heart of love, the magician's trick which, if we understand it, is no longer magical, no longer marvelous, no longer even interesting.

He took a last sip of water, chewed an ice cube thoughtfully, and got up to go into the bedroom to see whether his visceral reactions to their activities squared with his intellectual and aesthetic preconceptions. He approached the bedroom door, hesitated, then stepped through the doorway. In the demi-darkness he was able to make out their shapes on the bed. For an instant, he was uncertain about who was doing what to whom. Ah, yes, of course. Irene was on top, the aggressor, the initiator. Emily, lying back on the bed, still wearing her negligee but with the filmy gown spread wide to reveal her naked torso, was passive, accepting—as she had learned to be. Victor came close, to the side of the bed. Irene was naked, going down on Emily, kneeling between Emily's legs, her rump raised high. Victor cupped her buttock with his hand. He moved his hand to the inside of Irene's thigh. To her muff. To her vulva. Wet, of course. From the exciting wetness of Emily's cunt. Mirrors, mirrors.

He was hard. He could fuck either one of them. It would be especially pleasant, he thought, to put it to Irene while she had her ass sticking up that way and was eating Emily. But all in good time. He was merely male, had to husband himself as they did not. He sat down on the bed to watch. To touch. To stroke Emily's neck and breasts, and to kiss her while she groaned and sighed in delight from what Irene was doing.

Irene made Emily come. They shifted around and Emily repaid the favor easily, for Irene had excited herself in the mouthwork on Emily. Then

Irene invited Victor to join them to make Napoleon's hat. He lay on the bed. Irene lowered herself onto his cock. Emily knelt down over his face. He fucked one and ate the other, as they kissed each other and fondled each other's breasts, making the shape of the famous bicorne that gave the position its name.

SEVENTEEN

All night, and almost without stop. It would have been difficult for any two of them to manage, but with three, there were more possibilities, more combinations. Even extending himself, pacing himself to draw out his pleasure for as long as possible, Victor allowed himself at last to ejaculate into Emily's mouth. (Irene, at the time, had been eating Emily's pussy, and Victor had been eating Irene.) This put Victor on the sidelines for a while, but Irene and Emily were able to continue without him. He didn't feel at all excluded. He enjoyed watching them, even helping them along with a finger here, or on occasion, his mouth there. Irene brought Emily to a series of sharp, almost tearing climaxes. Victor, aroused by Emily's cries to a new readiness, fucked Irene while Emily watched. And on and on. There were pauses for champagne, for French toast, for coffee . . . But one way or another, they kept at it. At one point, Victor remembered how he had been lying on the bed, not quite asleep but not fully awake by any means, his head resting on Emily's ass, the smell of her sex a delicious tang in his nostrils. Irene, sprawled on the end of the bed was masturbating dreamily, alone. He had begun to imitate her, doing to Emily what she was doing to herself. And they had all roused themselves to another triple play. The sun was already up.

They were exhausted by then. And all three of them fell asleep. It was going on noon by the time Victor staggered into the kitchen to heat up the coffee that was left from one of their intermissions of the night before. He was standing there, leaning on the edge of the stove, waiting for the coffee to get hot but not wanting to let it boil. Irene came into the kitchen. She had not bothered to put on a robe. Her hair was frazzled. There were smudges under her eyes. But to Victor she had a glow, an earthiness that made up for the defects of her deshabille. Her full breasts, fuller than Emily's and only very slightly showing the sag of age (or of experience and use), were deliciously pale where her bathing suit top had covered them. "Good morning," he said. "You're looking gorgeous."

"I look a fright," she said, "but you're good to say so."

"What a splendid party," he said, pouring her a cup of coffee and then one for himself. "It's a shame you have to go back to New York."

She thought for a moment. She had already told him that she was giving up the house. Had given it up? She couldn't quite remember. But even if there was something of a risk, the gamble was worth it to her, because the alternative was obvious: to leave, as she had already said she was planning to do. "Yes, it is a shame," she said. "But I've given up the house. They have another tenant for it . . ."

"When are you thinking of leaving?" Victor asked.

"Tomorrow, I'd expect."

She watched Victor sip his coffee and consider. If it was going to happen, she knew, it would happen now. She sipped, waited, sipped again.

"Of course, if you wanted to delay . . . for a few days, even . . . you could come up the road and . . . move in with us?"

She raised her eyebrows as if surprised. As if just a little bit shocked. "What about Emily?" she asked. "What would she say?"

"Emily doesn't have a say," he retorted. "That's part of the arrangement. The foundation of it, in fact. Besides, my impression last night was that she enjoyed herself."

"She might feel different about it when she wakes up."

"But we could remedy that. She might feel the same about it by tonight. But she's not the point. You are. Wouldn't you like to join us? Just for a while?"

"It's tempting," she said, wondering whether the last four words had been added as a blandishment or as a limitation to the offer.

"If you get bored, you can always leave. We're old friends. And grown-ups."

She had won. It was what she wanted. Still, she could play him just a little longer. "Are you sure it's what you want?" she asked, not coyly.

"I know my own mind," he said. "Of course it's what I want. It'll be fun. Do say you'll come!"

"All right," she said at last. "For a few days. Until one or another of us begins to get bored."

"Is that really likely to happen?"

"Who can say?" Irene asked.

"I don't see it as much of a risk," Victor said, cupping her breast with his free hand. "After last night?"

"That was very nice," she agreed. "But it was a . . . what's the word? A crime of opportunity. This is more premeditated. And the rules will be different."

"What rules?"

"I have no idea. But there will be. We'll find out what they are."

"I'm game," Victor said, fingering her nipple.

"Not before I've had my coffee! That's the first rule."

Being no fool, Victor was perfectly well aware that there were risks in the new arrangement. He was sitting out on Irene's deck—she had gone inside to 'do something about this face'—and looking out at the water. He thought about risk and about its alternative. Irene had extracted from him early the evening before the admission that in some manner he was in love with Emily. He had been hooked. In that case, the object was to maintain his independence, to continue to consult his whims, to shore up by whatever means that crystalline objectivity with which the whole enterprise had begun. Otherwise, he knew, there would be no risk but an absolute certainty of ruin. Of hurt. To himself!

Assuming, for the moment, that he did so foolish

a thing as to consider the long-term prospects of his marriage, the outcome was unmistakably clear. In eight years, he'd be fifty-three—Emily would be coming into her prime. She'd be spoiled rotten. She'd have the handle end of the leash by then, and sooner or later would let it drop, finding among her lovers one to whom she happened to respond with special depth or richness. No way!

The worst risk, then, was caution. Even to be considering any duration of years was unsettling and appalling. It was far shrewder not to be shrewd, to use her in whatever ways the moment and his subconscious could suggest, and to assume that sooner or later there would be a break. He'd pay her off in dollars and walk away, getting off cheaply.

That Irene was willing to join them was therefore both threatening and comforting. The threat was that her presence might well speed up the reactions that otherwise would extend themselves over a longer stretch of time. The comfort was that Victor believed Irene to be fundamentally sane. Her perspective, her sense of proportion would be a help to him in this time of enthusiasm and distraction. He was confident enough not in himself but in her fundamental heterosexuality to suppose that if she had any deeper motives for accepting his invitation they had to do with him rather than with Emily, and if she was interested in him then he had little to worry about. More probable was the simpler explanation. Larry had left her, or had been dismissed, she was at loose ends; the opportunity had presented itself. What more was required?

How it would work was not at all clear. He rather doubted that it would work at all for very long. He'd suggested the few days not to limit the invitation, or even to coax her, but because he thought that was all any of them would be able to stand. The dynamics of a couple are complicated enough, with two separate realms of fantasy that reach out more or less blindly into the real world, to touch it, change it, and be nourished by it. Three separate heads and three different bodies all maneuvering in the same space? It would be chaos. But the old experiment had succeeded and he had managed to achieve the kind of domination he'd only dimly imagined with Emily. That success was enough to encourage him to try again, to see what would happen.

He finished his coffee and went back to the kitchen for another cup. Emily had woken up and was getting coffee for herself. Victor told her that he'd invited Irene to move in with them.

She nodded. She didn't say anything.

"It should be fun, don't you think?"

She shrugged.

They moved that afternoon. Actually, it was Victor who wound up doing most of the moving, driving back and forth with Irene's suitcases, liquor, and food.

It was probably a mistake for him to be doing this, but the forms of hospitality required it, and the last tag ends of the etiquette of the chivalric behavior of gentlemen demanded it. Irene was in the spare room, mostly because the closet there was empty. She could hang her collection of dresses and gowns from the chrome pole with Emily's admiring help. He lugged boxes and cartons with booze and food from the kitchen of the lower house, into the trunk of the car, and then into the kitchen of the upper house. He was sweating. Thirsty. Tired. Just a touch hung over. And they were in the second bedroom like a couple of sorority sisters, hanging up clothes!

Irene had picked the closet, saying, "I can put my things in there," as if it didn't matter. And maybe it didn't. But Victor was aware—and had to assume that she was also aware—that these preliminary dispositions, however casual or thoughtless, would be fundamental to the growth and development of the patterns by which they would, however briefly, be living. That Irene should be in the other room, and that Victor should flit between the two beds, the two women, the two bodies. . . was an attractive prospect. That he and Emily should share the big room and its king-size bed, inviting Irene to join them at their—or even better, his—pleasure was very close to what he'd had in mind in the first place. But it was also possible that he could be in the one bed, and Irene could be in the other, and that Emily would shuttle back and forth. Given the limitations of male sexuality, it was rather more likely, wasn't it?

He put away the last of the liquor bottles, then went to take a shower to cool off. On his way to the bathroom, he popped his head into Irene's room to tell Emily to get him a cold drink. But Irene intervened. "Don't be a boor! She's not your servant."

"She's my wife."

"All the more reason to show some courtesy."

"What are you talking about? Emily, get me a cold drink. Something with rum in it."

"Get it yourself," Irene snapped.

"I don't believe my ears. What is this? Some kind of feminism?"

"No, nothing of the kind. It's just good manners. Would you ask me to get you a drink, as if I were some sort of servant?" Irene asked.

Victor looked at Emily, whose head had been snapping back and forth like a spectator's at Forest Hills. "Emily is whatever I want her to be. I resent your interference. Emily, do as I say."

She hesitated. She looked at Irene.

"As I order. Now!" he said.

She went into the kitchen.

"What the hell is the matter with you?" Victor asked, now that he and Irene were alone. "You're undermining everything I've done with that girl!"

"Is it so fragile, after all?"

"It's early days to be testing it this way," he admitted.

"Well, then, I'm sorry. I didn't mean to upset you."

"Bitch!" he said.

"Of course," she agreed. "You've always known that, though."

Shaking his head, he went off to take his shower. In a little while, Emily brought him a cold rum punch. Victor turned off the water, stepped out of the tub, and took the drink from her. He took a large swallow, put it down on the vanity table, grabbed a towel and asked her, "What was that all about?"

"What?"

"Back there, in Irene's room."

"What in Irene's room?"

"That whole bit. The discussion . . ."

"I didn't say anything."

"But you didn't go when I told you to, did you?"

"I was waiting to hear what you and she were saying."

"Just remember, I'm the one you're married to," he said, drying his hair roughly. He took the towel off his head. "What have you and she been doing all morning?"

"I've been putting away her clothes. And she's been eating me."

So, that explained it. Irene just hadn't wanted to have her pleasure interrupted. Victor wasn't jealous, but he was mildly annoyed. He'd been lugging all that junk up the hill . . . He deserved a little consideration. He considered the idea of a prohibition against sexual activity except when he was present. But . . . Irene would say that he was being childish and selfish.

"How nice for you," he said.

"You're not angry, are you?" she asked. Mollifying? Defying? Reproaching him, perhaps, for having brought Irene into the house in the first place? For having impossibly contradictory expectations?

"No," he said. "I'm not angry. Of course not." He gave her the towel. "Dry me," he told her.

He turned around so she could dry his back.

They were discussing dinner. Anyway, Victor and Irene were discussing it. Emily sat quietly on the end of the bed in the large bedroom. They had been lying on the bed, all three of them, exhausted after a bout of sex that had begun with a simple enough game. Victor had gone from Irene to Emily and back, giving each one five thrusts; the point was to see which of them could make him come. The winner was to invent the next game, or determine the rules of the next bout. Or simply pick her partner. Irene, with her extraordinary vaginal musculature, had been able to bring him off easily. So, it was up to her. But she had asked about dinner.

"I suppose one of us can go and get something," Victor said. "Or we could all go out. There was a Japanese restaurant a few miles down the road. That ought to be okay. There's a certain standard below which Japanese restaurants seldom go."

"But it's so comfortable here," Irene complained. "Why don't you go out and get it. . ."

"Why me?" Victor asked.

"Why not?" Irene had asked. "Or . . . what if we send Emily?"

"Do you drive?" Victor asked.

Emily nodded.

"And perhaps she could pick up a man," Irene suggested. "The trouble with what we've got here is that in any good orgy, the men should outnumber the women by two to one. And we've got it the wrong way round."

"No, I don't think so," Victor said.

"Afraid?"

"A little, yes. It's . . . it's not what I had in mind."

"It's a way of testing her."

"It's dumb," Victor insisted. "I don't like it."

"I can see that. But look what will happen the

other way! Emily and I will be together all the time. You'll be relatively inactive, except as a voyeur . . ."

"And your way? Assuming that she brought back some stud. Or that you did. Or that you both did. I'd still be a voyeur most of the time, wouldn't I?"

"So? By that logic, it should make no difference."

"It makes a difference. It doesn't fit with my present mood."

"You do love her, after all."

"Yes."

"What I ought to do is take her away from you. For your own good."

"You can't!"

"Why not? What's keeping her? The money? I can pay her as well as you. The sex? I can give her more than you."

"I think she loves me."

"You're a fool!" Irene snapped. "You've tamed her for the moment. But that's all. She's tame for anyone now. For me. For a stranger in a bar . . . She has recognized her own sexuality, which is something that very few young women ever have to do. It's freed her, which is, considering your bondage fantasies, quite intricately ironic."

"Emily?" Victor asked, but he never got to express the question that was to follow.

"I won the game. I get to make up the rules of the next game. Emily and I will go to my room. You can come in when you have either an erection or dinner. Otherwise, you stay outside."

"Charming," Victor said. "And how long do you propose that we should play this game?"

"Let's say . . . twenty-four hours."

"And then?"

"And then it will be Emily's turn to pick the game."

He saw it suddenly clear. Could she, in twenty-four hours, win Emily away from him?

Perhaps. What the probability was, he couldn't begin to guess. But if it could be done that easily, or anyway that quickly, why did he want her? What good was she? If Irene was right about his being in love with Emily . . .

"All right," he said. "Why not?"

The Japanese restaurant was closed. He drove on to Kailua where there was a Colonel Sanders' chicken stand just across the road from the Kona Hilton. And he was in luck. They were having a special. Large signs proclaimed a reduction of a dollar on a barrel or a bucket of chicken on Tuesdays. And it was a Tuesday. He ordered a bucket and a couple of pints of cole slaw, took it away, and headed back to Punalu'u. Thinking. He could still go into their room. With the chicken. Or with an erection. Had that been merely an inadvertence on Irene's part? Or was it a part of the exquisitely arranged process—so that he should be allowed to see, even forced to see, the progress of her campaign to alienate Emily's affections. It was a legal phrase, but vivid, sticking in the mind. Should he stay away then? Could he imagine himself skulking around the house, his house after all, while the two of them were tangled together in that bed, playing on each other's nerves and flesh, awash in each other's juices?

On the other hand, the economics of the situation were not altogether encouraging. He had been more active, sexually, during the past week than he had been in years. How much more could he expect of himself during the next twenty-four hours? And what would be the effects of his probably diminished capacity? The abundance, the limitlessness of Irene's capacity, and of Emily's too, for that matter, simply could not be matched by any one man. Irene had been right about the proper proportions for an orgy. Still, if he could arrange matters so that he was a prize, so that his infrequent appearances would be the object, the goal of their strenuous exercises, he might yet come out with more authority and leverage than Irene expected. In the short run, anyway. In the long run, he just couldn't hope to compete.

It was humiliating. And he couldn't even blame Irene. Or Emily. The biology itself was unfair and whimsical. But that meant that he couldn't blame himself, either. Management was all. But Irene was such a fiendishly clever manager. The question was only what her object could be in this business. The sheer mischievousness? Or was she after him, using Emily only to drive a wedge between him and her? Or revenge, on Larry perhaps, so that Emily would be far beyond Larry's tolerance or abilities or tastes by the time Emily was ready to go back to him? Or all those things together?

He turned into the driveway and then into the carport. He picked up the two bags and carried them into the house. He heard giggling. And then gasping.

Well, they could probably use a break. The chicken, too, was finger lickin' good.

* * *

Emily had never known anything like it. But then, she'd never tried it before. She'd been afraid of it, worried that if she liked it, she'd become a dike. But Victor's occasional visits were reassuring. The fact that Irene could drive her out of her mind with pleasure didn't at all mean that she was unable to respond to Victor. On the contrary, after the exquisite caresses of Irene, the delicate nibblings, lickings, fondlings, strokings, and squeezings, it was especially good to have her cunt filled, to feel a cock inside her. She wondered idly why Victor never fucked Irene but always favored her. And Irene explained it to her, telling her that Victor felt threatened, that he thought it was a contest. Was that true? Or silly? Or true and silly? She hardly had the concentration to consider such questions. And she didn't much care. The result was the same, and delicious. She'd never been up that way, hot that way, for so long. And Irene, being a woman, knew Emily's woman's body better than any man could, how to surprise it, startle it, and coax it to orgasm, sometimes with a quick flick of finger or tongue that Emily couldn't believe would do anything, couldn't even imagine as effective, exhausted as she was, fucked out as she believed herself to be. But she was sensitized, engorged, the blood congested, the tissues quivering. And zap! Irene could touch her, ever so lightly, ever so briefly, and the sudden shudders would start all over again.

Irene talked to her. About herself. And that was reassuring, too, because it was clear that while Irene liked to make it with women sometimes, she was still no dreary lesbian, liked men, liked to remember which of them she'd loved and which of them she'd lusted for, and what it had been like. She told stories of her conquests that excited Emily and that calmed her, too, for Irene was not monstrous. Emily, therefore, could look forward to some of these same adventures, could for that matter participate in this one without thinking that anything terrible was going to happen to her. Indeed, as Irene maintained, sex improved the character, demonstrating not only selfishness but selflessness, because sex was in large measure a giving up of self, an abandoning of control and direction. "You give yourself," she said. "And the phrase is quite accurate."

Emily gave herself. To Irene, to Victor, to ecstasy, to delerious and endlessly protracted pleasure. And almost extinguished by the strenuousness of their attentions, she lay there utterly limp, drowsy, about to drift off to sleep, when Victor returned, ready to enter her again. She was barely aware of him, hardly sensible of the cock in her, unable even to move. She felt Irene's hands on Victor's shaft, helping him along. She felt Irene cupping Victor's balls and rubbing them against the base of her vulva. She heard as from a great distance Victor's grunt. She could not feel his spurt in her. She was too wet already. Or maybe it was a dry come with no juice left. She fell asleep.

In the morning, he was still there—not still in her but still there in bed. Either Irene had relented and had allowed him to stay or else she had fallen asleep herself. Emily woke to hear Irene order Victor to go and fetch coffee.

"Jesus Christ! I can't move."

"Either get coffee or get your ass out of here. Those are the rules."

"Yesterday's rules. Today's a new day, isn't it?"

"Get the coffee and we'll talk about it."

"Ah, shit!" he said. But he struggled to an upright position. And he left the room. Presumably to get the coffee.

When he was gone, Irene asked Emily, "You awake, dear?"

Emily nodded.

"You get to choose the rules today. You remember that?"

Emily nodded.

"Have you thought about what you'd like to do?"

She shook her head.

"You should, you know."

"Why can't we just go on the way we've been doing?"

"We could. Or we could move on."

"What would Victor like?"

"What would you like?" Irene insisted.

"I don't know."

"Do you want to be tied up again?"

"No."

"Do you want to tie me up?" Irene asked. "Victor?"

There was no answer. Emily was thinking about it. Afraid of it? Wondering what Victor would think and how he'd react? Or consulting her own whims and wishes—for the first time in a long time? Irene wished that there were something further she could say without risking the fragile bond of trust that had grown up between them. Or that Emily had more time . . . For Victor appeared with a tray and a pot of coffee. He had arranged the cups and saucers, spoons, napkins, and cream and sugar in a neat, attractive way. To show obedience? More probably, he was showing sarcasm. He even poured and served them.

"Okay, it's a new day. A new game," Victor said, pouring himself some coffee. "And we get to see how the old game came out, I rather imagine. Emily? What is it to be?"

"How would it be if we tied you up?" she asked. She had a gamine grin on her face.

"What an interesting idea!" Victor said. "How very original. Did you think of it? Or did Irene suggest it to you?"

"Listening at the door, then, were you?" Irene asked.

"Of course!" he admitted cheerfully.

"She suggested it. But it might be fun," Emily said.

"If anyone tells you what to choose, I will," Victor said. "I'm your husband. And I'm paying the bills."

"You're reduced to that already?" Irene asked.

"I'll thank you to keep out of this for the moment."

"Why should I? I've as much right to take part in the discussion as anyone. It's my ass as much as either of yours."

"I'm up to my ass with your ass!"

"Over your head, even," Irene quipped. She sipped her coffee for punctuation. "I'd tread carefully, if I were you. You're going to do something foolish—like making the girl choose between us. And you're not sure you're going to win, are you? You're not even sure you want to win. Or what winning is. So watch it. You can finish your coffee and go to the bathroom. Then we'll tie you up."

"No," Victor said. "No, you won't tie me up. And, no, she won't, either. And no, you're wrong about making the girl choose. She's already chosen. She's already done that, don't you see? She does whatever she does only with my permission. And I can take that back any time. I do take it back. From now on, you'll sleep in here. And she'll sleep with me. Just the two of us. In there. You understand, Emily?"

She nodded.

"You see? That's all there is to it. That's just fucking all there is to it."

"Is it?" Irene asked. "All that means is that if she stays here with me, the marriage is over."

"She's not going to stay here with you. Because you're not staying here. I think you've just about stayed out your welcome."

"All right, then. But she could come with me. The marriage would be over. But she'd be no worse off than she is. And in lots of ways rather better off, I'd expect."

"Yes, well, you're right about that, then. She gets to choose that. She gets to decide whether she's staying here or going with you."

"You're a fool, Victor," Irene said.

"Emily? It's up to you," Victor said. "Are you staying here with me? Or are you going back to New York?"

"Can I tie you up?" she asked, rather listlessly he thought.

He considered it. Was that a condition for her

remaining with him? Did he want to accept conditions? More to the point, did he want to risk being tied up? He had no idea how stable the girl was. She could have been harboring a grudge all this time. Or it could be an expression of some kind of love. He had no idea which. But he was afraid of it.

"No," he said.

"I'll go with Irene, then."

"Suit yourself," Victor said.

PART THREE

EIGHTEEN

On the plane, from Honolulu to San Francisco:

"Well, you've had a couple of hours to think about it. What do you think?" Irene asked.

"About what?"

"About anything! You can't go on this way, you know. Pretending to be a lump and acting passive. You did choose, you remember. First him. Then to leave him. What do you think?"

"I don't really know."

"Really, you do. You just can't admit to yourself that you know. It's as if . . . as if you were one of those huge boa constrictors—or are they anacondas?—with a great lump of meat bulging in its middle. You must either digest it or spit it out. You can't just go on this way."

"I know."

"And?"

"I don't know. What do you want?"

"No," Irene corrected her. "What do *you* want?"

Later, Emily asked, "How do we stand? You and I?"

"You mustn't rely on me for the long-term," Irene said after a moment's consideration. "I'm trying to help you. For your sake, partly. Victor's, too, partly. I have the notion that he was getting more deeply involved that was good for him. More than he could stand, comfortably, at any rate. And, I suppose, for my own amusement. I think of you . . . you should think of yourself . . . as a pupil."

"And what am I studying?"

"How to live," Irene said.

And later, Irene asked, "What about Larry? Are you thinking of going back to him?"

"I don't know whether I can."

"Of course. Neither do I. But do you want to?" Irene asked.

"It's . . . I was going go say it's safe. But it probably isn't. It'd be familiar."

Irene nodded.

"And I don't know that he'd want me. Or be able to take me. After what's happened . . ."

"That's a question, surely. I suppose you could conspire between you to . . . to forget it. To behave very carefully as if nothing had ever happened. No reference of any kind. You could deny it. Do you want to do that?"

"Yes. I don't know. No."

"There is no security," Irene said. "There is independence, which is strenuous. And there is false security. So many women think of men as rocks to which they cling like barnacles or mussels. The men leave them. Or just die. . . And they are back on their own, thrown back on their own resources."

"But haven't you been after Victor?"

"We're compatible. It would never do for me to . . . to rely on him. As things stand now, I have no idea how he'll feel. He may resent my taking you away. I mean, I'm sure he does now. But he may still resent it in . . . in a month. Three months. Men dream, you know. And they hate being roused to the real world. He may not forgive me. If not, then . . ." She made a gesture with her hand, a couple of lazy loops.

"Don't women dream too?" Emily asked.

"Oh, yes. But we daydream. We've been required by our inferior position in the world, by our powerlessness, to keep some sense of the world. We've been obliged to be realists."

"And you think Victor isn't realistic enough?"

"Enough for him. Whether enough to understand what I've done now . . . I don't know. If not, too bad."

Emily fiddled with the tab on her seat belt. "What would have happened if . . . if I'd stayed with him?"

"You'd have had a month, maybe. No more than two."

"You don't think I could have stood it?"

"I don't think he could have."

"So I was right?"

"You were right to follow your impulse. Whether your impulse was right or wrong . . . is a silly question," Irene said. "I'm tired. I shall try to take a nap." She pulled down the little shade and made her seat recline.

Realistically, then, or at least with as much realism as she was capable of bringing to bear upon the matter, Emily thought about her decision. Her impulse, as Irene had called it. That Victor had loved her in his way seemed to her to be true, and gave a dark poignance to their parting. No. . . a feeling of waste. Of needless waste. Spilled milk, over which it did no good to cry, but about which it was insane to feel good. He had loved her. She had responded to that love and, in her way, had returned it. But why had he not acceded to her request—or, yes, honestly, she was willing to call it a taunt, a dare—that he allow her to tie him up? She would not have subjected him to any awful indignities. She would have done for him as he had done for her. Not to him, but for him. With a tenderness and a delight . . .

He had not trusted her. Had not trusted himself to trust her. And in a weird way, that was worse than the way they'd started out, with neither of them trusting the other.

If only they'd been tougher, and had kept it free of emotion, of affection, they could have gone on. But the way things went . . .

"I had to leave," she said, not knowing that she had spoken aloud.

"Yes," Irene said. Not opening her eyes. "Yes."

Left alone, Victor had walked down to the lower house to ascertain the truth or falsity of the original premise—that Irene had given notice and that the lower house was already leased to another party. No one was around. No car. No answer to a knock. Or to a shout. Of course, he supposed, they could be out. Or delayed in their arrival. He trudged back up the hill, telephoned the real estate agency, and learned what he already knew anyway: that there had been no refund, no new renters. Mrs. Tarashoff had paid for two weeks. Could not have sublet without permission—and therefore, obviously, without the knowledge—of the agency. "I see," Victor said. "Many thanks."

So it had all been a hoax from the very beginning. And he had been incredibly blind. It was like the old joke about the fellow in the labor camp walking out every day with a wheelbarrow full of stones, where it turns out that he's stealing wheelbarrows. He'd been as blind as the guard in the joke. She's been after Emily. The whole time. How blind he'd been!

He packed in a desultory way. He was tired from his exertions of the previous days and nights, and he stopped to rest, feeling old and worn out. The clothes, themselves, seemed too absurd to have to bother with, their jauntiness and nattiness a kind of mockery of what he felt. He arranged them, nevertheless, in neat piles and put them in his suitcases. And lay down to rest. He slept for a while, woke, felt even worse, rather cottony in the mouth and dull in the head. He forced himself to complete the packing. He called the airport to make a reservation for a flight to New York. He called the agency to say he'd be leaving the key on the kitchen counter . . .

The woman at the agency wanted to know if the house had been unsatisfactory.

"No, the house was fine," Victor said. "It's . . . urgent business."

She regretted that there was no way that a refund

could be allowed. He told her that he understood. He was sorry too.

He poured himself a stiff gin, drank half of it, carried the suitcases down to the car, came up to finish the gin and leave the key, and then closed the door firmly so that the latch clicked.

It was all behind him.

Irene wouldn't have thought so. A realist, she knew that there are no final curtains, that plays and novels lie, and that whatever may be behind one, there are still results, unexpected reappearances, and curious renewals among the novelties ahead. Tired from the long flight, she opened the door to her apartment, held it wide, and waited for Emily to come in so that Charles, the doorman, could bring in the suitcases. "Here, in the hall, will do," she said. "We'll sort them all out in the morning. Thank you," she said, and she gave him a couple of dollars.

He touched his cap and said he hoped her trip had been enjoyable.

"Interesting," she said. "Thank you."

He closed the door behind him.

Irene looked at Emily. "You can take the guest bedroom, I think."

"Oh?" Emily was obviously disappointed.

"Don't be absurd!" Irene cautioned. "You're tired. I'm certainly tired. I need a long uninterrupted sleep. So do you, whether you know it or not."

"But I'll be staying here?"

"For a while, I expect so. You're welcome to stay here, at any rate. You may leave at any time. And eventually, you shall."

"Oh, no," Emily protested.

"Oh, yes," Irene insisted. "This is a temporary arrangement. But don't look so downcast. All arrangements are temporary."

"I suppose."

"Haven't you learned anything yet?" Irene asked. "You have your own bathroom. There are towels and toothbrushes. Whatever else you need, we can pick up in the morning."

"Most of my stuff is still in the old apartment. With Larry."

"I see. Well, you can get what you need tomorrow. If you're up to it."

They said goodnight in the hall. Emily looked so forlorn, so bedraggled from the long flight, that Irene kissed her on the forehead, like a mother putting a daughter to bed. Then she went into her own room. To bathe in her own tub. To crawl into her own crisp sheets and fall asleep in her own bed. Deliciously calm. But she was alert to the possibilities of the next day's errand. If she had to make odds, she would have supposed them to be about even that Emily would return to Larry. Maybe sixty-forty against.

The slight tilt had almost nothing to do with Emily. It was Irene's way of giving weight to what Larry would do and say, and what he could stand.

In the next room, Emily, in a strange bed, was less well settled. She was not secure about her place here in Irene's apartment and in Irene's life. She was thinking about Larry, whom she was afraid of seeing again. Or, no, not really afraid, but unenthusiastic. It would be an unpleasant scene. He would want her to come back. She would be reluctant . . . and there would be a long, stupid argument. The trouble was that eventually Larry would win, or would think he'd won. And she'd be back with him. She could imagine no other outcome. But would it last? Was Irene right about all arrangements being temporary? The possibility of Larry's defection or of his indifference or even distaste hardly bothered her. It was a more remote problem than that of the recurring images in her head—sudden unbidden snapshots of Irene's mouth and Victor's cock and her own body writhing on them, under them, and with them. What had those images to do with her life? How could they be included in a return to the simplicity and coziness she had known with Larry before any of this had happened? Or, even worse to consider, if that had been satisfying and fulfilling, why had she accepted Victor's proposal? To what undefined restlessness and discontent had he managed to address himself? She had to be patient with herself and hope that, in time, these visual reminders, these after-images, would blur to unbelievability and therefore to safety. She wasn't sure she wanted them to extinguish themselves altogether. All she wanted was that they should lose their power. Her breath, her heartbeat, her very skin tension were still in their thrall. She could see the hairs on Victor's balls. She could hear the squishy sound of his cock in Irene's cunt, and the quiver of anticipation in her own came back as a quiver of memory. And then he had pulled out of Irene and entered her, and she'd felt him, still wet from her, and hot from their friction, moving in her own body . . .

No, think about something else, about anything else. About being back in New York. About calling her agent, maybe. . . To work again. To do anything that would take her mind off these lurid pictures. Preferably, she could find something to do that would be absolutely exhausting and consuming, so that she would not have these intervals of imagination between the time she went to bed and the time she fell asleep.

The trouble, though, was that she was overtired. Exhausted and keyed up, at the same time. And turned on, goddam it!

Reluctantly, she put her hand down between her legs and started to masturbate. She tried to think of Larry. But it was Victor's face, and Irene's, and their bodies that swam like huge fish in the sea of her imagination.

She brought herself off. And then she fell asleep.

Larry was surprised when Emily showed up at the apartment, surprised to see her at all, and also surprised since he had expected the movers. Instead, there she was.

"Oh, it's you," he said. "Come on in."

She looked around. There were piles of boxes. All the books were packed. There were large cardboard wardrobes standing in a corner of the living room. "What's all this?" she asked.

"What does it look like? I'm moving."

"And . . . and my stuff?"

"I was going to have it stored. I was going to send you a note, letting you know where it was."

"Just like that?"

"Just like that." He stood there, working his jaw back and forth. "What did you expect me to do?"

"I thought we agreed to . . . to keep the apartment."

"Did we? It was a million years ago. Did we agree to keep it for a million years?"

"Is this what you want?"

"No, but this is what I've got. That bitch told me that you and Victor had come back to New York . . . I came back to look for you. You weren't here. You were still there, having yourselves a fine old time. The two of you . . . or was it the three of you? Was that the point of it?"

"Maybe," Emily said.

"Don't give me that shit. Was she there or wasn't she?"

"She was there. I meant that maybe that was the point. If that's what she told you."

"That's what she told me."

"I guess she lied," Emily said.

"I guess she did."

"So?"

"So?" Larry asked. "What happened?"

"She moved in with Victor and me. And then it broke up. I came back. Last night."

"Last night? I didn't see you last night. Where were you?"

"With Irene."

"Oh, great. That's just great!"

"What difference does it make?" Emily asked.

"None, I guess," he said, looking around at the boxes. He was going to clear out anyway. "You came back for your stuff?"

She nodded. "That's right," she said. "But I didn't expect to find you . . . running out. With your tail between your legs."

"Well, at least it's my own tail that's between my legs."

"What's that supposed to mean?"

"Forget it."

"What do you mean? You can't just walk out like this!"

"I can't? Why not? You did."

"That was temporary. This is permanent."

"Was it? Maybe you thought it was," he said, hurling himself into a small empty place on the sofa, knocking over a lampshade, and not bothering to retrieve it. "Maybe you thought it was just a temporary thing. Just a lark. But it wasn't. What we learned from it was permanent. Learning always is. You don't forget some things."

"You're sounding very fucking noble. You just didn't have such a good time with Irene. So you're blaming me. Don't give me any of that high moral tone. It's shit, and you know it."

"I didn't mean it that way. I meant . . . they're out of our league. I figured that out. You haven't. So maybe you're out of my league too. That's all. I'm not being moral. Just . . . practical."

"Bullshit!"

"Is it?" he asked. He picked up the lampshade and put it down, balancing it carefully on his pile of suits and sportcoats. His new camel's hair jacket was on top of the pile. "Maybe. Maybe not," he said. "Maybe you were right all along. Maybe we should have got married a year ago. Maybe it all would have been different. But we didn't. And this is the way things are now. It's no good pretending."

"We can go back."

"No. I wish. But no. I've thought about it. It wouldn't work. I couldn't take it and I don't think you could either."

"But this is crazy."

"Oh, yeah. You're only just now finding that out?"

She didn't try to answer. She stood there, looking around at what had been their life, packed away and ready to be shipped or stored. "Where are you going? A different apartment?" she asked him.

"No," he said. "I'm going home. Back to Pennsylvania. If I'm going to write, I can do it there as well as here. Better, maybe."

"Back to your folks?"

He nodded. "I haven't given notice to the landlord yet. If you want to keep the apartment . . . It's yours. You just keep on with the rent checks. And I won't have the movers move any of your things."

"You're really going back to the old small-town life and all that?"

"There's an apartment over the barn I can fix up. Nobody's used it for a couple of years. I can live there for next to nothing. And write more than I could here."

"And marry a small-town girl?"

"Maybe. Why not? A nice nobody who cooks and cleans and takes care of me. It makes a hell of a lot more sense than what you're doing. I'd be playing Victor's part, don't you see, instead of yours. And the Victors are always going to win."

"Very funny!"

"It's true. You look up to him. You're crazy, but you do. You don't look up to me. You never did."

"I loved you!"

"What's love got to do with anything? That only gets you so far. After a while, other things take over."

"What takes over?"

"I wish I knew. Look, no hard feelings?"

"Don't be an ass. Of course there are hard feelings. Anger and hurt and . . . and all the hard feelings in the world. I loved you, remember?"

"I guess so. I guess you're right. For what it's worth, I loved you. I still do in a way."

"You want to change your mind?"

He shook his head. "I've left you all the kitchen stuff. The toaster and all that. It's in one of the boxes in the kitchen. You'll have some unpacking to do, but it's all here."

"Thanks."

"I'll leave the keys on the kitchen counter."

"Do that," she said. She walked out. She slammed the door behind her.

She stood there, outside the building, blinking in the sunlight and feeling the same disorientation she had felt as a girl when she'd come out of a movie into the brightness of day. It wasn't supposed to have happened that way. He was supposed to have begged her to come back. And she was going to put it off just a little while longer. Probably that, or maybe even give in. Come back to him. But she'd asked, or come as close to asking as she could, and he'd said no.

Which left her alone. Defenseless. Afraid. She certainly couldn't rely on Irene. Or go back to Victor. She was on her own. At least she still had the apartment. A hole to run to, if she had to, but no more than that.

She walked to the corner, to Central Park West, to look for a cab. She'd always had the feeling, walking around New York, that at any time one of the cabs might come to a stop for her and that

Larry, its driver, would say hello or stop to buy her a cup of coffee. It had happened three or four times during the year. No more. Cabs passed her. She didn't have the heart to stick her hand out to hail one. She walked south to Central Park South. She could cross there, and walk back up to Irene's building. If she walked fast, the pounding of her heels on the concrete kept her from thinking.

NINETEEN

The reasonable and even obvious thing to do, Victor knew, was to call George Kern and start the machinery. And he got as far as picking up the telephone, listening to the dull drone of the dial tone, and getting his finger into position to dial the first digit. Several times he did this, and each time he paused, froze, thinking not of Emily, but of the humiliation that would inevitably result from his having to admit, even to a friend, even to an attorney, that the marriage had not lasted two weeks.

Well, it hadn't. And while no explanations would be required, there would hang in the air the unspoken questions, not from Kern the attorney, but from Kern the friend: *What the hell happened in two weeks?* To which Victor couldn't possibly reply. And to which, therefore, Kern would have to invent possible answers, drawing upon his worst fantasies and the general seaminess of life that he dealt with and eventually tucked away in those dried-blood-colored file envelopes with their labels in the upper right-hand corners. And what would be intolerable would be Victor's knowledge that the most bizarre and sordid guess Kern could manage would fall short of the truth. Kern would not suppose that after some days of bondage and orgies, Victor's young wife had run off with another woman.

Victor could hardly believe it himself. It made no sense. Emily had been having a good time, the best time in her entire life. They'd all been enjoying themselves and each other. What had gone wrong? But he could not reconstruct it in his mind with any certain clarity. Dreams and daydreams, on the plane and back home, in his apartment, alone in his big bed, seemed at the same time plausible and impossible. Had they done all those things? Had it been as good as he remembered? Better, better! In which case, it was insane for her to have left.

The actual issue had been silly, had been a joke. She had wanted to tie him up? He could not remember the tonality of the suggestion, having replayed the tape in his head so many times, each time with the controls set differently for different effects. But no version was convincing. He had declined . . . but had not utterly foreclosed the question. She could have argued. She could have insisted. If she'd really wanted to do it, she could have pressed the suggestion. But it had been put forth, he seemed to recall, as a pretext, expecting a negative reply, upon which, in turn, she could base her decision to leave. Or appear to. Because the decision must have been made on other grounds and earlier.

What he could hardly admit to himself was that

he missed her. And Irene, too, for that matter. They had all got on so wonderfully well together. But to hell with it. And to hell with both of them. He picked up the phone yet again, listened to the drone, fancied it was the noise of the wind making the wires vibrate over a long desolate stretch of prairie, and began to dial. He depressed the button on the cradle and dialed again. Not Kern's number, but Irene's.

"Well?" Irene asked. "You saw him. And?"

"Yes, I saw him," Emily admitted. "How did you know?"

"You look awful."

"I walked home. Very fast."

"What on earth for? Didn't you have any money? I suppose we'll have to consider money."

"It wasn't that," Emily said. "I wanted to walk." She told Irene about how she had found the apartment full of boxes and cartons, and how Larry was leaving the city to go back to his parents in Pennsylvania.

"Really!"

"Of course, really. Why would he do all that work of packing everything up? Just to scare me?"

"No, no. I believe you. I just find it interesting. He may be doing the right thing."

"He said that you and Victor were out of his league. And he thought I was too. Or I am now."

"And what did you say?"

"Nothing much."

"And what do you think?" Irene asked. "Is he right?"

"I don't know. I don't think so."

"About you? Aren't you out of his league—to use that depressingly hearty phrase from the sports page?"

"I'd have to think about it. Not yet, I don't think. But if I keep on this way, I will be."

"Exactly. The question is whether you want to be."

"It's too late. He's already gone by now."

"No, no. Not for him," Irene corrected her. "For yourself. You have to decide what you want. So long as you keep a white picket fence and a lawn and scrubby little children and a station wagon in your head, there's nothing I can do with you. On the other hand . . ."

"Yes? On the other hand?"

"If you aren't afraid to be original and to invent your life as you go along—as your venture with Victor suggested you might be able to do—then I can make something of you. It's up to you."

"I suppose so."

"You suppose what? That I can make something of you? I have no doubt of it. But you were upset to find that Larry was going home?"

"I felt responsible."

"Nonsense. It was his decision. He's a grownup. He's responsible for himself. As all of us are responsible for ourselves. And for all you know, it may be the making of him. New York is a terrible place for a writer to try to write. Good for a journalist, maybe, for not for a writer."

"You think he has talent?"

"My dear, I have no idea. If he does, he's done the right thing. If he doesn't, then it certainly doesn't matter where he goes."

"What have you in mind for me?"

"Are you interested?"

"Interested enough to ask," Emily said, defiantly.

"Good. A little spirit. I expected it would show itself. I'd begun to wonder. What I have in mind for you is a cruise."

"For me? I mean, you won't be along?"

"No, just you. And others, of course. The trouble with your marriage to Victor is that neither of you had any idea what you wanted. Your wants were limitless. And therefore impossible to satisfy. Given a more reasonable frame, of expectations and of time, you'd very probably do much better."

"You mean a cruise with a man?"

"Obviously."

"What man?"

"I haven't decided. Perhaps I shouldn't decide. Maybe we could make an evening of the decision. Have a party. I could invite a few friends and . . . auction you off."

"You mean you want me to learn how to whore!"

"One must cultivate one's natural talents, no matter what they are. The label, anyway, is too general. I think 'playgirl' is closer to the truth. Or companion. Or ornament."

"It's sordid, no matter what you call it."

"Sordid? Why? Is sex sordid? Or friendship? Or good food and expensive jewelry? Is life sordid? You have to push the questions back to the fundamental question and answer that one."

"Most people wouldn't consider it an admirable way of life."

"But they'd consider it enviable. And they hate what they envy, because it's inaccessible. They lack the beauty and the charm, and they lack the moral courage and honesty too, so they vilify what they can't have. Do you agree with them? Do you believe them?"

Emily wasn't sure whether she believed them or not, but she knew that to say so would be to insult Irene and, more important, to lose her friendship and patronage. And tutelage. "No," she said. "No, I don't."

"Good. We'll have a party, then, and auction you off. All the people I invite will be civilized, affable, and rich. Especially rich. We'll see what happens."

Emily was about to ask a question, had opened her mouth to do so, when the telephone rang.

"Would you get it, dear?" Irene asked.

Emily picked up the phone. It was Victor.

"Emily! It's Victor. Your husband," he added, as if to nudge her back to what he considered to be her responsibilities and domestic duties. "Are you all right?"

"I'm fine," she said. "But I don't want to talk to you."

"Why not? It can't hurt to talk. It could do some good."

"Could do *you* some good, maybe," she agreed. "But not me."

"Emily! Listen to me. Or, better yet, talk to me. What the hell happened? Why did you walk out that way?"

"I'll put Irene on," Emily said.

"Emily, wait!"

But she had already put the phone on the table, had announced to Irene that Victor was calling, and had walked away, to leave the miniscule voice wheedling and cajoling out of the earpiece like an excited chipmunk with the gift of speech, as in a Disney film.

Irene picked up the phone. "Victor? It's Irene," she said, stopping his complaints at once. "You just get back?"

"I got back yesterday. I was tired."

"Of course."

"Emily's all right?"

"Oh, yes. She's fine."

"And you?"

"I'm fine, too, thank you."

"Why did she leave? Why did she go with you? For that matter, why did you take her away?"

"As the saying goes, 'If you've got to ask, you'll never get to know.' "

"Don't give me wisecracks, Irene, please!"

"Well, it's true."

"I want to see her."

"Oh, of course. I have no objection whatever. As a matter of fact, we're giving a party. Probably tomorrow night. And a few friends will be coming by. You might drop in if you're free. She'll be here."

"There's a hook in it. I can tell that much," Victor said.

"Of course! Emily's the hook. Or the bait. Or the prize. It's an auction."

"An auction?"

"Is there something wrong with the connection? Or with you, dear? An auction! Emily is up for bids."

"You're kidding."

"Come by around eight thirty or nine, tomorrow evening, and see if I'm kidding."

"Don't be ridiculous!"

"Don't you be ridiculous. You don't have to bid,

after all. And you'll get a chance to see her, which is what you called about, isn't it?"

"If she changes her mind about talking to me, tell her I'm at home," Victor said, changing the tack of the conversation.

"I'll tell her," Irene promised. "See you tomorrow, I trust."

"Over my dead body."

He slammed the phone down. Irene hung up rather less emphatically. She was looking at Emily who was grinning approval. " 'Over my dead body,' he said. But I shouldn't be surprised if he showed up," Irene told Emily, who positively beamed, feeling her power and loving it.

The rest of that day and most of the next were an impressive display of organization and energy. Irene could have managed perfectly well by herself, of course, but by including Emily in the planning, she was allowing Emily to learn how these things are to be orchestrated, the way they are all brought together to make an illusion of effortless style, ease, and grace—not so much to impress the guests with the elegance and efficiency of the hostess, but to flatter them, to allow them to believe for the time they spent in her apartment that this was a perfectly natural extension of the grace and ease of their own lives, that this was what they naturally appreciated and deserved.

The caterer, first. Because it's cheaper than keeping a cook full-time, and unless one lives a terribly regular life, much more sensible. You lay on what you need when you need it. Flowers. Very good candy. It's pointless to put out anything less than the best candy. Allow three pieces per guest. Some won't eat any, but those with a sweet tooth will take up the slack. Nuts. Champagne—the best Californian is perfectly adequate, better than a lot of the ordinary French champagne, and cheaper. Only a few will notice, anyway, and they'll be proud of themselves for being able to tell. Ordinary booze for those who dislike champagne. A good liquor store will send more than you need and take back any unopened bottles, so order a lot. Irene had a woman come in to polish all the silver, a man to do the windows and the floors that needed waxing. The caterer would have people to serve supper, and they could manage the bartending as well.

Meanwhile, they had to attend to themselves as well, to set up appointments at the hairdresser's, a wash and set for Irene and a complete styling for Emily. The manicurist for both of them. And for Emily, a dress, something elegant and yet simple, not too sophisticated but still suggestive. And shoes.

Interspersed with these preparations, there were the invitations to extend, which Irene did in her bedroom, making telephone calls, checking her lists, consulting her notebook with private numbers, and notations of the best times to call or of code words to alert her guests through their secretaries, their Answerphone machines, or their companions of the moment. "These are complicated men," she explained, "leading complicated lives." She made a checkmark on her masterlist to indicate an acceptance and went on to the next call. It took her several sessions at the telephone to round up the likeliest group of six men for her "intimate little evening."

"What about Victor?" Emily asked. "Do you really think he'll come too?"

"It's likely. I can't guarantee it, but then I can't really imagine him staying away. Do you want him to come? He's not likely to outbid some of the others, especially having just spent a week in Hawaii with you. Besides, some of these people have more money in income than Victor has in capital."

"In that case," Emily said, "yes. I hope he comes and loses out, and . . ." She didn't have to finish the sentence. Irene knew exactly what she meant. Had counted on it, in fact.

They found something even better than Irene had imagined for Emily to wear. At one of the little specialty alcoves in Bloomingdale's, they'd passed a mannequin up on a pedestal. The mannequin had been dressed in a gauzy white caftan with a large butterfly embroidered in shiny gold thread. The butterfly seemed to be inching up, or perhaps, poised on the slight shelf of the figurine's hip, to be about to take flight. Irene had stopped suddenly, staring at it. Emily had looked, struck herself by the rightness of it, and had agreed aloud, "Yes." The white was for the ceremony; the caftan suggested slavery; the butterfly suggested the freedom of whimsy, delicacy, unpredictability, and beauty. There was only the one sample, the one on the mannequin. The rest of the order hadn't arrived. Irene insisted that Emily be allowed to try it on. And of course it fit. Perfectly. Not a thing needed to be done to it. "Charge and take," Irene said, flicking her plastic card onto the counter like a chip onto the cloth of a casino table.

The dress was perfect, the exactly right touch with which to harmonize all the other effects and gestures that came together to flatter and to impress the six guests who arrived promptly, all within fifteen minutes of one another, eager to be beguiled and diverted from the ordinariness of their extraordinary lives. There was an executive vice president of a conglomerate that owned a film studio and a publishing house as well as other duller but more reliably profitable enterprises in natural resources, mostly uranium and natural gas. There was a Wall Street wonder—or anyway, former wonder—who had made six million dollars in one delirious spasm of pyramided risk, and who now sat on advisory boards of mutual funds and advised them about investments. There was a Brazilian banker, and there was a Saudi businessman whose business it was to buy things for his relatives and friends back home. There was a Greek whose father was a shipowner. And there was an American with a French surname and a British accent whose grandfather had been one of the great robber barons, accumulating a fortune that staggered his heir's well-developed talents for its—and his own—dissipation.

They ranged in age from the late thirties to the late fifties. The Arab and the Greek wore dinner clothes. The conglomerate executive wore a business suit. The others were informally dressed, establishing themselves at various places on a spectrum between elegant and funky. Irene, who was wearing a hostess gown in gold, welcomed them all, introduced them to Emily, and saw to it that they were supplied with drinks and canapes.

They were all Irene's old friends. Emily wasn't quite clear about what the relationships had been, whether all or some of them had been her lovers, or merely friends of lovers. Their poise and sophistication made it difficult to tell much about them. They were all the kind of men who have a confidence that allows them to be at ease in almost any situation. Obviously they all knew each other, or some of them knew others. Nobody did anything so crude as to talk business, either their own business or that of Irene's evening. Quite naturally, they engaged Emily in conversation. And she followed Irene's instructions, speaking of herself as little as possible, but telling the truth if the occasion arose, as from time to time it did.

The caterer, Mrs. Whiggins, sent word to Irene that dinner was ready. She seated her guests. There was a rather formal meal, as Irene had intended. The food—a country terrine, a poached salmon with dill, and a crown roast of lamb—engaged and rewarded the attention of the guests. Emily ate rather delicately, not nervous but keyed up, alert, and looking at one and then another of the men, the guests, the bidders. All things being equal, whom would she choose? The Arab with the dark eyes and the full, almost pouty lips? The Greek, who looked to be almost as old as Victor, and who quite possibly was wearing a toupee? The man from Wall Street with the coke spoon on a gold chain around his neck? The Brazilian, who was rather short but very muscular, and who smiled sometimes in such a way as to suggest that there was a wonderful joke he'd thought of but couldn't tell. Did it make any difference?

It wasn't until coffee was served in the living room—Emily pouring for the gentlemen—that Irene explained the rules of the auction. There were to be three rounds of bidding. The first two would be with written bids, proposing periods of time and amounts of money, together with any other relevant information—about travel, or specific expectations of performance, sexual or otherwise. After the first round, the times and amounts of the two high bids would be announced. Those wishing to participate in a second round would be invited to do so. The third round would be *viva voce,* with the two highest bidders invited to remain to pursue their bidding with whatever additional money or other persuasions they could bring to bear. Was this agreeable? Were there any questions?

"Is this an unreserved auction?" the Greek asked, rather languidly Emily thought.

"Practically speaking, no," Irene said. "I'm confident that there will be at least one reasonable bid. And no reasonable bid will be refused."

"And the terms?" the Arab asked. "Cash? In advance? Afterwards? And to whom?"

"To me," Irene said. "In advance, but to be held. In case of dispute, my arbitration will be final. Agreeable? I can't see how else to do it. And you know me."

"Fine, fine," the Arab said.

"In that third round," the robber baron's grandson asked, "who decides about the nonmonetary considerations? You or Emily?"

"We'll consult," Irene said, "but the final decision will be hers."

"Your part in this is what?" the Wall Streeter asked. "Agent? Friend? Broker?"

"Friend," Irene said. "The money will go to Emily. All of it."

Emily was surprised by this. At least the expenses, the cost of the party, she had expected to repay, if there were enough money to allow her to do so. But certainly this was the wrong moment to argue about it. Irene was already distributing little white cards with their matching envelopes, enclosure cards from a florist perhaps.

Emily collected the cards at Irene's signal. She handed them to Irene who took them into the bedroom. Emily followed her. She watched from the doorway as Irene, sitting on the corner of the bed, opened the little envelopes.

"Well?" Emily asked.

"Not bad," Irene said. "Three blanks. They may just be waiting for the second round. Or they may not be interested. Or they may be interested, but not just now."

"Why not now?"

"A man might have other plans. Or might want to wait to see how you did with one of the others . . . Anything's possible. Don't take it personally."

"It's difficult not to."

"Difficult, perhaps, but necessary. You've been offered a trip to Rome and Istanbul and a thousand dollars. You've been offered a cruise of the out islands of the Bahamas and a minimum gift of five hundred dollars. And a part in a motion picture. That's from Dick, obviously. He doesn't specify what the salary is. Still . . ."

"That's terrific. They're all terrific!"

"Why not?" Irene asked. "We'd better get back."

They took their seats in the living room. Irene was about to announce the results of the first round of bidding when the doorbell sounded.

"Would you get it, dear?" Irene asked.

Emily went to the door, opened it, and saw Victor standing there. He was wearing a sport coat and a shirt open at the neck. He looked haggard. Emily stood aside to allow him to enter, but for a moment he didn't move. He just stood there, staring not at her but at a point over her shoulder.

"Well, come on in, Victor," Irene called.

He lurched into the room. The other men stood. Irene introduced them all, using their first names. Evidently, Victor knew some of them.

"So, you weren't kidding, were you?" he said, when the introductions were completed. "I figured you might go ahead and . . ." He broke off. It was unnecessary to finish the sentence anyway. He sat down in one of the empty chairs.

Irene summarized the results of the first round of bidding. Emily passed out a second set of cards, giving one to Victor. He took it, held it, and stared at it as if he were trying to read something from its blankness. He looked around the room, his gaze bouncing from one man to the next, watching them as they made their little notations on the small cards they held in their hands or propped against a thigh, writing with a Mont Blanc, or a Cartier's Must, or, in the case of the Arab, an old-fashioned barrel pen in gold. Victor didn't reach into his pocket for a writing implement. He just sat there.

"Need a pen?" the Wall Streeter, who was sitting in the next chair, asked him.

"Yes, thanks."

Victor accepted the offered pen, a silver Sheaffer, unscrewed it, and scribbled quickly. He returned the pen and put the card into its envelope.

Emily went around the room collecting the

cards. Again, she and Irene retired to the bedroom.

"What did he offer?" Emily asked, the minute the door was closed behind them.

"Who? Victor?" Irene asked.

"Yes, Victor. What did he say?"

Irene opened all the envelopes and examined them to find Victor's. "What I expected," she said.

"And? What's that?"

"The old arrangement. To be continued."

"Oh. Is that all?"

"It was pretty generous."

"Yes."

"Is that what you want?"

"What are the other offers?"

"I'll get to them. What about Victor?"

"No," Emily said, not even pausing. "Not Victor."

There were two blanks this time. The offer of Rome and Istanbul and a thousand dollars had been repeated, by the Arab. The robber baron had raised his five hundred to nine hundred, and had specified that the cruise in the Carribean would last at least a month. The Brazilian had offered two weeks in Estoril and the use of a villa there with two servants for a minimum of six months.

"Alone?" Emily asked.

"Yes, of course. The bank probably owns the villa. You can figure out what the equivalent would be in money."

"And the movie offer?"

"Is repeated."

"What should I do?" Emily asked.

"You have to decide. I can answer questions for you, give you information—or anyway my best guesses. But the decision has to be yours. Otherwise, you'd . . . you'd be missing the point. It's your life. Your opportunity."

"The Hollywood offer . . . You think it's legitimate."

"Of course not. But it's real. I mean, he'll give you your chance. What you do with it, and what the luck of things will bring . . . no one can say. He has no idea, himself. But he'll do what he says he'll do. It may not be much, but it'll be something."

"It's that or . . . or Estoril and the villa."

"All right. I'll call them in. You're sure?"

Emily thought for a moment—ten seconds, perhaps—and then nodded. "Yes, those two."

Irene went out to announce the results and to invite the Brazilian and the conglomerate executive inside.

Victor stood up. "Excuse me," he said.

"I'm sorry, Victor," Irene said.

The other men were looking at him, the two successful candidates and the other four.

"No, no. I meant . . . I'm not feeling well," he said. "My congratulations, gentlemen." He took a step toward the door, stopped, turned back, and said to Irene, "Thank you for inviting me. I . . . send Emily my best wishes."

He turned away and continued to the door. He fumbled at the doorknob for a moment, managed finally to get it to work, and let himself out.

In Irene's bedroom, there was a conversation that lasted no more than five minutes. Irene had been right in both cases. Her guesses had been correct about the villa in Estoril, and about the part that she might expect in Hollywood. The Brazilian was gracious and suave, but he had unpleasant, calculating eyes. Either because of the look of those eyes, or perhaps because of her ambitions to be an actress, Emily chose Hollywood. It was agreed that Dick would send a plane ticket the next morning for a flight that afternoon.

The two men and the two women in the bedroom returned to the living room to rejoin the others, all of whom had been waiting to celebrate the decision with a new bottle of champagne.

TWENTY

In the morning, Irene called Victor to invite him for coffee. To say goodbye to Emily.

"Damn you!" he said.

"That's hardly responsive," she pointed out. "Will you come or not?"

"I'll be there in five minutes," he said, obviously unhappy about it, but unable to refuse.

In a little less than four minutes, he was at Irene's door.

"It was Emily's idea," Irene said. "But I'm glad you came."

"Oh?" Victor asked.

"Yes," Emily said. She handed him a cup of coffee. "Black with a little sugar, right?"

He nodded and thanked her.

"I wanted to tell you . . . why," Emily said.

"I'm curious to hear," he said.

"I was falling in love with you. And . . . and you were falling in love with me. Or I thought you were. But it wouldn't have lasted. And sooner or later, the break would have come and . . . and it would have been worse. For me."

"I doubt it."

"Oh, yes," she said. "I couldn't have stood it. I could hardly stand it as it was."

"I see. You just didn't go off with Irene . . . for Irene's sake?"

"No. She was there. She helped. But that's all."

"So, which is it? Estoril or Hollywood?" Victor asked.

"Hollywood."

"I thought it would be."

"You approve?" Emily asked.

"Of course not. You'll fail, probably. Most people do. Even people with talent."

"But I'll have had my shot at it."

"That's true," Victor said. "If you ever find yourself stranded . . . call me. I'll be able to help you out a little."

"Thank you," Emily said.

"No strings," Victor told her.

"I know."

"Are you satisfied?" Irene asked Victor.

"With her? Yes. With you? No."

"What have I done?"

"What haven't you done?" Victor asked back. "Or, more to the point . . . why have you done what you've done? I can't figure it out."

"It was just my meddling instinct."

"I don't believe you. Not for a minute," Victor said.

"Some toast?" Irene offered.

Emily packed. She called the moving and storage company to arrange for them to come and pick up all the things that Larry had packed. A messenger arrived with the airplane ticket.

Victor had sat around all this time, watching, listening, occasionally talking, and drinking coffee.

"I suppose we'll be getting a divorce now?" Emily asked him.

"Yes."

"I'll let you know where I am."

"Thank you."

"I have a couple of hours before I have to leave for the airport."

"Oh?" Victor asked. It sounded as though it might be an invitation to a farewell bang. He hoped not.

Whether it had been or not, Emily retrieved the moment by saying that she probably ought to take a nap. She hadn't slept well the night before. And Dick would be meeting her at the plane. "So," she said, "I guess this is goodbye." She kissed Victor on the cheek. Then on the mouth, but a dry, brushy kiss. And she went into her room, Irene's guest bedroom, to lie down for the time that remained to her.

"I'm tired too," Irene said, once Emily had left her alone with Victor.

"I'll leave if you like."

"No, no. Not sleepy. Not even physically tired. Tired of . . . of games. Do you know, I'd been to bed with everyone here last night? Including Emily, but she hardly counted."

"And?"

"And? It's very wearing. I'd begun to think so a while back. That was . . . that was why I did all this."

"To get rid of Emily?"

"Yes. To have you to myself. If you want me."

"You and I?"

She nodded.

"You've gone to a lot of trouble."

"Some."

"Suppose . . . suppose I say yes. What am I saying yes to?"

"I don't know, exactly. One never does, does one?"

"Do I give up my apartment? Move in here?"

"Not necessarily. No, I shouldn't think so."

"Or do we get married?" Victor asked. "I mean, once my divorce goes through?"

"No, certainly not."

"Just . . . play it as it lays?"

She nodded.

"Then there's no question," he said. "Of course. I'd be honored."

There are ceremonies by which such proposals are solemnized. In this instance, Irene went to her desk, opened the middle drawer, and gave Victor the key to her apartment. He put it on his key ring. And that evening, after they had driven Emily to LaGuardia and had returned to Manhattan, he stopped off at his apartment to get a key for her.

A year later, they had news of their protégés. Larry had finished a novel, had managed to find a publisher for it, and had a few brief but respectful notices. The book sold only six thousand copies, but it wasn't bad at all. Emily had a bit part in a film, playing the housewife who was attacked by the space creature. She showed about thirty seconds of terror and a fair expanse of thigh before she died.

"Unbelievable," was Victor's verdict as they left the theater.

"The picture? What did you expect?"

"No, not the picture. That whole business. In Hawaii, I mean."

"People do odd things, sometimes," Irene said. "We're better than we think, and worse. So much depends on the occasion."

"I can hardly imagine it now," he said. "We're safe now, aren't we?"

No, of course not, she thought. But she didn't tell him that. She simply took his hand. For comfort and for luck. And together they walked north on Third Avenue.